This is not a fairy tale, though there are Fairies in it. And Kings and Queens, and Princesses and Princelings, and magic that comes from faraway places not found on any map...

For Zander and Orlie

First published in the UK in 2022 by Usborne Publishing Ltd., Usborne House,
83-85 Saffron Hill, London EC1N 8RT, England. usborne.com
Usborne Verlag, Usborne Publishing Ltd., Prüfeninger Str. 20, 93049 Regensburg,
Deutschland, VK Nr. 17560

A CIP catalogue record for this book is available from the British Library.

Trade paperback ISBN 9781474964395
Waterstones exclusive paperback ISBN 9781803707570
05326/1 JFM MJJASOND/22

Printed and bound in Great Britain by CPI Group (UK) Ltd, Croydon, CR0 4YY.

MagicBorn

PETER BUNZL

The Fair Isle
Heart of the Forest
Tree of life
Old Ruins
Pool
Spring
The Greenwood Forest
Hut
Bell
Stepping Bones
N
W
E
S
To The Dead Lands

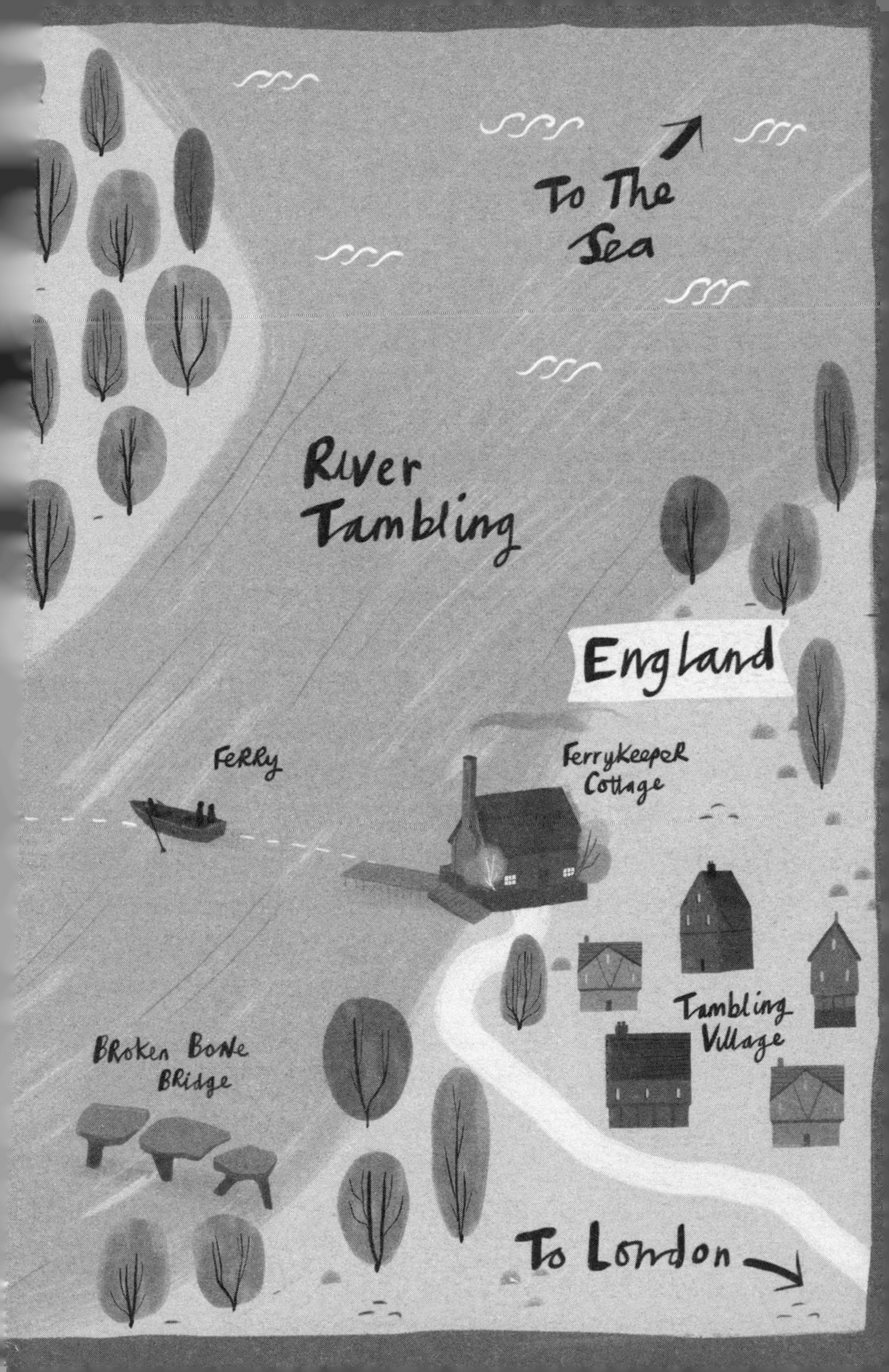
To The Sea
River Tambling
England
Ferry
Ferrykeeper Cottage
Tambling Village
Broken Bone Bridge
To London

"Remember, remember all that is lost.
The first days of spring, and the last winter's frost.
The trees that were saplings, the birds that were eggs.
The dream-lives of children tucked up in their beds.

Fairy tales long forgotten, bring them to light,
as the sun in the morning makes daytime from night."

~ Traditional Fairy remembering spell

Prologue

This is not a fairy tale, though there are Fairies in it. And Kings and Queens, and Princesses and Princelings, and magic that comes from faraway places not found on any map.

When you make a list like that, your story can't help but sound extraordinary and adventuresome. But this is not a tale of that type. Nor would it befall most people if they lived for a thousand years.

This is a story of discovering yourself a stranger in a strange land, with nothing but the words in your head, the charm round your neck and the wild hope in your pocket to see you through. And it does not begin with the usual "Once upon a time…"

Instead, it starts far off, and rather like a dream: on a cold winter's night in 1726, at full moon, on the thirteenth stroke of midnight, in the Greenwood, on the Fair Isle, in the furthest reaches of England, where there was and there wasn't a Wild Boy running through the trees…

The woods were deep and the woods were dark, but the Wild Boy was not afraid. Not of the forest. As he weaved between its bare branches, over the deep snow lying on the ground, he smelled burrowing insects, hibernating mice, scurrying squirrels, barn owls scouring the sky and restless seedlings curled deep underground.

This Wild Boy was ragged in appearance. Black curly hair poked from beneath the fur hood of his coat. His darting eyes – one green, one blue – were set in a round face, white as paper. He pursed his lips in concentration as he stumbled forward, clutching at frosted tree stumps. A single wolf's tooth was sewn to his collar, and his torn coat-tails flew out behind him.

The first remarkable thing to observe about this Wild Boy was that he possessed the shadow of a wolf. It danced on the white drifts as he ran.

The second remarkable thing to observe about him was that he wore a stone that looked like an almond-shaped eye with a hole through its centre, threaded onto a leather string around his neck.

The Wild Boy could not recall where he'd got this charm, nor who had given it to him. Truth be told, he couldn't even remember his own name. That's if he'd ever had one. He felt as if an enormous, confusing storm was rolling along behind him, and an unnameable fear was brewing in his belly. His cheeks stung with tears as he scrambled onwards, muttering a spell:

"Tail, snout, pelt, paws. Wings, fins, teeth, claws. Shake me, change me, magic art. Make me the creature of your heart."

Magic seeped from within the Wild Boy, making his limbs heavy and long. His hands and feet became furry footpads, and he fell to all fours, leaving paw prints in the snow. His fingernails clawed. His face lengthened. His nose sharpened and became a snout, and his tattered coat grew around his body like a pelt.

He had become a wolf.

The wolf swerved around trees and ruined buildings, and all at once came upon a magnificent great oak growing through a stone floor. The sight of its branches reaching up like fingers to grab the sky filled the wolf with fear. Why it was frightening, the wolf couldn't say. In his head, he had not the words to compose such thoughts. All he knew was that this tree was dangerous and he must not go near it.

He skittered nervously away and broke into a gallop, leaving the tree and its surroundings behind.

Somewhere, somehow, at some time or other in the not-too-distant past, he had gone hopelessly astray. Got terribly lost. But up above, the stars were sparkling, and the moon shone full and bright.

The wolf looked at the moon and the moon stared back at him, beaming like a proud pockmarked parent. Smiling its celestial smile.

The wolf opened his jaws wide to reveal a mouthful of yellow teeth and gave a joyful growl.

The growl became a bark, then a roar, and finally a howl as long and loud and fierce as the night itself.

AWHOOOOOOOOOOOOOO!

1

Storm Girl

The river was wet and the river was wild, but the Storm Girl was not afraid. Not of the crashing waves, nor the clink of the ice that sat atop the freezing cold water like broken shards of glass.

She wasn't afraid of the mermaids her nearly pa, Prosper, the ferry keeper, told her swam in the river. Nor the giants her nearly da, Marino, told her stalked the mountains, smashing glaciers with their bare fists.

She wasn't even afraid of the Fair Folk, who, legend had it, danced in the ruins around the great old oak tree at the heart of the forest, once a year at winter's end, on the thirteenth stroke of midnight.

Nor was she afraid of the fact that the villagers were whispering that wolves had returned to the Greenwood, and that a wolfish creature – half-boy, half-cub – had been spotted howling at the moon by local charcoal-burners.

The Storm Girl wasn't scared of any of that…at least, that's what she told herself. And in the daytime those assurances held. Yet when she lay alone in her bed on these cold winter nights, thoughts of those strange and magical creatures brewed a squall of anxiety inside her.

Then she told herself they were only myths and legends, old wives' tales. Just stories… But stories can have a ring of truth to them, like the peal of a bell. Sometimes that truth is so deafening it can wake the dead. Other times it's barely loud enough to stir the hidden secrets inside you.

The first remarkable thing to observe about the Storm Girl was her name:

Tempest.

It was an odd name with a wild and stormy nature, and Tempest was as tempestuous as it suggested. Plus, she was rather unkempt in appearance. Her mousey hair fell like a stream over rocks and tangled on the shoulders of her red cloak, which she'd had for longer than she could remember. Her nose was as sharp as the craggiest rock in the river, and pointed boldly wherever she wanted to go. Her brow was as high and rugged as a cliff, and was often furrowed in deep thought.

But there was a clean-cut truthfulness to her, fresh as broken stone. You could tell what she was thinking in each of her shining eyes – one green, one blue – and in every corner of her strong-willed face.

The second remarkable thing to observe about Tempest was that she could talk to the robin on her shoulder.

The robin's name was Coriel. Coriel's eyes were dark as coal and were constantly looking about for danger while she fluffed her grey-brown plumage and plumped the red feather pinny she wore across her chest.

Tempest sometimes had to mother Coriel, but most of the time Coriel mothered Tempest. That little bird was the most matronly creature in the young girl's life. Apart from Prosper and Marino.

Tempest kept the fact she and Coriel could speak together secret. Most people in the village where she lived were wary of magic abilities, even small ones like talking to a bird.

The third and most remarkable thing about Tempest was that she had lost her memory. She could remember nothing before Prosper and Marino had plucked her from the river, just over two years ago. Not who her real family was, nor where she'd lived, or who had cared for her before she met Prosper and Marino.

Coriel couldn't remember either. The little robin's sharp mind drew a blank when it came to the before times. "*I don't recall anything from our past, little gannet,*" she would whisper to Tempest. "*Not a dicky bird. I feel clueless as a chick straight out the egg when I try to think of it.*"

In the days following the Almost Drowning, Tempest and Coriel lived with Prosper and Marino in their home, Ferry Keeper's Cottage. Tempest would let her mind whirl back through half-forgotten memories, shaking them up like shards of broken mirror. Sadly, she could recall next to nothing.

There was one tiny physical clue to her past, however: a small piece of bone, carved into the shape of a cloud, that Tempest wore on a leather thong around her neck. The Bone Cloud had three words engraved on its back, written in the same secret language Tempest spoke with Coriel.

From your mother

That message was enough for Tempest to know her real family were somewhere and missed her.

Holding the Bone Cloud in her hand, she could sense small details about her mother. The smell of her, sweet as tree sap. Her ears poking through her long, straight, silver hair like leaves frozen in ice, and her dark eyes, deep as still water.

Her mother must have given her this beautiful necklace out of love...and maybe one day she'd come and find her.

It was sad to be left with these few faded memories, but Tempest blew on their embers in the hope that soon they'd blaze into a roaring fire of remembrance.

Those first weeks and months at the cottage drifted by slowly like the flotsam of the river. Prosper and Marino were kind and treated her as if she was their own daughter. Each day that Tempest was with the couple, she learned more about them.

Marino was very talkative. He was always full of song and chatter, which floated through the house and garden like birdsong.

Prosper kept his cards close to his chest. He could be quite grumpy, especially on land, but he loved the river.

Under their tutelage, Tempest became a natural sailor. Soon she could row and steer their little ferry boat, *Nixie*, like an expert. Tempest could swim already – she must have learned sometime in the past – but Prosper and Marino taught her stronger strokes that she could use in dangerous currents.

A year passed, then two. On the second anniversary of their meeting, on the winter solstice, the couple threw Tempest an Almost-Thirteenth birthday party. There was smoked fish, and all the food and jollity they could muster on their meagre earnings. Almost-Thirteen was how old Tempest thought herself to be, if she counted up the vague number of real birthdays she sensed she'd had. Though, for some reason, she felt her actual birthday was in spring.

For a present, the couple gave Tempest a tiny wooden rowing boat with three painted figures in it. Prosper had whittled the piece himself with his knife, and Marino had painted it with tiny horsehair brushes. The figures looked exactly like each of them. Tempest even wore her red cloak. The boat was just small enough to fit in the palm of her hand.

"This is our gift to you," Prosper said.

"If, one day, your parents do return…" Marino said.

"Or if you have to go away for any other reason…" Prosper added.

"Then," they both chimed in, "you'll have it to remember us by."

"Thank you," Tempest said. "I'll treasure it always."

She knew she would, for it had been given with love, like her mother's necklace.

"There's something else we've been meaning to talk with

you about," Marino said, as Tempest turned the little boat around in her hand.

"You've been here for two years now," Prosper said in his straightforward way. "And we're still not sure where your parents are. Perhaps they want to come back, but aren't able to. So until they do, or if they don't return, we thought..."

"We thought you could stay with us on a permanent basis," Marino added soothingly. "As our honorary daughter."

"But only if you want to," Prosper continued. "Coriel too," he said, stroking the little robin, who was sitting on the table's edge. "What do you think?"

Tempest didn't know what to say: both of her worlds were unexpectedly colliding like a sudden breeze on a calm day. She'd always thought her parents *would* return, so she hadn't really considered what she'd do if they didn't. Now she knew she must face that possibility, but something was still stopping her.

"Can I have some time to think about it?" she asked.

"Of course," Marino said.

That night Tempest dreamed of a stormy curse that cut the land in two. She was on one side of the river, in the daytime. Her real mother and family were on the other, at night.

Tempest couldn't see their faces. They were too far away.

She waded into the river and tried to swim across to them, but suddenly the black waters of the Tambling clenched like a fist around her, its strong current dragging her down to the Dead Lands below on the riverbed.

Half-remembered garbled words floated in her mind as water gushed endlessly down her gullet, until she felt as if she would drown.

She woke scared, thrashing and drenched in sweat. Coriel was circling around her head, squawking in alarm, until Prosper and Marino arrived.

"I had a nightmare," Tempest explained tearfully, as Marino dried her face with the corner of the blanket.

"What was it about?" Prosper asked.

"The Almost Drowning." Tempest settled nervously back into her bed. "I was searching for my family in a terrible storm. I saw them on the far bank, and waded into the river to swim across to them. But then I started to sink deeper and deeper, just like I did in real life, and I couldn't get out or escape my fate."

"But you did get out," Marino reminded her, stroking her hand. "We saved you, remember."

"I know," Tempest said.

"My dear Storm Girl," Prosper said. "Some difficulties can feel immeasurable on the surface, but in your depths you carry something stronger."

"What's that?" Tempest asked.

"Stillness." Prosper smiled.

"Own that stillness," Marino advised. "Let it fill you with power. Then you'll know the truth of who you are."

"Whatever you're missing, my love," Prosper added, "whatever you've lost, remember your troubles are only passing. Even in the raging of life's biggest storms, there is always a tranquil calm space available to you, if you look hard enough."

"Right here." Marino touched his chest. "Beneath your worries, in the depths of your heart, underneath."

Tempest considered their words over the next few weeks, and their offer for her to stay on as their daughter. She had always imagined going home to her real family at some point. But, after all this time, she could see that Prosper and Marino were probably right. Her real family might not return for her.

That didn't mean they didn't love her. There could be umpteen other reasons that they hadn't come. Perhaps they couldn't afford to take her back, or maybe they just weren't able to because she had drifted so far away from them downriver.

A small seed of sorrow grew in her belly as she considered

these thoughts, but another part of her wondered how she could possibly miss what she couldn't remember. Still, she could never quite close the door on the idea that her mother might one day reappear to claim her.

The last evening she thought about all this was in the final week of winter. It had been snowing heavily along the river. Unseasonably late for such weather. The snowstorm lasted through the night. It didn't even stop the next morning when Prosper and Marino were due to go to the nearby town of Miles Cross.

Even so, the two ferry keepers didn't think of cancelling their trip. This was the day they had to renew their Ferryman Licences for the coming year, and their appointment in the town hall had been booked for months. Tempest and Coriel were to stay behind to look after the cottage. Tempest decided that when Prosper and Marino returned that evening, she would tell them about her decision to accept their proposal, and become their honorary daughter. She couldn't wait to see their faces when she told them.

"Promise me you won't take the boat out alone on the river today," Marino said to Tempest, when he and Prosper were finally ready to depart.

"I won't," Tempest replied. "I promise."

"Good girl." Marino gave Tempest a hug and kissed the top of her head.

"Not even if you hear the naiads calling," Prosper said, as he took down his coat from the hook on the back door. "*Nixie*'s a strong boat, but even she couldn't save you from being dragged down by river sprites on a stormy, snowy day like this."

"And if that happened," Marino said, buttoning up his winter jacket, "we might never see you again."

Tempest hugged Prosper and Marino goodbye.

"We'll be back this evening," Marino said.

"If anyone comes to be ferried across to the Greenwood," Prosper added, "tell them they'll have to wait for the storm to pass. In the meantime, you'd best secure the boat."

With that, he and Marino left to fight their way through the snow to Tambling village and catch the stagecoach to Miles Cross.

Tempest had set herself plenty to do that day, so she wouldn't be sitting around nervously awaiting their return. But they didn't need to worry about her going out on the river, she thought as she washed the breakfast things in a big stone trough. The truth was she never took the boat out solo. The Tambling River stretched like a scar in her mind between the Greenwood and Ferry Keeper's Cottage, and being on its treacherous waters reminded Tempest of the Almost Drowning.

She spent the rest of the morning after Prosper and Marino left tidying the cottage. Then she got ready to go outside. She put on her boots, lined with wild rabbit fur, and her red woollen cloak, and placed the three painted figures in their little wooden ferry boat in her pocket. Coriel flapped to Tempest's shoulder and jumped into the hood of her cloak. She curled up in a ball to keep her feathers dry as Tempest opened the front door and, with her cloak billowing out behind her, Tempest set off into the snow.

Out in the bluster by the riverbank, she set to swabbing *Nixie*'s deck. Tempest loved *Nixie*. The way she sat primly and confidently in the river no matter what it threw at her. Tempest trusted the little ferry boat with her life, just as she did Prosper and Marino. Some days the three of them, along with Coriel, rowed *Nixie* to the mouth of the Tambling River, where its crystal waters met the clouded salty ocean. There they would see storms far out at sea – thunder and lightning that roiled in the distance – while all around them the waters were calm and clear, as if they made their own weather.

By lunchtime, the wind was whisking a constant stream of fresh flakes giddily through the air. Tempest had cleared all the ropes and boxes from the pier and secured *Nixie* in preparation for the growing storm. She was about to head indoors when Coriel flapped from her hood and gave her a warning nip on the ear.

Tempest turned to see a carriage drawn by a pair of brindle mares approaching through the stream of spiralling snow.

It was driven by a coachman in green livery and a tricorn hat. Smart strangers like him rarely called at Ferry Keeper's Cottage, especially not in winter. Strapped to the carriage's roof, among the bags and boxes, was a large, ominous-looking cage, whose iron bars glinted oddly in the afternoon light.

Coriel fidgeted on Tempest's shoulder. "*Have a care, my little Stonechat,*" she whispered softly in Tempest's ear. "*Something wicked this way comes!*"

And Tempest shivered in agreement.

2

Devil's Bargain

"WHOA!" cried the coachman, manoeuvring the carriage down the lane, and stopping it alongside the heavy drifts that had settled beside the cottage. Holding his hat against the wind, he stared with concern at the icy river blocking the end of the road, and the dark sky full of snow that swirled around the pier.

The coachman's face was white with ruddy cheeks and a large purpling nose, and he wore a grey wig rammed on tight beneath his hat. He hadn't noticed Tempest, or Coriel. They were hidden out of sight on the far side of the pier, by the corner of the cottage.

Tempest squinted up again at the coachman's cage.

Its iron bars looked sturdy enough to hold a wild beast, maybe even two. Any creature trapped in there would probably never escape.

The sight of it didn't make her want to show herself. She stayed where she was and watched the coachman as he leaped from the driving seat and ran to open the carriage door.

From inside the carriage came a hacking cough that sounded like a death rattle.

"Why have we stopped?" asked the cough's owner.

"There's no bridge, Your Lordship," the coachman answered.

"We'll see about that," came the rough reply. "Get the step."

"Yes, Your Lordship." The coachman placed a small step in the snow beneath the carriage door and bowed his head, waiting for whoever was inside to descend.

The horses nickered and shuffled their hooves in the snow.

Tempest's heart thumped loudly. She stared hard at the brilliant square of darkness inside the coach. She'd never met a Lord. She always imagined them to be wise and warm, yet the voice of this one was cold and brittle.

The boy who jumped from the carriage was not what she expected at all. He had deep brown skin and tightly-coiled black hair, and wore a smart blue-and-gold jacket with a knapsack slung across his chest.

Tempest hadn't seen many people with the boy's complexion in these parts. Only a peat and charcoal trader and his wife, Adofo and Yaba Fremah, who came up occasionally from the city of London to buy stock. The pair were friendly with Prosper and Marino, and would pay for Prosper to take them across the river.

This boy's britches were pristine and his boots, which were polished to within an inch of their life, looked like they had never seen a drop of mud.

The boy stood beside the coachman, fidgeting, hugging his arms and stamping his feet. He wasn't the Lord it seemed, for both he and the coachman stood waiting for someone else to appear.

Tempest waited too.

The air in the doorway congealed into the face of a man, with deep-set eyes cast in shadow. His face was sharp and pinched and, as he leaned out of the carriage, Tempest saw something swinging about his neck.

A tiny charm necklace: a ring of thorns carved from polished wood. Tempest's heart leaped at the sight of it, for it looked similar to the charm her mother had given her.

The Lord with the charm necklace unfolded himself from the carriage doorway like a praying mantis. He was tall and thin and narrow of waist, and his shoulders and chest were couched in a jacket of shiny silken green, part-hidden by a long black woollen travelling cloak that flapped about in the high wind.

He dipped his head carefully so his neat wig would not catch on the top of the door frame as he descended delicately onto the snowy ground. He took a few brisk paces, looking about.

The coachman hurried back to the carriage and threw blankets over the horses' steaming flanks.

The boy fidgeted with the strap of his knapsack.

Tempest held her breath and watched, intrigued to see what the Lord would do next. She was far more used to the plainly clothed local people, who made their living in the forest across the river in the summer months, and had none of these strangers' fineries. She wondered where they were from.

Neither the Lord nor the boy nor the coachman seemed to have noticed her or Coriel in their hiding place. The Lord didn't seem to be paying much attention to anything. He gazed past the end of the pier, across the river, towards the far trees. It felt as if he was imagining something on the other side, lurking in the Greenwood.

Suddenly, the Lord turned and strode towards Ferry Keeper's Cottage.

"*Sweet woodruff!*" Coriel whispered. "*What's he up to?*"

"Is there anybody there?" the Lord called, knocking on the cottage door with a gloved hand. "I think there is!" he said, answering his own question. Then he added in a sing-song voice:

"Look lively, do your best. Open the door and greet your guest!"

Tempest didn't want to reveal herself, but something about the strange phrases the Lord had used compelled her to. His words seemed to contain fish hooks pulling her from where she was hidden, down the pier.

"What a splendid specimen of *Erithacus rubecula*!" the Lord said, as she stepped out of the shadows.

"A what, sir?" Tempest asked, walking up the snowy pathway.

"A robin." The Lord gave a crooked smile. "A splendid robin."

Coriel hid herself in Tempest's hair. Tempest wrinkled her nose. The Lord smelled like dead creatures left out in the rain.

"Is there a bridge?" the Lord asked. "We need to cross."

"'Fraid not," Tempest said. "Your Lordship," she added, out of courtesy. Despite the fact she'd willed herself not to be polite, the Lord's manner seemed to compel her to.

"Shame," the Lord said. The polished wooden charm

around his neck glistened, as if hit by a sunray. But there was no sun. The sky was overcast. Snow fell.

The coachman attended to the horses. The boy stood by the river. Both snuck worried glances at Tempest, checking she was all right.

"Odd that there's no crossing," the Lord continued. "There's a bridge on my map." He held out a yellowing paper.

Tempest took it, before realizing with shock that it hadn't been in his hand a moment before. Where had he conjured it from?

She peered at the map. The details were all there. The Greenwood Forest, the ruins round the great old oak, the River Tambling, Ferry Keeper's Cottage and the inlet to the sea. But near the bottom was a large stone bridge, spanning the river. A bridge that hadn't existed in her time here, or in the lifetime of Prosper and Marino. Two words were written over it:

BoNe BriDGe

"Your map's wrong, Your Lordship," Tempest told him.

"Nonsense!" the Lord cried. "Maps don't lie. Bridges don't disappear. Not in King George's England." He snatched the map back and jabbed it with a finger. "The

Bone Bridge starts here and proceeds across the river. Where is it?"

"There." Tempest nodded at a handful of crumbling pillars poking from the icy waters near the riverbank. "They say a rare and magical current pulled it down a hundred-and-thirty-three years ago. It was never rebuilt. Not enough call to go to the Greenwood. Nothing but ruins and trees there. But there's another bridge, further upriver. About thirty miles, as the crow flies."

"We must cross at once." The Lord stared at the boat. Tempest wondered what his hurry was. "Is there a ferryman?"

"My pa and da. They're up the way in Miles Cross." She pointed back along the road down which the carriage had come. "They'll be back this evening."

"Can you take us?"

"I'm not supposed to go out on the river alone."

"Shame." The Lord waved a hand over the map and it disappeared, replaced by a leather purse. "This might change your mind." He opened the purse and counted twelve gold coins into his gloved palm, whispering as he did so:

"For the ferry keeper's daughter. Enough to see us 'cross the water."

Tempest was spellbound. This Lord was offering her more money than she'd ever seen. More than Prosper or Marino could earn in a lifetime. If she accepted, it would be enough to keep the three of them and Coriel for years to come.

The Lord jingled the coins persuasively in his palm.

"Take the money if you feel. Perhaps we can make a deal?"

"*Don't do it, little house martin!*" Coriel cawed agitatedly in her ear. "*It's fool's gold and only a fool would take it!*"

Tempest ignored Coriel's warning. She was being overprotective as usual. The coachman and the boy were still watching her apprehensively, but she ignored them too.

Prosper and Marino weren't due back until that evening. The ferry trip would be over by then. Yes, the snow was closing in and the wind was against them. Yes, even the two ferry keepers would have second thoughts about pushing the boat out in this weather. But Tempest was a good sailor. She made up her mind. Twelve gold coins was too much to turn down.

"All right, sir," she said finally. "I'll do it."

"I knew you would," the Lord replied.

Coriel screeched in alarm. But Tempest had given her word. Once she'd done that, she never changed her mind.

"The wind'll blow us off course, Your Lordship," she explained. "Strong currents are against us, so it'll take longer than usual."

"My apprentice will help row." The Lord counted six gold coins into Tempest's palm. "Half now, and half when we return," he explained. He put the purse away and walked off to talk to the coachman. "Get the cage, my man!" Tempest heard him say, and then, more quietly: "Take the carriage and wait upriver, along the road, be sure to keep out of sight."

As Tempest put the coins in her pocket, the apprentice boy glanced anxiously at her, then at the large iron cage the coachman was untying from the carriage roof.

"My name's Kwesi," he said gruffly, adjusting his knapsack. He was about the same age as her, but an inch or two shorter.

"My name's Tempest," Tempest replied. "Pleased to meet you, Kwesi."

"I wish we could've met under better circumstances," Kwesi replied.

He seemed to want to say more, but the Lord had turned from supervising the coachman. "NOAH!" he cried. "Fetch my bags! We're going on a little trip."

"Yes, Lord Hawthorn." Kwesi bristled.

Tempest must've looked confused, for he whispered a hurried explanation.

"Noah's not my real name. It's my English name, the one I was given. The one *he* calls me. Kwesi's what I'm truly called. It means 'born on a Sunday' in my mother tongue, the language of my homeland."

Tempest watched Kwesi hurry back to the coach for the bags. She wondered how he'd come to be apprenticed in England. She couldn't understand why Lord Hawthorn didn't use Kwesi's real name, but something about the scared look in the boy's eyes made her certain it wasn't for pleasant reasons.

A wave of fear rose inside her as she watched Lord Hawthorn supervising the coachman unloading the horrible cage from on top of the coach. She suddenly wondered if she'd made the right choice agreeing to ferry this Lord and his apprentice across the river.

3

Rough Crossing

Tempest clutched the ice-cold oar in her fist. Her hands were raw from rowing and each stroke was like trying to crunch through broken glass. Her hair blew in her eyes and a blizzard of snow blasted her face.

Coriel shivered in her hood and Kwesi sat at the starboard oar beside her, his teeth chattering loudly.

Tempest wasn't sure how long they'd been on the water. Already it felt like for ever. It was as if the river didn't want them to reach their final destination. Strong currents and a high north-easterly wind kept dragging them down towards the estuary. Tempest had to keep steering *Nixie*'s prow upriver, aiming it back towards the far bank and sculling hard to keep them on track.

"That's the spirit," Lord Hawthorn said cheerfully. "Keep up the good work. I would help you, but I need to save my energies for the hunt."

Hunt? Tempest wondered once again why Lord Hawthorn was here, and what he intended to hunt in the Greenwood on such a wild and inhospitable day. She examined him as he sat in the bow, wrapped in his black woollen cloak, one gloved hand steadying the cage.

Never before had she met a grown man who would let two children row him across a tumultuous river without bothering to lift a finger. It brought clouds of anger to her chest and she whispered so to Coriel.

"*He's nothing but a common ragwort,*" Coriel replied quietly. "*You shouldn't have taken his money.*"

"*I couldn't help it,*" Tempest whispered.

It was true, she couldn't. It wasn't just the coins – something in the Lord's honeyed words had compelled her to accept his deal. It made Prosper and Marino's warning melt away like vanishing snowflakes. From that moment, she'd even found that she was no longer afraid of the river. Her fear had dissolved as soon as they had stepped into the boat, replaced by a kind of false bravado that she knew she didn't really possess. It made her wonder if she had agreed to this trip because Lord Hawthorn had somehow tricked her?

She touched the Bone Cloud charm necklace her mother had given her and prayed it would keep her safe from any more deceptions the Lord had planned for this crossing.

The surface of the water grew choppier. Waves jumped over the sides of the boat, scattering shards of slush into the hull. When the ice slopped over Lord Hawthorn's bag and the tips of his polished boots, he finally leaped into action, raising his arms and shouting into the blustering breeze:

"Clouds split. Rains break. River calm. Storm abate."

As Lord Hawthorn finished speaking, the blizzard began to die. Soon the little rowing boat was engulfed in silence. Such a silence! The kind Tempest imagined one might find at the heart of a hurricane. Then the snow stopped falling and the fog on the surface of the river lifted, splitting like a curtain to reveal a clear path before them.

A *spell!* Tempest thought, in amazed disbelief. She was astounded. She'd never seen someone perform magic before. She hadn't even been sure that spells really existed. Not the kind you said out loud, anyway. There was her speaking with Coriel, but she'd always thought of that as more of a unique skill.

Magic was what Lord Hawthorn had used to trick her on the pier, Tempest realized, and the shock of that almost made her drop her oar.

The disgust she'd had for Lord Hawthorn a moment before was suddenly mixed with a sliver of begrudging admiration. His manner was charmless, but his sorcery was powerful.

Even though it felt somewhat taboo, she began to imagine what she would do if she had such power. Find her family for starters, then help Prosper and Marino by calming the river every day. Finally, she would bridge the gap in her memory and uncover her forgotten past.

When she next glanced at Lord Hawthorn, he was slumped in his seat, taking deep, ragged breaths. His big weather spell seemed to have drained a dram of life out of him.

For a long moment he looked winded and off colour, but then he finally regained his breath, and all of a sudden seemed mighty pleased.

"See that, Noah?" he crowed. "That's the work of a real sorcerer! A lowly apprentice like yourself could never achieve such spells. Not in a thousand years. Even if you were to pay attention in all your lessons!"

Kwesi didn't answer, just kept his head down and kept rowing. But in the shape of his shoulders and the hunch of his back, Tempest saw a dormant anger brimming within him that was as deep and wide as the river.

The light was starting to fade as they neared the far bank. It had taken longer than Tempest expected to reach the Greenwood side. Prosper and Marino would probably have arrived back at Ferry Keeper's Cottage by now, and be worrying where she'd got to. She'd best hurry and drop these two off so she could return home to them.

She lit the lantern in *Nixie*'s bow and peered onwards.

The old bell appeared through the half-light, hung on its wooden gallows above the pier. They were within a boat's length of it.

The bell had a clapper rope so travellers stuck on the Greenwood side could fetch the ferry keeper over. The gallows always reminded Tempest of one of Prosper's old stories, about a man who ferried people's souls to the underworld to meet the Grim Reaper.

Tempest stared at Lord Hawthorn. Swathed in his black cloak with only his skeletal face peeping out, he looked rather grim and reaper-ish himself. She brushed that thought away and brought the boat alongside the pier.

Tempest and Kwesi climbed out onto the boards and made good the boat.

Lord Hawthorn offered no assistance; instead he stepped out then skirted the hut on the riverbank, muttering to himself:

"**Glow light, make darkness bright**."

As Tempest watched, a small and eerie globe-like lantern appeared and floated a few inches above his hand, pulsing softly.

"*What's that bristly oxtongue up to?*" Coriel whispered.

Tempest tracked the Lord's movements in the corner of her eye, watching distrustfully and in disbelief as the magical globe light bobbed above his head.

Lord Hawthorn sniffed the air and stepped towards a scraggy line of trees. It was as if he was searching for some invisible, intangible thing, carried on the breeze.

"He's here!" he shouted, turning towards a path that led through a gap in the trees. "I can smell his power. Noah, fetch the cage!"

"Yes, Your Lordship," Kwesi mumbled, hunching over further. He had been shrinking into himself the whole afternoon, Tempest noticed.

"Stop daydreaming and help him, girl!" Lord Hawthorn commanded.

A sudden fuzz filled Tempest's head, and she found she could not disobey.

She and Kwesi returned to the boat for the heavy cage and carried it to the end of the pier. Tempest's hands were stiff from rowing, making the cage cold and awkward to carry. Tempest wondered with horror who the *he* was Lord Hawthorn had mentioned and whether the strange sorcerer intended to lock that person behind these bars?

"What's this for?" she asked Kwesi softly, but he didn't answer.

They placed the cage in a clearing opposite the hut. Then Kwesi hurried back alone for Lord Hawthorn's bag and his own knapsack. As he pulled them from the boat he almost slipped on the icy pier.

"Careful!" Lord Hawthorn strode over and snatched the bag from him. "You'll smash my vials! Don't damage my Grimoire!"

"*What are vials?*" Tempest whispered to Coriel. "*What's a Grimoire?*"

"*Vile and grim items, my little goosander,*" Coriel said, cocking her head. "*Vials are glass jars to store magical ingredients. A Grimoire's a powerful spell book.*"

Tempest wondered how Coriel knew such things. She wished, not for the first time, for her past to be clear to her. To understand what her and Coriel's lives were like before now. Perhaps, she thought, the little bird had once belonged to a powerful sorcerer like Lord Hawthorn? Maybe Tempest had lived with such a sorcerer too? Her mother, or father? And through their magic, she and Coriel had grown to understand each other. Could the little robin's knowledge be from a forgotten memory somewhere deep in that shared past? It was something to consider.

"We'll stay here until my work is done," Lord Hawthorn announced.

If this was another spell, Tempest was having none of it.

"As you wish," she said. "But I'm going home, Your Lordship."

She peered across the river. Ferry Keeper's Cottage was hidden by the encroaching dark. Thunder crackled overhead. The storm Lord Hawthorn had banished with his earlier magic was making its way back over the water towards them. Even he couldn't dismiss the bad weather for ever it seemed. Pretty soon the sleet and snow would make landfall.

Tempest felt nervous about taking the return journey alone in such a storm, but she didn't want to wait either. Not while they completed whatever dubious deed Lord Hawthorn had in mind. She needed to leave immediately.

She pointed at the bell hanging above the end of the pier. "When you want my pa to come and get you, ring that. He'll be over right away."

"No," Lord Hawthorn said. "That wasn't our deal." He cleared his throat and spoke in his sing-song voice again:

"You, young lady, will stay right here. Wait with Noah. Is that clear?"

Tempest could tell by his rhymes that he was trying to use more magic against her. She felt a sudden strong and compelling urge to obey Lord Hawthorn. An urge that was not her own. She shook her head to ward it off. But the Lord's spell was strong and stuck fast, clinging to the edges of her mind like a dogged parasite.

"It doesn't work like that," she snapped angrily, attempting to fight it off. "The ferry keeper never waits."

Lord Hawthorn sneered and replied once again in his hypnotic way:

"Yet that is what *you* will do, because I paid and told *you* to."

Tempest dragged her teeth apart and tried hard to speak once more. She wanted to disagree with him, wanted to rebel, but despairingly she realized that her will was no longer entirely her own. Her once clear thoughts had become muddied like silt stirred up in the river, and she couldn't find the words inside herself that she needed to refuse his request.

Lord Hawthorn's fist clutched something that looked like a small shell.

"Noah, I hold your will within my hand. You must do as I command."

The Lord smiled knowingly. "My orders are: make sure this girl does not renege on our agreement."

"Yes, Your Lordship," Kwesi replied. His voice was plain and monotonous. Tempest realized Lord Hawthorn must have him under some sort of powerful enchantment too.

"Very good," Lord Hawthorn said. "Let the hunt commence!"

The Lord slung his leather bag over his shoulder and marched off into the dark alone, striding through the snow with his pulsing ball of magical light weaving above him.

"*Good riddance,*" Coriel snapped, primping her wet feathers. "*I hope that's the last we see of that pignut.*"

Tempest couldn't agree more. With Kwesi at her side, she watched as the Lord and his magical light faded into the Greenwood Forest. Then, suddenly, full darkness fell around them.

The storm hit soon after that, the snow returning with it. It was as if the bad weather had been waiting for Lord Hawthorn to disappear. Tempest bundled her damp cloak tight around her, stepped to the end of the pier and rang the bell to let Prosper and Marino know where she was.

A flash of light on the far side of the river, like a distant firefly, told her that they had got her message.

The pair wouldn't be able to come and collect her, for there were no other boats nearby on the river. And she wouldn't be able to get back to them, not tonight, in the dark and the storm. But at least they would know she was safe…for now. That was worth something, she supposed, even if they would chide her dearly on her return for taking the boat out against their express instructions. And here she was alone with an unknown boy, in the Greenwood, waiting for the terrifying Lord Hawthorn to return with his quarry.

She glanced at Kwesi shivering beside her. He was standing up straighter. Tempest was sure now that he was here against his will. With Lord Hawthorn gone, his face looked more open and friendly. Tempest didn't have many friends in Tambling. She felt a sudden and odd sort of kinship with him – both of them ensnared by Lord Hawthorn's magic and stuck here in this raging gale, alone in this dangerous, isolated forest.

"Well," Kwesi said at last, "I suppose we'd better make do." He gave her a small grin, as if to say, *Look at us! How on earth did we end up here?* It was the first time Tempest had seen him smile since they'd met that afternoon.

"Come on," she said, as a barrage of icy hail began to pound down around them. "We can wait in the hut."

4

Bread, Cheese and Truths

The hut was little more than a roof and four walls. A simple shelter with a stone fireplace, a table and two chairs, where any wood-collector, forager or charcoal-burner caught this side of the river could shield themselves from the inclement weather.

It was rarely used in the cold months, as no one liked to come to the Greenwood before the ice and snow abated, or, as legend had it, before the last winds of winter were danced away by the Fairies. In the last three months, since the gossip of a wild wolf-boy living in the forest had begun, people were even less inclined to come.

Tempest pushed open the creaking door and she and Kwesi stepped into the cool, dry darkness.

Coriel flew to the mantel and perched there, puffing the water from her red feathered chest and quietly preening.

Hail pounded in the chimney breast, like someone angrily drumming their fingers on a ribcage.

"Make yourself at home," Tempest told Kwesi, hanging her wet cloak on the back of the nearest chair.

"Thank you." Kwesi folded his soaked jacket and placed it over the back of the other chair. His knapsack he put carefully on the table.

They stood warming their hands in their armpits until they could finally feel them again.

Then Tempest busied herself trying to light the fire. There were logs and kindling and dry leaves in the fireplace and a flint and steel in the box under the table. But when Tempest tried to strike the flint to the leaves, she found it damp. A spark would not come.

"Here, let me." Kwesi took the flint and steel from her and crouched by the hearth, striking it a few times. He had more strength in his wrist than her and was able to get a flicker of a spark.

"Come on!" he muttered. "Light, you blasted thing!"

Finally, one of the sparks jumped from flint to leaves, to logs and wood.

Tempest watched as the flames began to lick away happily, spreading into a roaring fire.

Kwesi stood and dusted himself down. "Do you have anything to eat?"

Tempest shook her head. "If I'd known we were going to be staying, I'd have brought something." Her stomach grumbled loudly in agreement.

"You can share my food." Kwesi took a flask and a napkin from his bag. "Molly, my friend, smuggled these to me when she heard I was coming on this trip," he explained, as he neatly unfolded the napkin in the centre of the table. It was full of bread and cheese.

"Thank you," Tempest said. "Who's Molly?" she asked as she broke off a piece of bread.

"Someone who looks out for me," Kwesi answered.

Tempest had many more questions, but at that moment her hunger took precedence and she just ate. The bread tasted a little stale, but it quietened the rumblings in her stomach. The cheese was strong, nutty and delicious. She didn't recognize its flavour, but she gobbled it down, saving a few crumbs for Coriel, when the robin had finished drying herself on the mantel above the roaring fire.

"So, if you're Lord Hawthorn's apprentice," Tempest said to Kwesi as they ate, "was that a magic spell you cast on the flint to light the fire?"

Kwesi laughed. "It was no spell. I can't do magic without my Talisman. Lord Hawthorn has that."

Tempest didn't know what he meant by *Talisman*, and she didn't want to ask, in case he thought her a fool.

But Kwesi saw the frown on her face and told her anyway. "A Talisman is a charm that focuses magic," he explained. "Like a magnifying glass can focus rays from the sun. But it only works if the owner of the Talisman has magical ability in the first place. To cast a spell, the owner must touch their Talisman with their bare hand, or wear it against their skin."

It was strange to hear someone talk about magic so freely and knowledgeably. Tempest was learning a lot today, and the more she heard, the more complicated it sounded. Still, the details intrigued her. She couldn't help herself; she needed to know more.

"Can anything be a magical Talisman?" she asked. "Can anyone do magic with one?"

"Not anyone," Kwesi replied. "Only someone 'Magicborn'. That means someone born with magical ability. And, no, not anything," he replied. "A magical Talisman is crafted for its user by another sorcerer. It's made from an object gifted to them by someone they love, that's usually associated with their ancestors. At least, that's what I've been told and, given my own story, I'm inclined to believe it."

It was a fair amount to take in. Tempest stored the

information away in her head as they finished up the last of the bread and cheese. They washed everything down with mouthfuls of water from Kwesi's flask.

By the time they were done, their coats had dried in the heat of the fire. Kwesi packed everything carefully away, and put on his jacket for warmth. Tempest wrapped herself in her red cloak for comfort. She yawned contentedly. The meal had made her feel tired.

Coriel flapped over and perched on the edge of the table.

"Is it a him or a her, your robin?" Kwesi asked.

"She's a hen." Tempest blinked her eyelids, trying to ward off the heavy feeling of sleep. "Female robins are called hens."

"I like her red chest. Can I feed her?"

Tempest wasn't sure. These were odd circumstances. She couldn't be certain how the little robin would react to a boy they'd just met. "I'm usually the only one she lets do that," she told Kwesi. Though he had asked *very* politely.

"*Can he feed you?*" Tempest asked Coriel.

"*Of course, little waxwing,*" Coriel chirruped, hopping between them.

"Go ahead," Tempest told Kwesi, shrugging off her flutter of nerves.

Kwesi picked a few crumbs from the table and, with some trepidation, offered them up to Coriel in his palm.

Coriel leaped up and perched on his fingertips, pecking at the morsels.

"She likes you," Tempest told Kwesi. "Her name's Coriel. She's been with me since I can remember."

"Hello, Coriel," Kwesi cooed with a soft, tired grin.

"*Hello, little marsh harrier!*" Coriel chirruped back, although only Tempest knew what she was saying.

"So you two can talk?" Kwesi asked.

"We've always been able to," Tempest explained sleepily. "Most people just hear Coriel's chirrups, but I hear her words."

"Who taught you?"

"Perhaps my real mother?" Tempest shrugged. "Or maybe my real father… Who knows? I lost them, but if I ever find them again, I'll ask. I don't remember learning, I just know everything Coriel says."

"*Not that you ever listen, my ruddy duck!*" Coriel twittered, flitting from Kwesi's palm to Tempest's.

"What did she say?" Kwesi asked.

"That I don't listen."

Kwesi laughed. Tempest joined in. All of a sudden, both of their laughs became big yawns.

"I think you're a good listener," Kwesi admitted, hugging his jacket tight around him and shifting uncomfortably in his seat. "It's sad that you don't know your parents. I lost my mama and papa too. They died."

"I'm sorry," Tempest said. She wanted to ask how, for she sensed there was more to his disclosure than he'd revealed, but she could hear the sadness in his voice and she didn't want to pry. Besides, he didn't owe her his story. Nobody owed anybody that. Least of all Kwesi, with the hurt he held in his voice. The Bone Cloud necklace itched against her chest. She pulled it out and hung it over her shirt.

"I promise I won't tell His Lordship about you speaking with your robin." Kwesi sniffed and wiped his nose with a handkerchief from his pocket. "Or about your Talisman."

"My Talisman?" Tempest asked, confused.

"That." Kwesi nodded at the necklace. "It hums with magic. Weakly for me. And Lord Hawthorn probably wouldn't have noticed; he doesn't listen. But for you, that magic must feel strong."

Tempest took the carved Bone Cloud charm in her hand and found Kwesi was right. Now that she was concentrating on it solely and completely, in a way she'd never quite done before, she could feel something. A very soft buzz of energy that echoed in her hand and in the back of her head like a small bee. So her mother's charm was a…Talisman? She could feel that this strange discovery was true, but it threw up so many more questions. Questions about herself and her past, which Tempest knew Kwesi couldn't possibly answer. She was grateful to him anyway. Excitement bubbled in her chest. To think she was the owner of a magical item like that. She turned her Bone Cloud Talisman over and reread the message on its back.

From your mother

She'd mouthed those words a thousand times. They were carved deep into her memory, deeper than they were in the bone. But this time they took on a new significance.

Tempest let the Bone Cloud Talisman drop; felt it bounce light and hard against her chest. Despite its scariness, this trip had been one of discovery. She was learning new and surprising things about her past and future. Things that were beginning to make her view her life in a completely different light.

"What's *your* Talisman?" she asked Kwesi.

"It's a Sunray Shell," Kwesi replied. "Mama gave it to me when I was born. Papa was already gone. He died fighting the slavers when they first assaulted our village."

Kwesi paused and gulped back his sorrow. Tempest felt a shiver of shock run through her. She reached out and gave his hand a soft squeeze, like Marino would sometimes do after her nightmares. She waited patiently for Kwesi to continue, listening carefully, not just to his story but to his body language, and the long silences that seemed to speak of his past as fully as his words did.

"Mama was alone and pregnant with me when the slavers came for a second time," Kwesi said at last. "This time they succeeded. They stole Mama and many others away from our country. Mama tried to fight them like Papa had, but they caught her anyway.

"Later, as she was waiting in chains to be taken aboard the slavers' ship, she saw a glinting shell with a hole in it half-buried on the shoreline of our Akan homeland. It was small and slicked with sand, but Mama heard Papa's voice, along with a chorus of ancestors telling her, '*This is a gift for your son. Pick it up.*'

"As Mama took the shell, its magic hummed in her hand. I kicked inside her and she felt her belly thrum with an energy stronger than she'd ever felt before. Then she knew with certainty I would have great powers, and that the Sunray Shell was destined to be my Talisman.

"A week later, in the hold of the slavers' ship crossing the Atlantic, I was born. My magic means I remember every detail of that terrible night, as well as each small thing Mama told me in the precious little time we had together."

Kwesi stopped and took another shaky breath.

"In the hours after my birth, Mama and I were crammed in beside our countrymen, as a violent storm ravaged the Middle Passage and nearly sank the slavers' ship. Water flooded the lower decks. The ship was listing terribly, and my countrymen and my mother might've drowned. But, just at the moment of my birth, the ship righted itself and everyone survived. The slavers too, unfortunately. When they discovered I had been born during the storm, they wanted to throw me overboard. But because of the Captain's superstitions I was spared.

"The Captain decided I was a good-luck charm since at the moment of my birth, the ship had weathered the storm. So he ordered that I should be kept alive. Mama was not so lucky. She was bleeding heavily and would not last the night."

Kwesi blinked hard, scrunching away tears.

"For a long time Mama battled to remain with me, cradling me in her arms, whispering tales of her and Papa. How they'd met and fallen in love. How Papa had built their house, and brought people together to make a great village.

"Mama was not a sorcerer, but she was an excellent storyteller and her words contained enough magic that night to weave their way into my memory for ever. The last thing she did before she passed was to tie the Sunray Shell around my neck. I felt her soft hands place it gently against my chest. Her fingers pulsed with care and power.

"'I name you Kwesi,' she said. 'This Talisman is a gift from me and your papa, and your many ancestors. Take it and use it to do great things. And when you are old enough, I promise you that your courage and your magic will be the gifts that set you free.'

"Mama smiled at me one last time," Kwesi said sadly, "and then she was gone. I had only just come into the world, in terrible circumstances – the worst a person could suffer, and I had endured a great loss – but I had three great gifts from my parents: my name, a Talisman blessed with love and magic, and my life. I did not yet know it, but such treasures are rare for those born under such terrible ill-fated circumstances. That was twelve summers past, but magic keeps all memories, as curses do hide them."

Tempest was shocked. She had never heard a story tangled with such horror. "I'm so sorry," she said, but the words seemed far from enough to acknowledge his suffering.

"How long has Lord Hawthorn had your Talisman?" she asked.

"Six years. He took it when I became his apprentice. He uses it to control me and steal my power." Kwesi ground his teeth angrily. "No person's life should be owned or controlled by another, nor should their magic. It should be theirs and theirs alone, and they should be free to do with it as they please."

His Lordship was quite the most horrible man, Tempest thought. Though the ship's Captain and the slavers who

Kwesi had encountered after his birth sounded even worse. Then Tempest remembered the cage, and what Lord Hawthorn had said when he'd stepped from the ferry boat. "He's looking for someone out there in the woods, isn't he? Someone else with magical abilities, he can imprison too?" she asked.

Kwesi chewed his lip. He seemed to be deciding whether to tell her the truth or not. Finally he whispered, "It's a Wild Boy."

"A Wild Boy?" Tempest repeated. "You mean the wolf-child the charcoal-burners say first appeared here three months ago? The one the villagers have been gossiping about?" She had thought that gossip a new version of an old woodland wives' tale, but Lord Hawthorn appeared to have heard it too, and it had brought him here, to the Greenwood...

"A week ago, Lord Hawthorn's wife had a vision," Kwesi said. "The vision told her someone with great power had appeared, many, many miles away, in the Greenwood. Then gossip reached Lord Hawthorn that a Wild Boy had been found here. He wants to capture him and make him one of his apprentices at Kensington Palace."

"Kensington Palace!" Tempest sat back in her chair in shock. "So that's where he comes from! What on earth does he do there?"

"He's the Royal Sorcerer to the King," Kwesi said.

"Crikey!" The possibility that someone from the Royal Palace, a place Tempest had only heard about from Prosper and Marino, a place so distant from her life it might as well have been in another world, had come here to the Greenwood was the strangest thought of all. And yet, here they were...the Royal Sorcerer and his apprentice – held against his will.

"I knew Lord Hawthorn *seemed* important," Tempest said. "But I didn't know he was *that* important." She brushed a hand across her face to regain her composure. "That means you're from Kensington Palace too, Kwesi. Surely, in some ways, that must be a good thing?"

"It is not," Kwesi said. "It is a bad thing. Everything at the palace is rotten to the core."

Tempest was shocked by this revelation. She'd never considered that life at the Royal Court might be sour, or rotten, but the strength of Kwesi's words left no room for doubt.

Coriel had finished pecking up the crumbs on his palm and on the table. She flitted to the back of Tempest's chair.

"So you think the Wild Boy would be better off here, in the woods?" Tempest asked.

"It doesn't matter what I think," Kwesi said. "Lord Hawthorn has set his sights on capturing this boy, and he will stop at nothing to do so." He stared into the fire. "I probably shouldn't say this, because I wouldn't wish the Royal Sorcerer's apprenticeship on anyone, but at least if this Wild Boy came to the palace, I'd have a friend with magical abilities like mine. Together, perhaps, we might be able to defeat Lord Hawthorn and help each other get out. I've tried a few times, but I'm not strong enough alone. But with planning, preparation, and a little help, I'm convinced I can make it happen."

It was an understandable hope, Tempest supposed. Though one that she felt would be hard to fulfil. She felt bad for bringing Lord Hawthorn to the Greenwood. He had dazzled her with his money and tricked her with his magic and she hadn't known the extent of his schemes at the time, or that he meant to keep the Wild Boy as an apprentice against his will, just as he'd done to poor Kwesi.

If she'd been more familiar with the forest, and hadn't promised Prosper and Marino not to go there at night, Tempest might've thought about heading off to warn the Wild Boy of the terrible danger he was in. But it was dark out, and she had no tracking skills. Even Coriel wouldn't be able to find the boy on a night like this. They would put themselves in danger too. The best option was to stay where it was warm, in the safety of the hut and hope that the Lord failed to find him.

Tempest ached to learn more about Kwesi's life as the Royal Sorcerer's apprentice, and about the palace, and the rest of his past. But Kwesi had fallen silent, and Tempest didn't want to ask things that weren't hers to ask.

The apprentice boy glanced nervously once more at the shadows in the corner of the room. It was as if he thought Lord Hawthorn was hidden in those dark places, listening, and could step out of the wall at any time.

Now that she'd learned a little more about Lord Hawthorn, Tempest felt as if such things might well be possible. She gave an involuntary shiver.

"I'm tired," Kwesi muttered. "Let's get some rest."

"All right," Tempest agreed.

There were no beds, just the two chairs and a couple of blankets in the box. Tempest fetched them out and placed another log carefully on the fire. She gave one blanket to Kwesi, keeping the other for herself.

Settling back in her seat, she thought about the Wild Boy and his great magical powers. She imagined him running through the woods; Lord Hawthorn hunting him, following his footsteps through the snow. How had such a boy ended up in the Greenwood? What was his history? Prosper had often told her tall stories of stormy children raised by wolves and Fairies. Maybe that was part of the Wild Boy's tale?

Tempest thought about Kwesi losing his father before he was born, and his mother on the slavers' ship, then ending up imprisoned with the hateful Royal Sorcerer. She thought about his hope that a friend with magical abilities might be able to help him escape.

She thought about herself and the mystery surrounding her own life. She talked to Coriel, which was an enchantment that she'd no control over. Did that mean she was more than just an ordinary girl rescued from a river by strangers? Had she been ignoring something that had been there all along? For now, she knew nothing of spells, or magic, or Talismans. Nor how to find out more about them when she was stuck out here in the wilds.

She stared at her companion through half-closed lids. "Night, Kwesi," she whispered. But he was already asleep, breathing heavily. So, after a pause, she said, "*Night, Coriel.*"

"*Goodnight, little dunlin,*" Coriel twittered, hopping onto the chair arm. "*I'll keep an eye out for trouble while you're sleeping.*"

"*Thank you.*" Tempest snuggled beneath her blanket and inched her chair towards the fire.

This was the first time she'd been away from Ferry Keeper's Cottage since she'd arrived there. It was an odd feeling to be spending the night in a hut, a river's width from Prosper and Marino. Especially with a dangerous Royal Sorcerer nearby, hunting for a boy prowling in the woods.

Tempest hoped Lord Hawthorn wouldn't capture the Wild Boy and that he'd be left alone to live in peace and do as he pleased. After all, she said to herself, as she settled down to sleep, not all who wander in the Greenwood are lost. Some are there because they call it home.

Almost Drowning

The Storm Girl was sinking in the depths of the Tambling River.

Her Bone Cloud Talisman floated before her face and her heart thudded in her chest:

Thud!

Thud!

Thud!

Aching for those she'd lost.

Down.

Down.

Down.

She drifted.

Almost drowning.

She flailed her arms in desperation and her red cloak billowed behind her, as she opened her mouth to speak:

"To the rivers, the oceans, the lakes and the sea. Heed my request…"

But the water washed the spell away.

"*Never mind the magic, my little waterlogged partridge!*" twittered a voice far above. "*SWIM! KICK! LIKE YOUR LIFE DEPENDS ON IT!*"

The Storm Girl's lungs ached. Her limbs burned, but the red robin was right. She had to try. She thrashed her legs and windmilled her arms, struggling for the surface.

But the current held her tight in its grip, refusing to let go.

The Dead Lands were closing in. The Storm Girl felt them near. This would be the end of her.

Then a pair of big, heavy, calloused hands grabbed her by the scruff of the neck

and pulled her

up

up

up

dragging her…out!

She broke the surface, choking and gasping for air. As she tumbled free into the light, she coughed, vomiting water, and found herself in the middle of a bright winter's day. Odd. She could've sworn it was night when she'd fallen in.

The hands yanked her over the wet curved side of a boat and were helped by another set. A pair of concerned, new, mystifying voices buzzed around her and she collapsed onto dry boards, surrounded by two sets of heavy boots.

She opened her eyes some moments later to discover that she was in a rowing boat with two strangers, floating in the middle of a sparkling river.

A stout rosy-cheeked man with wrinkles around his green eyes and red hair streaked with strands of white sat holding one oar. Another fellow with greying blond curls sprouting from beneath a tricorn hat held the other. Grave concern filled his blue eyes.

The rosy-cheeked man clucked and gave a helpful, hopeful smile, as hc asked something in a language the Storm Girl wasn't familiar with. The Storm Girl assumed the rosy-cheeked man wanted to know if she was all right, so she nodded and smiled, first to him, and then to the hat-wearing man.

"We saw your robin making a fuss over the water," said the rosy-cheeked man.

"And knew something terrible was afoot," added the hat-wearing man.

The Storm Girl understood nothing they said and did

not respond, but the rosy-cheeked man spoke some more. "Do you speak English?" he asked.

English. The Storm Girl recognized that word. The red robin had said it to her before. It was the language people spoke in England.

"*Coriel!*" she cried in delight to the robin sitting on the gunwale. "*We're not in the Dead Lands, we're in England!*"

"*Didn't I tell you we'd make it, my ringed plover!*" chirruped the red robin proudly. "*Didn't I say we'd escape? My fussing even alerted these humans, who saved you from drowning.*"

Coriel was right. They had made it! Though from where, the Storm Girl couldn't say.

There was somewhere else, another place she'd been and people she'd been with before she'd fallen in the water. Family, not far off, who she couldn't quite remember. She felt that the other place where they were was only a sliver of a distance away. But she'd no idea how to get there, or why she'd left.

She shivered and coughed up more handfuls of water.

The rosy-cheeked man put a blanket round her shoulders. "I'm Marino," he said, touching his hand to his chest. "This is—"

"Prosper," the hat-wearing man interrupted, pointing at himself.

The Storm Girl realized they were telling her their names.

"*Tempest,*" she replied.

Prosper and Marino smiled and nodded at her and then at her little bird.

"*Coriel,*" said the red robin, but Prosper and Marino didn't understand. The Storm Girl thought perhaps this was because of the way words came out differently with birds.

"Let's get you both to safety," Prosper said, and he and Marino took up the oars and rowed the Storm Girl and the red robin across the river, towards a stone house on the far side.

Prosper moored the boat alongside a small pier and Marino climbed out and offered the Storm Girl his hand.

As Prosper clambered onto the pier behind them, he gestured at a grey stone house.

"Our home," he said. "Ferry Keeper's Cottage." He pointed at both of them. "We're the ferry keepers."

The main room of Ferry Keeper's Cottage had a table and chairs, a small double bed, and a fireplace with a pot and trivet and a warm fire burning in the hearth. There was a single window and a door in the rear wall that stood ajar, revealing the edge of a small, dark anteroom beyond.

Marino bustled about and produced some dry clothes from a chest: a heavily patched shirt and grey woollen trousers, which he handed to the Storm Girl. Then he and

Prosper stepped into the other room so that she might change in peace.

The Storm Girl took off her wet things, which seemed to be made of crumbling leaves, and put on the fresh outfit. The sleeves fell over her hands and the trouser legs swamped her feet.

When Marino and Prosper came back in, they stared open-mouthed and giggled.

"I'm afraid they're a bit too big," said Marino, helping her fold back the cuffs and turn up the trousers. "They used to be mine. But perhaps you'll grow into them."

The Storm Girl frowned and stared back at them. She could feel a warmth that radiated between the pair like the sun on a summer's day.

Marino fetched three bowls of bubbling soup from a cauldron over the fire. He placed a bowl down in front of the Storm Girl and one each in front of himself and Prosper.

"Eat up, before it gets cold," he told them.

The Storm Girl snatched up her bowl and tipped the soup into her mouth. It was a broth with chunks of fish and vegetables, hot enough to burn her lips. She finished it quickly in three long, large gulps, and gave a burp.

"Tastes better than river water, doesn't it?" said Marino.

"A lot better!" Prosper laughed.

The Storm Girl didn't understand, but she smiled and

nodded as she fed the red robin a few drops of broth from the end of her finger.

Soon, with the delicious soup in her belly, the warm, dry clothes round her body, and the hot fire on her face, not to mention the earlier terror of the Almost Drowning – the Storm Girl felt tired enough to sleep for a hundred years. She yawned loudly.

"Sleepy?" asked Marino.

Prosper got up and handed her a blanket from the chest. Then he and Marino showed her through to the back room. A small window looked out onto the river and a snug, narrow bed with a straw mattress nestled behind the chimney breast.

"You're welcome to stay here for as long as you need," said Prosper.

"For ever, even, if you like," said Marino.

"Well, at least until we find out where you're from," added Prosper. "And who your family are. Maybe they're farmers upstream?" he suggested. "I might head up to the village and make some enquiries."

The Storm Girl blinked at them both blankly.

"Do you really not understand anything?" Prosper shook his head. "Never mind," he said, waving at the bed. "Get some sleep."

He and Marino left, shutting the door behind them.

The Storm Girl listened for a moment to them clomping about in the next room, then she stepped over to the tiny window and looked out.

"*What do you see, little meadow pipit?*" asked the red robin perched on her shoulder.

"*A wood on the other side of the river,*" answered the Storm Girl.

The sun was setting and the water was orange. So were the bare trees on the far bank.

"*Maybe we come from there?*" the red robin suggested.

"*Maybe we do,*" the Storm Girl agreed.

The two of them had not been alone when they'd tumbled into the water, of that much she was certain. She felt sure whoever had been with them would come and look for her eventually. But more than that she could not say.

She walked over to the bed and put a hand on the straw mattress. Was it to sleep under or in?

"*What am I supposed to do with this?*" she asked.

"*Make a nest in it, I think, my little lapwing,*" replied the red robin.

The Storm Girl climbed into the bed and pulled the blanket over her. She shifted in the straw as the red robin had suggested, until she felt herself sinking comfortably into its warm embrace.

The red robin hopped down beside her and nestled in her hair.

They lay still for a short while like that, until they both fell asleep.

The Storm Girl dreamed of walking in the Greenwood in the spring. Sheets of rain followed in her wake, as if she was making her own weather. Little creatures hidden in the branches and the bracken stared at her with apprehensive eyes, bright yellow as coltsfoot blooms, and the trees and plants bent as she passed as if bowing to a Princess. The Storm Girl trod ancient paths in her dream, searching for a family she knew was out there, but who she'd since entirely forgotten.

5

A Wild Guest

"*Wake, my tufted vetch!*" Coriel shrieked, tapping Tempest's head with her beak. "*Someone's stalking in the Greenwood!*"

Tempest brushed Coriel from her tangle of hair. Her jaw throbbed from grinding her teeth in her sleep and her arms ached from yesterday afternoon's rowing.

She'd been dreaming about the Almost Drowning again, she realized, and her first day with Prosper and Marino in Ferry Keeper's Cottage. But there was more; images lingered in her head, of old paths and odd creatures, blurred and far-off, as if Tempest was looking through the wrong end of a telescope... What was Coriel talking about? Something outside?

Tempest sat up and looked about. She was not in her cosy bedroom at home, as she had supposed, but in the hut. Kwesi was still asleep in the chair beside her, snoring lightly. The cold, grey dawn shadows obscured his face. The hail had stopped and the fire had gone out, but otherwise nothing was out of place.

"*Are you sure someone's outside?*" Tempest asked Coriel.

"*Sure as eggs is eggs,*" Coriel twittered. "*I can feel it in my feathers, little storm bird. By the dog's mercury.*"

"*Maybe it's Lord Hawthorn?*" Tempest suggested.

"*What are you waiting for then?*" Coriel landed on her blanket. "*An army of weasels to back you up?*" She pattered fearfully across the hills and valleys of Tempest's knees. "*Go to the window and see what that scabious man's doing!*"

"*All right. All right.*" Tempest sighed.

Mustering her meagre supply of courage, she brushed the blanket aside and crept to the window. Coriel swooped ahead and pressed her tiny beak to the glass. "*No sign of the pignut, my house martin. We must've been wrong.*"

Tempest wiped away the condensation and stared out. Coriel was right, the clearing *was* empty. A near-full moon stared down from the sky, pale as a peeled apple, its ghostly face fading in the dawn light behind the far trees.

Tempest was relieved Lord Hawthorn hadn't returned. A part of her hoped he'd been eaten by wolves. She was about to go back to her chair when she got the sudden and unaccountable sensation that someone was watching her.

"*What's the matter, little fulmar?*" Coriel whispered.

"*There is something out there,*" Tempest said. "*I can feel its eyes on me.*"

"*Bedstraw and hogweed, my pied wagtail,*" Coriel said. "*It's my ragged-robin talk that frightened you. I was cracked as broken eggshells to think—*"

"*No,*" Tempest interrupted. "*You were right. Look.*" She pointed to the shadows of the farthest fir tree, where a pair of dark shining eyes were fixed on the hut.

"*Knotted knapweeds!*" Coriel said. "*What is that?*"

Tempest wasn't sure. Her pulse pounded like a stormy sea in the confines of her chest.

"*Should we wake Kwesi?*" Coriel asked nervously.

"*Not yet,*" Tempest said. She wasn't sure who the eyes belonged to, but something in her heart told her she must face their owner alone. The eyes blinked. The creature must've realized it had been spotted for, within seconds, it had disappeared.

"*Great black horehounds!*" Coriel gasped. "*It saw you!*"

"*Or you.*" Tempest shrank from the window, hiding her face in the shadows.

Coriel hopped onto Tempest's head and paced anxiously through her tangled hair, her tiny claws pricking into

Tempest's skull as she stared through the glass from her new vantage point. "*It can't possibly have seen me, little grebe. I'm small as a walnut husk.*"

"'*Course it's seen you, Coriel. Your belly's bright as a red berry.*"

"*Scarlet waxcaps!*" Coriel muttered. "*Where's it gone?*"

For a while they saw nothing, then a snout emerged from the far side of the fir tree, and a wolf bounded from the woods. Its body was small, but it looked strong and confident in its gait.

Ducking beneath a tree limb, it slunk across the clearing. As it stepped from the shadows and approached the hut, its shape changed.

Soon it was no longer a wolf at all, but a boy.

A boy moving on all fours wearing a wolf-skin coat.

"*Hound's tongue and dog roses!*" Coriel twittered from atop Tempest's head. "*The Wild Boy!*"

"*So it is.*" Tempest pinched herself to check she wasn't still dreaming. She peered at the Wild Boy, and then over her shoulder at Kwesi, who was still dozing in his seat.

When she glanced back through the window, the Wild Boy was standing up straight on two legs. The wind ruffled his fur coat. A single wolf's-tooth button was pinned to the neck, clasping it shut. Beneath it he wore tattered clothes, patched together like the leafy green canopy of a tree. His arms dangled down by his side. As he raised them, his front paws uncurled into hands and pushed back his hood, revealing a head of curly black locks.

In a leap and a bound, he was at the hut door. Tempest half-expected him to knock, but instead he scratched his fingers across the wood and whined softly.

Before she knew it, she had clasped her red cloak tight around herself and stepped forward to open the door for him.

"Welcome," she said softly.

"*Squinancywort and bugloss!*" Coriel cried, alighting nervously on her ear. "*You're supposed to keep the wolf from the door, little redstart. Not welcome him in! Doesn't matter that he's boy-shaped now, for all you know, he might be angry enough to huff and puff and blow the hut down!*"

The Wild Boy stepped through the door into the hut. His face was smeared with mud and mottled from the cold. Beneath his loose dark curls, his bright inquisitive eyes took in the room. Tempest's heart leaped. He'd one blue eye and one green one, like hers. "Don't be scared," she whispered. "We don't want to hurt you. We want to help."

The Wild Boy hadn't understood. She tried to take his hand, but he backed away, startled, furrowing his brow and pinching his lips.

It was a familiar expression, though Tempest couldn't

say why. She spoke again, quietly, so as not to frighten him or wake Kwesi. "A Lord from the city is searching for you. He wants to take you away."

The Wild Boy said nothing, merely growled. His coat stank as if it was alive.

"*What's wrong with him, Tempest, my rock dove?*" Coriel asked.

"*I don't know,*" Tempest admitted. "*I don't think he knows English, Coriel.*"

"*I understand you now, Storm Girl,*" the boy said. "*And you, red robin. And I am* not *angry enough to huff and puff and blow the hut down!*"

Tempest gave a surprised gasp. She stared at the boy. He could speak their language, and he knew her and Coriel's nicknames! Could he be from their past? But, if that were the case, she'd remember him, surely? And Coriel would too. After all, the little robin had been with Tempest in her old life.

"*Did you say 'English' before?*" the Wild Boy asked. "*Is that what you speak?*" He laughed through his teeth. "*Greenwood save us! This isn't the Dead Lands. It's England!*"

Dead Lands...there had been something about the Dead Lands in Tempest's dream, but she couldn't quite remember what. She noticed a charm around the Wild Boy's neck. An eye-shaped hag stone with a hole through its centre, threaded onto a leather necklace. Could it be a Talisman? One thing was certain. The Wild Boy *was* magic. For he had stepped from the woods a wolf and through the hut door a boy.

Tempest touched the Bone Cloud Talisman round her neck and felt the soft hum of it beneath her red cloak. She wanted to show it to him, but she couldn't make herself. She lacked trust in him. And yet, he seemed so familiar. The colour of his eyes, the shape of his face, the way he shifted from leg to leg as if he didn't quite belong in this world. He was her opposite. Her reflection. She felt like day looking in the mirror and finding night.

"*A Royal Sorcerer is looking for you,*" she warned again. "*He plans to take you away.*"

"*He's a terrible man,*" Coriel added. "*A thin gutweed of a fellow. But powerful. We advise you to go far away from here, little stonechat, before he returns.*"

"*I smelled such a man,*" the Wild Boy said. "*Creeping between the trees. He smells of death.*"

"*Doesn't he, though,*" Coriel agreed. "*He has cruel intentions. Stinks of them like a stinkhorn fungus!*"

"*He's gone now, red robin,*" the Wild Boy crowed. "*I lost him deep in the woods. He thinks I'm still a wolf.*"

Tempest felt a sliver of relief at this news. But still, she wondered how the Wild Boy knew hers and Coriel's secret nicknames. And how he spoke their private language... She'd yet to learn his own name, but the more they spoke, the more certain she was they'd known each other in her past, that place which only existed as a blurred muddle inside her head. She needed to find out more at once, and to impress on him the desperate danger he would be in when Lord Hawthorn returned.

6

Riverside Revelations

"*You knew our secret nicknames*," Tempest insisted. "*The ones we used to have for each other: Storm Girl and red robin. Tempest and Coriel are what we're really named. What are you called?*"

"*I don't recall*," the boy replied, shaking his head and his curly black locks.

"*Why not, little snow bunting?*" Coriel asked.

The Wild Boy shrugged. "*I just don't.*" He didn't seem to find it strange to be talking to a bird. "*I've been flickering between forms like a candle flame for three full moons. Sometimes wolf, sometimes boy. Because of that, I don't recollect much of anything.*"

Tempest's heart jumped. Missing memories: it was

another similarity between them. Since the day Prosper and Marino had pulled her from the river, Tempest remembered nothing of her own past. But, facing the Wild Boy, she felt sure a part of it was standing here before her. If the Wild Boy couldn't remember his name, perhaps she could?

"*Why don't we guess what you're called?*" she suggested. "*You could say which name feels right.*"

"*All right,*" the boy replied.

Tempest considered what sort of name he might have. She needed one that sounded like it belonged to him. She scratched her head, but could think of nothing. Just to try felt overwhelming. But she was sure his name was somewhere in the back of her mind. Was it John, Paul, George, or Richard? None of those sounded right. Coriel could see Tempest struggling.

"*How about Robin, my little grey partridge?*" she suggested. "*Could he be called Robin?*"

Tempest wrinkled her nose. "*I don't think so, Coriel. That doesn't sound right.*"

"*It doesn't,*" the Wild Boy agreed. He'd just noticed Kwesi sleeping in the chair. "*Who's this?*" he asked, leaning towards him.

"*Kwesi,*" Tempest said.

The Wild Boy straightened up. The hag stone round his neck glinted.

They mirrored each other in their eyes, Tempest realized, but maybe also in their temperaments. Like his stone he was craggy and wild, and she too was stormy and wild. But beneath this, there was a certainty that they could also be strong and steady. She felt it."*Your name might be Thomas. It means twin in ancient tongues.*" He smiled. "*I like this name,*" he said. "*It does feel like it might be mine. Good guessing...I think.*"

Tempest was about to reply, when Kwesi sat up in his seat. "Who are you talking to?" he demanded woozily. "I heard a stranger's voice." Rubbing the sleep from his eyes, he blinked them open. "Crikey!" he cried, jumping to his feet. "It's the boy!"

"His name's Thomas," Tempest said. "That's what we've decided."

"Lord Hawthorn's looking for you," Kwesi warned the Wild Boy. "You won't be safe around us."

"*Kwesi is apprentice to Lord Hawthorn,*" Tempest explained to Thomas. "*The Royal Sorcerer.*"

"*The man you keep saying wants to capture me?*" Thomas asked. He seemed rather calm about it, Tempest thought, considering the warnings she'd given, and the danger Lord Hawthorn posed.

"He'll be back soon," Kwesi warned. "You should tell Thomas to go, if he values his freed—"

But that was all he was able to say. For, as if he'd been

magically summoned, suddenly there was Lord Hawthorn. He appeared stealthily in the doorway like a shadow looming large from darkness when a candle flicks across a wall.

"You've captured my Wild Boy!" he cried in delight, and he crossed the wide space between them in the blink of an eye and snatched up Thomas's Hag Stone Talisman. As Lord Hawthorn ripped the Talisman from around Thomas's neck, Tempest glimpsed a message engraved on its underside:

From your mother

The same words that were written on her Bone Cloud. She gasped. Who was Thomas? What was their connection…? But she'd no time to wonder further, for Lord Hawthorn was clutching Thomas's Talisman in his palm and whispering a spell over it:

"Bind and tie, make him cower. Hold his will within my power."

Lord Hawthorn squeezed the Hag Stone hard, pushing his magic into it with his fist, and Thomas screamed and doubled over, as if he was being crushed. "Quiet!" Lord Hawthorn admonished. "You're coming with me." He grabbed Thomas's arm and wrestled him out into the snow.

"*Stop him, my swift!*" Coriel cawed, swooping off after them.

Tempest and Kwesi scrambled for the door. Outside, Lord Hawthorn was dragging Thomas through the snow. Thomas put up a good fight, but he couldn't win. Lord Hawthorn was stronger, and he had Thomas's Talisman.

"*What's the plan, little kingfisher?*" Coriel twittered.

"What should we do?" Tempest asked Kwesi as they raced across the clearing.

"I can't do anything," Kwesi said. "Lord Hawthorn has me in his power. But you can resist his hold. Focus on your Talisman. Use your magic."

Did she really possess magic? Proper spell magic? Tempest's thoughts trailed off like creeper fronds. She had no plan. No spell was coming. Maybe if she just shouted?

"LEAVE HIM ALONE!" she screamed at the top of her voice. Reaching Lord Hawthorn, she pounded his back with her fists.

Kwesi joined her, his mouth agape at his own audacity.

Still grasping Thomas in one arm, Lord Hawthorn turned and muttered a spell at them:

"Cease, desist, begone, beware. Sling my assailants over there."

He waved his free hand and Tempest and Kwesi flew backwards and landed with a puff of snow in a heap on the far side of the clearing. By the time they'd stood and dusted themselves down, Lord Hawthorn had already opened the cage and wrestled Thomas into it. He slammed the door shut, muttering a Locking Spell to make it unbreakable:

"Lock tight. Strength and might."

"*Tempest! Kwesi! Coriel!*" Thomas screamed. "*Save me!*"

But Lord Hawthorn was chanting again:

"Slender bars. Silver-bright. Weigh nothing. Be light."

He picked up the cage as if it and Thomas were mere feathers and marched with it out along the pier.

They had to do something. Tempest took Kwesi's hand and they darted towards Lord Hawthorn, who was stowing the caged Thomas in *Nixie*'s stern.

"NO!" Tempest shouted, her voice hoarse and shaking. "You're not taking him!"

Thud! Thud! Thud! went the Bone Cloud Talisman against her chest. She felt the power that buzzed through it pulsing stronger and stronger. Energy began breaking free from somewhere deep inside. It fizzed through her hair and arced from her fingertips.

"Careful!" Kwesi warned, snatching his hand away from hers.

Tempest felt her power surge inside her. A haze of burning words filled her head, tripping off her tongue like molten gold:

"Tide rise. Clouds gather. Floods come. Rain batter!"

Plumes of icy water rose in columns as high as the sky

and splashed over *Nixie*'s prow, soaking Lord Hawthorn and knocking him sideways. Kwesi gasped. Thomas stopped rattling the bars of the cage. Tempest's mouth fell open.

Had *she* done *that*?

"You!" Lord Hawthorn cried in startled surprise. "You're magic!"

A flash of pain broke in Tempest's temple and thundered through her body like a tidal wave. Sweat poured from her brow. Heat radiated off her, melting the snow on the pier.

She stepped towards Lord Hawthorn and the icy waves rose around him again, writhing and frothing, until she could no longer control them.

Tempest swayed, clutching the humming Bone Cloud Talisman, trying to direct the magical storm inside her outwards. But it was too strong...

"Focus your magic!" Kwesi warned. "Or the blast could knock us all out!"

Lord Hawthorn was turning away, muttering words, fighting the tidal waves and the storm. It wouldn't take much to overwhelm him. She needed one more surge of power.

But she couldn't find it.

There was nothing left to hold onto.

No stillness. No anchor. No focus.

"*Coriel!*" she wailed in a frightened voice. "*What's happening to me?*"

Coriel flitted in agitated circles. "*I don't know, little turnstone!*"

Tempest's head spun dizzily. She threw her arms wide for balance, but the world had other ideas.

The hut and pier and river tipped sideways. Water gushed through the forest. Trees waved their branches and leaped into the sky as if their roots were on fire. And Tempest fell…

down,

down,

down…

Until her head pounded the ground, and…

everything went **black**.

Naming Day

On a Fair Isle, in the Greenwood, on the first day of spring, a newborn baby boy and girl lay side by side on a blood-red blanket in a crib of bulrushes. Their arms and legs entwined as they slept together beneath a great ancient oak tree called the Heart of the Forest, whose five lofty limbs clutched at the sky.

The baby boy had curly black locks. His face was as smooth as a worn pebble and as still as a shadowy pool. His right green eye and his left blue one flickered with concentration. Wild unreadable thoughts swam in their depths like rainbow-coloured fish.

The baby girl was his opposite, his twin, the day to his night. She had a face as proud as the river and a nose as sharp as flint. Clouds of feeling clashed like a thunderstorm behind her right blue eye and her left green one, as if there was a squall of emotion whirling inside her that never ceased.

Behind the crib, on a throne of branches, sat a silver lady wearing a high crown of stag antlers, bird wings, briar twigs and green shoots. She was the Fairy Queen and the twins' mother. She wore a silver necklace threaded with a single golden leaf and a cape sewn from fronds of ivy, spotted with wild flowers.

Beyond the bower stood a palatial Throne Room that was both indoors and out at the same time. Weeds and mushrooms grew between the cracked floor slates. Windows cut through thicket walls. Trees held up a canopy of leaves, through which dappled sunlight seeped. Guests fair and foul, with tree-bark skin, deer-snout noses, ram's-horn ears, bird-feather hair and furry eyebrows milled about.

A black raven was sitting on the shoulder of a woman in a voluminous red dress with writhing silver briar-bush hair. The woman wore a white diamond brooch at her breast, and looked so like the Queen she could only be her sister. She watched the two babies with intent.

"Your Majesty," she said, in a sing-song voice, plucking a single bloom from the roof canopy. "This flower marks the first day of spring, which means tonight's full moon marks the end of winter."

The guests in that hallowed hall cheered.

"It is also the naming ceremony of your twins," the Queen's sister continued, dipping the flower into a crystal pool of water in the bowl of an old tree stump. "May the Greenwood bless them."

She handed the flower to the Queen, who took the bloom and poured a drop of water from each petal onto the heads of her two children, anointing them.

"I name you Tempest," said the Queen as she sprinkled the water over the baby girl. "My Storm Girl. My wild sky. My daughter of the water."

The Queen took out a charm necklace with a piece of bone carved into the shape of a cloud and engraved with three words:

From your mother

"I gift you this Bone Cloud Talisman," she said as she hung the necklace round the baby girl's neck.

The baby girl gurgled and cried in reply.

Next, the Queen turned to the baby boy.

"I name you Thomas," she said as she sprinkled the water over his head. "My Wild Boy. My Twin. My ragged rock. My son of the sun."

She took out a second charm necklace. A hag stone

carved into the almond shape of an eye, engraved with the same three words as his sister's gift.

"I give you this Hag Stone Talisman," said the Queen as she hung the necklace round the baby boy's neck.

The baby boy stayed silent. Inside he felt calm, but his mama had said he was her wild son of the sun, so that is what he supposed he must be.

Finally, to both her children, the Queen said, "This palace, this garden, this green wood, this river, will be your home. In this magical realm, you are welcome, now and always...until the end. May the blessings of the Fair Isle be upon you. May the trees and the mountains, the woodlands, the streams, the oceans and the untamed world be with you both, from this moment and for ever."

The watching guests cheered and threw their dried flower petals in the air, until there was an abundance of falling blossoms and it felt like all the blooms of spring had come early.

When the last dried petal hit the ground, the crickets in the tree canopy of the palace's roof struck up a chirping tune, the birds joining them with trills. The frogs and toads among the rocks and shingle added their croaking to the serenade.

Then, with toothy smiles, open jaws, hands clapping, fingers clicking and claws beating time to the music, the guests made merry and danced. Even the Queen joined them.

In between each reel and jig, the Fairies of the court queued to pay their respects to the newborn twins. Soon the line was so long it stretched out the door, around the pool and into the Greenwood beyond. As each Lord or Lady approached the twins' bower, their name was called out by Hoglet, a tiny man with hedgehog spines, who spoke with a deep booming voice that was larger than he was.

"Her Grace, Lady Primrose Cowslip – Baroness of the Midge Marshes. Madam Angelica Hogsweed – First Lady of the Periwinkles. His Grace, Lord Mayfly-Peasmould – Earl of Walnut Husk. Her Grace, Lady Holly-Blue – Countess of Bedstraw. Sir Argus Firebrat – Knight of the Order of the Dung Beetle."

The twins soon tired of meeting new people. No matter that they were polite, it was too much to take in. They felt like bursting into tears.

Finally a tiny robin with an apron of red feathers perched on the edge of their crib.

"Thank you for receiving me, my little sedge warblers," she trilled. "My name is Coriel, and I'm the right-hand bird to your mother. I bring you many feathered blessings. May your plumage be bright, your song clear, your flight true and your nests without thorns."

The twins beamed at the red robin. Neither of them could form the words to reply, but they understood the tone of love her chirrups contained and were filled with joy. The robin puffed her feathers gratefully in return. She was supposed to leave then, having said her piece, but something stopped her.

Another grand announcement by Hoglet.

"Her Grace, Lady Hawthorn, Duchess of Stalactite and Stalagmite. His Grace, Sir Auberon Raven, Lord High Commander of Birds."

The robin hid in the crib and watched the Queen's sister approach, her hair a tangle of writhing, living twigs and hawthorn branches.

"Look at these two darlings," the Queen's sister cooed, stroking both twins under their chubby chins with a long pale finger. The white diamond brooch pinned to her chest flashed in the moonlight.

"Do you know," she told the twins, "today is my Naming Day too. And your mother's. Everyone's, in fact. We are all one hundred and twenty years old! That's how long it's been since the Fairy Kingdom was last born anew."

"Are you telling them a story?" the black raven asked, alighting on her shoulder. "I'm sure they love stories. Aren't they the most precious, perfect little lambs, Milady? I'm so glad they're safe here."

The Queen's sister laughed. "How very thoughtful of you, Auberon."

"Consider what terrible dangers could befall them in other worlds," cawed the raven. "Or what trials they might face, if they *accidentally* took your place in thirteen years' time, at the next appeasing of the Hundred-and-Thirty-Three-Year Curse." He paused and looked at her meaningfully, one beady eye open, one closed in a raven's wink. "Maybe then you could be free?"

"Auberon!" The Queen's sister laughed. "What a suggestion! To seal the fate of the Queen's own children like that! Two such lovely babies. Anyway, we cannot change the Curse. What is written on the tree is what must be."

"It would only require one small alteration, Milady," croaked the raven. "Hardly a change at all. And memories are short in Fairyland. Years hence, no one would even remember what the Curse originally said." He foraged with his beak under a wing, plucking thoughtfully at his feathers. "But, why worry? That's still many moons away. I feel sure, by then, the Fates will have lent you a hand. Though, there's no harm in helping them."

"Perhaps you're right," said the Queen's sister. "It is better we assist in shaping events."

She stepped to the back of the bower, where something was carved into the tree's trunk.

As she passed her hand over it, it lit up, revealing a strange and terrible Curse.

"At the chiming of the thirteenth hour,
At the plucking of the thirteenth flower,
On the hundred-and-thirty-third Naming Day...
In the Greenwood Forest,
By the Tambling River,
On the Stepping Bones...
The Queen will sacrifice a life
Of a single sister
Born in strife
And given to her as kith and kin.
To save her Royal soul and skin,
She'll cry cold and bitter tears,
But will rule Fairyland for a hundred-and-thirty-three more years..."

While the raven kept a lookout, the Queen's sister touched one hand to her brooch and the other to the Curse. Then she whispered a Deception Spell.

"Trick and scheme. Save my skin. Make the bearer of this curse a twin."

Stealthily, the red robin swooped over to the tree trunk to see what she had done.

When the little bird read the Curse, she ruffled her feathers in shock. A single word in it had been altered: ***sister*** had become ***twin***.

And with it, the fate of the two babies was sealed.

A worried look came into the red robin's eyes. She flitted back to the crib and whispered through her beak, "Awful tidings, little puffins. They have changed the Curse! She changed it! A terrible thing will happen to you. On your thirteenth Naming Day, one of you will—"

But that was all she was able to reveal, for the Queen's sister and the raven had returned to the crib. And when the Queen's sister heard the red robin tweeting her secret to the babies, she quickly cast a second spell:

"Sticky beak. Never tell. Keep my secret dark withheld."

The Fairy Queen returned from mingling with her guests. The red robin flew at once to her shoulder and tried to tell her of her sister's deception, but found she could not. As the Queen stepped towards the crib, her sister spoke quietly, pointing a single finger at her back and casting a third spell.

"The Curse is changed. You'll never know. The truth is lost. The lie will grow."

Then the Queen's sister and her raven returned to the party, leaving the red robin twittering madly at the Queen, unable to tell her the truth.

The Queen grew so frustrated with the little bird that she swept her up into the air with an angry flick of her wrist. "Don't chirrup at me so, Coriel!" she admonished. "I've had a long day and need some peace and quiet."

The little red robin flitted to a nearby branch and had to watch as the Queen scooped up the baby boy and girl and took them to a corner, far, far away from the madding crowd, so that she could nurse them in private and in peace.

Cradled in his mother's arms, the baby boy wondered what the red robin had been trying to tell them. But he soon lost track of those thoughts as he tasted his mother's warm milk. Then the long day and the guests and everything the Queen's sister and her raven had said and most especially the warning from the red robin all slipped from his mind, like a blanket falling on the nursery floor, and were forgotten.

By the time the baby boy and girl were full of milk and sleeping peacefully, the full moon had risen high in their nursery window. Then the Fairy Queen returned the babies to their crib and floated off to join the Fairy Court, dancing in the end of winter and the start of spring.

7

Capital City

Tempest dreamed she was in a grand old oak tree. Her mother was standing at the base of the trunk looking up. All around her was a terrifying party filled with dancing creatures who raged ever onwards.

"Come down," her mother said, her face masked by waving leaves.

Tempest tried to climb towards her, but no matter how far or how fast she descended the tree, her mother didn't seem to get any closer. Then, suddenly, Thomas the Wild Boy was there beside her, swinging from a branch and kicking his feet in the air.

She woke giddy and elated, gasping for breath, and

ragged and empty inside.

She'd done magic by the river, she remembered, and then she'd fainted. She hurt horribly, as if her organs had been scooped out, jumbled, and put back in tatters, and her brain had been pierced by a shard of lightning.

Hard iron strips pressed into her back. Her head throbbed and her limbs felt numb, and she didn't know if it was the magic or the dream that had caused such feelings. She rubbed her face and anxiously opened her eyes.

She was crammed with Thomas into the cage, strapped to the top of Lord Hawthorn's carriage, careening along a foggy road, and over potholes that made her bones rattle like the oars in *Nixie*'s oarlocks.

Tempest stared around. Through the bars, she could see the broad back of the coachman covered in his warm cloak, driving the horses onwards at a fast pace. Kwesi was huddled next to him, hugging his arms and shivering in his thin blue-and-gold jacket. Tempest assumed sitting up top was his punishment for disobeying Lord Hawthorn.

"You're awake!" Thomas said, shakily. He was curled up, trembling in his fur coat on her far side.

"*Thank the Greenwoods!*" Coriel cried, popping her head up from where she was nestled in Thomas's hood. "*We were so worried! You looked sick as a guillemot that's guzzled a bad guppy!*"

"*Coriel, you're with Thomas!*" Tempest said, in shock. "And, Thomas, you spoke English!"

Kwesi turned in his seat and spoke secretly to them. "I taught Thomas some phrases while you were passed out," he explained in a whisper. "He's been teaching me some of your language too. *Haven't you, Thomas?*"

"A few words," Thomas said in English. "*You've been sleeping a long time,*" he explained to Tempest in their own language, as she rubbed her aching head.

Coriel hopped from Thomas's shoulder onto Tempest's, squishing her beak into her red feathery breast to guard against the cold. "*That old toad rush, Lord Hawthorn, caged you with Thomas and rowed back across the river,*" she chirruped. "*Then he moored* Nixie *behind the tumbledown bridge.*"

"*He summoned a fog to hide us while he called the coachman,*" Thomas added.

More sorcery! Tempest had managed to cast one spell and it had knocked her unconscious. Lord Hawthorn had to be very strong to do so much magic with such precious few consequences. But then he was the Royal Sorcerer, she supposed. To have got that position, he must be more powerful than most.

"*That pair of bogbeans drove off so fast with you both in the magicked cage,*" Coriel added, flapping to Tempest's ear, "*I hadn't time to fetch Prosper or Marino. And I couldn't leave you,*

Tempest, my little shelduck…not when I didn't know where you were going."

Tempest was relieved no one else was hurt, but Prosper and Marino would be so worried when they found out she was gone. She imagined them searching the river and woods for her. They'd have no idea she'd been taken by Lord Hawthorn, so how would they stand any chance of finding her? She felt terrible.

She put her fingers through the cage bars and covertly tapped Kwesi's back. He turned slightly, listening, and Tempest crawled close enough to whisper through the bars so he could hear. "Where are we going?"

"Kensington Palace. Home to King George," Kwesi replied, just loud enough for Tempest to make out what he was saying over the creak and jangle of the coach, but not loud enough so the coachman would hear.

"Ken-sing-ton Pall-lace," Thomas mumbled, tasting each of these new English syllables as if it was a ripe berry. "*Who's King George?*" he asked.

"*The ruler of England,*" Tempest answered. "What'll happen to us there?" she asked Kwesi.

"Oh, I imagine Lord Hawthorn has plans for you," Kwesi replied with a shudder.

"Plans?" Thomas parroted with a frown of incomprehension.

Tempest didn't like the sound of that. Maybe her magic could protect them? If she could learn to use her Talisman… She clutched at her neck, feeling for the buzz of the Bone Cloud charm beneath her cloak, but it wasn't there. A lurch of panic shot through her.

"Lord Hawthorn has it," Kwesi said. "And Thomas's Hag Stone Talisman. There's no way for either of you to escape him. He'll take your magic and use it for his own ends, just like he did with me."

Tempest felt in the pocket of her cloak for the coins, but they were gone too.

"*He took those as well, my little redstart,*" Coriel twittered.

The crook! Tempest's hands were still scrabbling around in her pocket when she found something else. Small and lumpy and carved from wood. She took it out.

Thomas's eyes widened with interest when he saw what it was. The three painted figures in their little wooden boat. Tempest's one gift from Prosper and Marino. Thank the Greenwood she still had that! Lord Hawthorn probably thought it had no value. But it did to her.

Tempest put the boat in her lap so that the three figures looked like they were rowing across the red river of her cloak. She imagined Prosper carving the wood, and Marino painting the boat. And remembered what they had said to her on the day they had given her their gift.

"If you have to go away for any reason, you'll have it to remember us by."

Tempest longed for them now. She treasured their memory along with their gift. It was given with love, and it was the only thing, apart from Coriel and her new-found friends, that was keeping her from being overwhelmed by despair.

By evening, the carriage had slowed and the wind dulled its bluster. Along the roadside the snow was melting, exposing patches of mud. Tempest felt exhausted. A cold hard tiredness had seeped into her bones from the whirl of the journey, the burn of the magic and her constant chattering fears.

Her belly ached and her mouth felt dry with thirst. She licked her chapped lips. Thomas's stomach grumbled. Up front, Kwesi was also holding his tummy in hunger. Coriel chirruped agitatedly in Tempest's ear.

Soon squares of light rolled by, candles in windows, twinkling like stars. Thousands of them.

Tempest realized they were in a city.

"London," Kwesi called back at them, above the noise.

"Lun-Dun," Thomas repeated, copying Kwesi's English.

"That's right!" Tempest said, smiling at him. Despite the

scariness of their situation, Thomas was learning fast, recognizing words just as she'd done when she'd first arrived in Tambling. Funny to think, she hadn't recalled learning to speak so quickly until this moment. The memory made her even more certain that there was some deep bond between herself and Thomas.

She looked around, taking in the view. She'd never been to the capital city before, but she'd heard about it from Prosper and Marino, who'd both lived in London when they were young. Prosper had talked of the docks and piers and boats and the raucous fish markets. And the many different people from all over the world he'd met while working as a Thames ferryman. Marino had spoken of the smart squares, stone monuments, and the magnificent cathedral he'd glimpsed while running errands as a household servant.

They'd met because Prosper ferried Marino across the Thames every day. They had fallen in love with life on the river and with each other. So they'd come back to Tambling together, and Ferry Keeper's Cottage where Prosper had grown up.

If Prosper and Marino had been here with Tempest under different circumstances they could've shown her round the city where they'd found each other. But they were not. Tempest was lost and scared in the dark, in a cage with Coriel and Thomas, somewhere in the middle of the city.

Soon they swept along a road as wide as a river, which was crowded with carriages. Bridles jingled, horses neighed and hay, rubbish and snow filled the gutters. In any other circumstance, Tempest would've been excited by the activity but her dread pushed all that aside. She jigged about, worry churning inside her. The sights and sounds coursed past in a gale.

A few roadside peddlers stood in the cold selling unfamiliar-smelling food. A handful of people walked the street. A lamplighter with a flame on a long stick lit lanterns on poles along the pavement. Tempest tried shouting to them, but her voice was hoarse and tired and barely reached beyond the bars. Thomas shouted too and rattled the cage door. But no one seemed to notice.

"Can't they see?" Tempest cried, in despair. "Can't they hear us?"

"The cage is cloaked in an enchantment that makes it invisible," Kwesi replied over his shoulder. "Only people who know it's there can see it, or who's inside."

So that was the trick – more magic. And it meant no one would come to their rescue.

The carriage turned down an imposing avenue. One side of the road was filled with grand houses and bright windows, the other was a park of tall trees, gauzed in fog.

Suddenly, a pair of heavy scrolled-iron gates loomed

from the mist. A guard in a red uniform with a black hat saluted the carriage and opened the gates to let them pass.

As they rattled down a long driveway, Tempest glimpsed silhouetted trees and high stone walls.

In the distance, a spiky dark shape reared against the skyline, its high crenellated roof was peppered with chimney stacks and squat windows, whose panes glinted in the moonlight like precious jewels set in a crown. Kensington Palace…it must be!

Tempest anxiously turned the little wooden ferry boat with its three painted figures over in her hands. She felt adrift in a stream of uncertainty. Unsure of what to do next, or where to turn; trapped in a strong current she had no control over, with no way out.

She wished that the two ferry keepers were here with her, to help her face whatever came next. Marino so calm and collected, Prosper so sure of the right thing to do. In her whole life, she realized, she had never missed her home more. She had Coriel though, and Kwesi and Thomas too. She put a shaking hand on Thomas's arm and smiled to cover the twitching butterflies in her stomach.

Spring Spells

The years ran like rabbits in the Greenwood, and the Wild Boy and the Storm Girl grew from babes to toddlers, into walkers, then runners. They raced everywhere together, skipping and jumping and cartwheeling through the forest and around the edges of the Fair Isle.

They were growing constantly. Their clothes, sewn from leaves and cobwebs and magic, had to be replaced each season. One thing did stay the same, however: the necklaces their mother had gifted them. They wore those Talismans everywhere, never taking them off.

Every year at the start of spring, the twins would each pick a flower as a memento of their first Naming Day. Their mother would keep these flowers pressed in a book. "One bright bloom for each bright year of your life," she would say, when she got it out to show them.

The rest of the time she was cold and distant. She kept out of their way and never played with them in their nursery. She never ate dinner with them in the palace in the evenings, nor walked with them by the river in the day, nor climbed trees with them in the forest at sunrise, nor swam with them in the pool at sunset. Mostly she was away, busy with her queenly duties, and when she wasn't she seemed to want to keep her twins at arm's length.

Luckily, the red robin was more motherly, and looked after them instead. Whenever they went exploring, the little robin would tag along and tell them stories of their first Naming Day and how special it was.

"So much pomp and pageantry, my puffins, so many Fairies and sprites and animals, visiting from near and far... So many worthy gifts brought for you two beautiful baby-chicks in your nest. Such dancing in the ballroom, under stars and over stone, such gaiety at your naming, and the burgeoning of the first blossoms."

But the thing the Wild Boy remembered most from that golden afternoon was the robin's warning, even though she'd never mentioned it to them again:

A terrible thing will happen to you on your thirteenth Naming Day.

"What did you mean by that?" the Wild Boy would ask.

"Oh nothing, my gorgeous greylag geese," the red robin would reply, twitching uncomfortably like she had fleas in her feathers. "Cuckoo things come out of my beak sometimes. Verbal worm poo. Forget you heard me trilling about it!"

And so, for a time, they did.

Each year, on the first day of spring, Fairies from across the Kingdom gathered in the great hall of the palace, on the Wild Boy and Storm Girl's next Naming Day.

Then the Queen's sister would pick one Naming Day Flower from the palace's roof-canopy of leaves and gift it to their mother and everyone would dance the night away beneath the season's first full moon.

In the weeks after their Naming Day, when flowers sprouted and there was fresh magic in the air, and when the rest of the Fairy Court had gone home, the Queen's sister and her black raven would stay a while to teach the Wild Boy and the Storm Girl the ways of magic.

"Magic is energy, my precious lambs. A gift of Life Force from the ancestors. Some Fairy folk have it. Some do not. Your Talismans help you focus that energy into the world, which is why you must wear them always."

"Magic is about balance," said the black raven. "Make it

rain here and there'll be drought there. Transform yourself into a huge beast for a day, and it'll take great power to return you to your own form tomorrow."

"Remember," said the Queen's sister, "magical energy drains from one place or another when it's used."

"Why does that matter?" asked the Wild Boy.

"Because the bigger the magic, the bigger the cost," counselled the black raven.

"When there's less life in the outside world to draw from," continued the Queen's sister, "for example, in the dead of winter, or far from nature, then your Talisman takes the energy it needs from inside of you instead, and you get tired and ill."

"Or worse," added the black raven.

"Worse how?" asked the Storm Girl, aghast.

"If you cast a dangerous spell that you're unprepared for," replied the raven, "it can kill you. The big, uncontrolled magic will suck out your heart and soul and drain every drop of life in your body."

The Wild Boy shivered.

The Storm Girl shuddered and thought of their mother. Perhaps the Queen had done too much magic and lost her heart and soul and that was why she was so cold to them? Or perhaps there was another reason?

"I won't EVER cast such spells," she swore.

"You won't have to," said the Queen's sister. "I promise you, while you remain in Fairyland, no harm can come to you."

The black raven cawed a guffawing laugh at this, and the Storm Girl noticed apprehensively that the Queen's sister had her fingers crossed behind her back.

Then it was time for the actual lesson.

The Queen's sister taught them all kinds of magic, but the Storm Girl's favourite spells were always to do with the weather. She could make the sun shine, or clouds gather. She could make fog, snow, showers and drizzle. Her most treasured spell combined snow with thunder:

"Snow spiral, thunder clash, blizzard blow, storm crash."

It created something new. The Storm Girl called it thundersnow and claimed she'd invented it.

The Wild Boy's favourite spells were to do with shape-shifting. He could change himself into any creature and talk with animals in their own languages – not just with the red robin, but also badgers, hedgehogs, foxes, wolves and frogs. His most favoured spell turned him into a wolf:

"Tail, snout, pelt, paws. Wings, fins, teeth, claws. Shake me, change me, magic truth. Make me into a Wild Wolf."

When the Wild Boy returned to his own form, he'd tell

the Storm Girl, "If I wasn't a child of the Fairies, I'd be a wolf-cub."

And, often, when no one else was about, that's what he'd become.

At the start of the summer, the Queen's sister and the black raven would leave for another year. Then the Wild Boy and the Storm Girl would practise their magic alone, throughout the summer months.

The red robin helped. She couldn't do magic herself, but she'd watched the Queen and her sister for years and knew the theory of it. She offered as much advice as she could from her tiny bird brain.

In late autumn, when the leaves turned brown and fell from the trees, they'd stop spell practice. This was a time to conserve energy, not a time for big magic.

"It's like your aunt said, my little grebes," counselled the red robin. "In winter, when growth slows, magic must too. Doing too much in the barren months is dangerous! Magic must await the spring."

So they climbed trees instead.

One day, near midwinter, the Wild Boy and the Storm Girl dressed themselves in their finest furs and climbed up into the magnificent and ancient oak tree called the Heart of the Forest. The Heart's roots grew through the tiled floor of the palace and its twiggy fingers held up the palace roof. The twins sat down in the crown of the tree, on the highest limb, let the cold pinch their cheeks, and dangled their feet, tapping the trunk with the heels of their boots, which were made of bark and moss and lined with scraggy old sheep's wool.

The Storm Girl found a woodpecker's hole. Something glinted inside it in the dark. She reached a gloved hand in and pulled out a wolf's tooth. "Look," she said, showing it to the Wild Boy. "You should have this."

"Why?" he asked.

"As a present. You could sew it onto your coat like a button," his sister suggested. "To keep the wind from blowing it open. And to remind you of your wolf-friends when you can't see them."

"Thank you." The Wild Boy took the tooth. No one had ever given him a present before. Not since his first Naming Day. "I shall treasure it," he said and promptly dropped it.

The tooth bounced off the trunk and landed in a shady bower.

The Wild Boy and the Storm Girl, with the red robin flapping at their side, climbed down quickly to retrieve it.

As the Wild Boy bent to pick up the tooth from the floor of the bower, he saw faint words carved into the trunk of the tree:

"At the chiming of the thirteenth hour,
At the plucking of the thirteenth flower,
On the hundred-and-thirty-third Naming Day...
In the Greenwood Forest,
By the Tambling River,
On the Stepping Bones..."

Moss grew over the rest of the words, hiding them. The Wild Boy and the Storm Girl tried to tug lumps of it away.

"What does it mean?" the Wild Boy asked the red robin.

"Nothing, my little greylag geese," reassured the robin, fluttering nervously around. "Leave it alone, please...it's some scrambled, shaggy old Curse!"

"What Curse?" asked the Storm Girl.

"I've said too much, little warblers." The red robin's eyes darted everywhere but at them. She snapped her beak shut.

Then the Wild Boy knew that this was what she had been hiding from them. He snatched the moss away as quickly as he could, and read the rest of the words inscribed into the bark:

"The Queen will sacrifice a life
Of a single twin
Born in strife
And given to her as kith and kin.
To save her Royal soul and skin,

She'll cry cold and bitter tears,
But will rule Fairyland for a hundred-and-thirty-three more years..."

The Wild Boy finished reading and felt sick.

One of them was cursed to die. This was the reason their aunt and her black raven were always secretly laughing at them. This was the secret the robin refused to speak of, and the answer to why their mother was so cold and distant to them.

"This was what you tried to warn us of on our first Naming Day," whispered the Storm Girl shakily.

The red robin nodded. "The Queen's sister cast a spell over me so I couldn't tell you, my little goosanders. But now that you've learned the truth on your own, that spell on me is broken."

Then the red robin told them the rest of what she knew of the Curse – what would happen on the first full moon of spring, on their thirteenth Naming Day. How the Queen had to sacrifice one of her family to the river and the Dead Lands every hundred-and-thirty-three years, in order that she might live. How that sacrifice was destined to be the Queen's sister, until the sorcerous Fairy had changed the Curse and cast a devious spell over the Queen to stop her realizing.

The Wild Boy and the Storm Girl listened in shock until the little bird had finished.

"But now that we've broken your spell, can't you tell the Queen what happened, surely?" the Storm Girl asked. "That you saw her sister change the Curse with magic all those years ago?"

"The Queen would never believe me over her sister," replied the red robin. "Never."

"What about us?" suggested the Storm Girl.

"She wouldn't believe you either, my little swallows," said the red robin. "The spell her sister cast over her was unbreakable. The Queen will never learn the truth of what was done that day."

The Wild Boy sighed deeply. "Then," he said, "we have no choice. We must run away, leave this place, and never come back."

He could see that the Storm Girl wasn't so sure, but he knew with certainty that there was no other option.

"If we stay," he told her, "one of us will die."

The Storm Girl realized he was right. They'd have to hide from their aunt and the black raven and from their mother and the Fairy Court, and the Greenwood and the Fair Isle and the entire world of Fairyland and everything they'd ever known and held dear, if they were to escape their deadly fate. And the only place it would be safe to do that was in a land far, far away.

8

Kensington Palace

Cold seeped into Tempest's bones. Hunger gnawed at her belly. She and Thomas stared through the bars of the cage at the sight before them.

They were approaching a large two-storey building whose brick sides were filled with tall sash windows. Gleaming candles flickered behind their warped glass.

The horses slowed to a walk, pulling the carriage through a wide archway into a snow-strewn courtyard, overlooked by a clocktower. The coachman yanked on the reins and brought them to a stop.

Tempest noticed a woman on the far side of the courtyard standing with two red-coated guards. She was tall and pale and wore a highly embroidered dress with a black diamond brooch pinned to her breast. On her head was a grey wig that fluttered with pink ribbons, and on her shoulder was a white raven, with a beak as sharp as a scythe.

The raven opened that beak and gave a loud "*CRAWW!*"

"*Fluff and pin feathers!*" Coriel whispered from her hiding place in Tempest's hair. "*Who in the Greenwood is that?*"

"*I-I don't know,*" Thomas replied.

Tempest shuddered and clutched the little wooden ferry boat with its three painted figures closer. The sight of the woman and her raven set off an uncomfortable nagging feeling inside and sent a cloud of anxiety scudding through her senses.

Suddenly, the carriage door swung open. Lord Hawthorn jumped down from the side of the coach and said out loud:

"Magical cage, cloaked in stealth. Remove your charm, reveal thyself."

Tempest felt a shimmer of magic run round the cage bars as if a spell was being lifted.

The guards down below gaped open-mouthed as the cage and its occupants became visible to them, appearing as if from nowhere.

"You're back, Milord!" the woman called out. "And you've found new apprentices, I see."

"Two, my dear Lady Hawthorn," Lord Hawthorn replied,

taking her arm. "A Storm Girl and a Wild Boy. Now I have multiple apprentices to assist me in my research, just like the old days. Instead of the one disobedient one." He glared up at Kwesi sitting on the driver's seat, next to the coachman.

"As befits you, beloved husband. You are the Royal Sorcerer, after all!" Lady Hawthorn glanced at Thomas and Tempest. "Welcome, new apprentices!" She grinned like a tiger intent on eating a flock of small birds. "Welcome to Kensington Palace!"

The white raven did not smile, but stared at them with beady red eyes.

"How fares the King?" Lord Hawthorn asked his wife.

"His Majesty is well, dearest," Lady Hawthorn said. "He requests you greet him in the Presence Chamber at once."

Lord Hawthorn's loud sigh made Tempest wonder what the Presence Chamber was.

"Must we, my precious?" he asked. "I've barely arrived. I'm weary from my travels, and my clothes smell of the road."

"*And of dead fish,*" Coriel whispered from Tempest's hood.

"The King was most insistent, my love," Lady Hawthorn said. "He saw your carriage on the driveway. He requested you bring the new apprentice. I'm sure he'll be delighted to learn there are two."

Lord Hawthorn sighed. "I suppose we must accommodate the old fool's wishes, my dearest, if I am to continue my work." He turned to the guards. "Escort the new apprentices from the cage to the Presence Chamber."

Tempest and Thomas were suddenly shaken around as the guards hurriedly manhandled the cage from atop the carriage. As it hit the ground, Lord Hawthorn muttered a spell to undo the charm on the lock. The cage door swung open. Tempest barely had time to take in what was happening before she found herself wrestled through it along with Thomas, and forced to her feet.

Behind the guards, she glimpsed the burly coachman and a worried-looking Kwesi jump down from the carriage. On the far side of the courtyard, Lord Hawthorn and his wife were already stepping through an open doorway.

The guards hustled Tempest and Thomas across the courtyard after them, while Kwesi hurried at their heels, glancing across to see that they were all right.

Soon they were in a long stone gallery where their footsteps echoed across cold flagstones like Tempest's racing heartbeat.

Tempest tried to stay calm. She told herself she must be brave in this new world, but inside she was falling apart. "*I don't like this place,*" she murmured to Coriel in her hood.

"*Neither do I, little redshank,*" Coriel answered.

"*Nor me,*" Thomas replied. His shoulders were knitted, and he cut a fragile figure in the dark.

Kwesi remained silent and did not join in their conversation, but when Tempest and Thomas glanced nervously at him, he gave them both a friendly and reassuring smile.

The guards ignored their chatter. They arrived at an opulent stairwell, filled with marble and shining stone the likes of which Tempest had never seen. Square glass boxes hung from the ceiling. Each contained a chandelier with eight spitting candles that illuminated wall-mounted coats of arms and statues in alcoves. As the guards escorted them up the stairs, Tempest peered at the statues. Up close, she could see they were all an illusion painted on the plaster, and she didn't know what to make of that.

At the top of the staircase, Lord and Lady Hawthorn were waiting with a large, bald gentleman with a jowly round face and arched eyebrows. He wore a silken red jacket trimmed with fur, and a fine green waistcoat embroidered with flowers and gold ferns.

"That's Mehmet," Kwesi whispered. "The King's head servant. He's Turkish. When he was young, his country was at war with King George. He was captured and taken from his homeland, just like me. He helps me, whenever he can."

Mehmet beamed warmly at Kwesi, Tempest and Thomas.

Lord Hawthorn frowned at the guards. "I said bring the *new* apprentices," he snapped. "Not the old!" He pointed at Kwesi. "This one's in disgrace!"

Mehmet tutted, not at Kwesi but at Lord Hawthorn.

The guards looked around at everyone confused. They didn't know what to do.

A fanfare of trumpets blasted behind the doors.

"Never mind," Lord Hawthorn growled. "It's too late now. We'll take him in." He turned to Tempest and the others. "Bow to the King when you enter."

"And under no circumstance speak to His Royal Majesty," Lady Hawthorn warned.

"Not unless the sovereign chooses to converse with you first," Lord Hawthorn said. "In which case you're to address him as 'Your Majesty'."

"Try to answer as briefly as possible," Lady Hawthorn added. "And never turn your back on the King."

Tempest's head swam. It was too much to take in on top of everything else. She glanced fearfully at Kwesi, and then at Thomas. She hoped he'd understood. She hadn't time to explain it to him. She thought for a moment about turning and running, but the Hawthorns and the two guards had made a wall of bodies, trapping them as Mehmet opened the doors.

Coriel nuzzled in her hood, and the little bird's warmth against her neck gave her the dose of courage she sorely needed, as the doors to the Presence Chamber swung slowly open.

Summer Stories

By the start of summer, pennycress and silverweed flowered in the Greenwood. Every day the Wild Boy thought of the frightening secret he and his sister had uncovered in the bower.

He'd always wondered why their mother didn't care for them. Why she was never around – not to clean their cuts when they scraped their knees climbing trees, nor to dry them off when they pushed each other in the pool, nor to tell them bedtime stories. Now, at last, thanks to stumbling on the hidden bower and reading the secret Curse carved into the bark of the Heart of the Forest, he knew why. Their mother had always known of the evil Curse, and had cultivated her cold indifference so that, when the time came, it would be easier for her to choose which of the two of them to sacrifice.

The Wild Boy was determined that would not happen. An escape plan had been brewing in his mind for some time. One day he told the Storm Girl and the red robin about it. "We will run away, and shake off our fate like a winter coat in spring. Reach the far side of the Tambling River and leave Fairyland behind for ever."

The Storm Girl still didn't want to go. She couldn't believe that anything bad would happen to them here, in their home. She thought the words of the Curse must be a mistake, but she was curious about what lay beyond the river. So she finally agreed to run off, for a little while.

"I'm certain it's all a terrible misunderstanding," she said. "But we can go and have an adventure and then our mother will bring us home, where we will be safe from harm. Surely, she will not want one of us dead."

The Wild Boy wasn't so certain. He had a feeling their mother was the one he was running from. A mother who was as frosty as a winter's day all year round wouldn't be the one to spare them when the time came. In the end, he realized, they would have to save themselves.

That afternoon they ventured beyond the last reaches of the Greenwood and down to the riverbank, and looked out, trying to discern a way across.

The river curved around to the sea in one direction and upstream in the other. Its black waters marked the boundary between the Fairy Kingdom and who-knew-what on the other side. The river was enchanted, filled with swirling currents and swathed in a constant fog, so that you could never see what was on its furthest shore. There was one landmark on the nearside bank: a line of broken white stones. They had once been a crossing called the Bone Bridge that led from the Fair Isle to a land far, far away. A hundred-and-thirty-three years ago, a great storm had pulled the bridge down. And now only its slippery stones remained: big white rocks called the Stepping Bones that rose like humpbacked sea creatures from the black waters of the Tambling, stretching out from the shore in a rough T-shape that stopped abruptly somewhere midstream, where the very last and largest Stepping Bones rose from the waters, barely visible in the fog.

"What's beyond the Bones on the far side of the river?" the Wild Boy asked the red robin, as the three of them considered how to get across.

"Why England, of course, my tawny owl," replied the red robin. "Everybody knows that!"

"What's England?" asked the Storm Girl.

"Another land," said the red robin. "Much like this one."

"Who rules it?" asked the Wild Boy, thinking of their

mother, who, as Queen, was always doing some ruling or other. Every moment of her day in the palace and the Greenwood and the Fair Isle seemed taken up with Royal duties.

"A King named George," said the red robin.

The Storm Girl laughed. "That's a funny name for a King."

"Isn't it, though, my little pochard?" said the red robin. "He's called George the First, because he's the first King of England with that name."

"What's England like?" asked the Wild Boy. "Can we escape the Curse there?"

"I don't know, my little gadwalls," said the red robin.

"Well, I'm going to go and take a look." The Wild Boy strode towards the riverbank. "If it's a place I can be free, then I want to see it. I want to discover what's beyond the edge of Fairyland."

"The grass is not always greener, my little fulmar," said the red robin wisely.

"I don't care about the grass!" said the Wild Boy. "I want to find parents who'll love me as I am. I might even visit the King of England. He's sure to want to greet a Fairy Prince." He took his sister's hand. "Will you come?"

The Storm Girl pondered this. "I suppose," she said at last. "If you promise we'll be happy there. And safe."

"I promise," said the Wild Boy, without a second thought.

"How do we get to England?" he asked the red robin.

"Great mulleins!" The red robin peered carefully around. "I-I don't know if I should say."

"I command you to," said the Wild Boy. "So does my sister. We're Royalty. You have to do as we ask!"

"All right, little tree sparrows!" the red robin relented. "I'll tell you, but you must swear by all the gypsywort in the Greenwood not to let anyone know it was me. I'd be in trouble otherwise."

"We swear," said the Wild Boy and the Storm Girl together.

The red robin flew to the Wild Boy's shoulder and whispered in his ear. "You must cross the Stepping Bones."

"Is that all?" asked the Wild Boy.

"No, that's not all!" twittered the red robin. "It's not a straightforward journey, little wheatear." She shifted uneasily. "Fairyland sits at a crossroads. It's connected to other lands by magical doorways. To get to England, you have to walk across the Stepping Bones, open such a doorway at the end of them and step through it."

"Open it with what?" asked the Storm Girl. "A key?"

"No, not a key." The red robin shook her head. "You must cast the Opening Spell. You must say it on the last Stepping Bone. If you get it wrong, or miss the doorway, or step the wrong way, you'll sink to the Dead Lands, down below, at the bottom of the river. Death rules there and no one ever returns."

"That sounds awful," said the Wild Boy. Leaving was starting to seem as dangerous as facing the Curse.

"Every journey has its risks, my little ringed plover," replied the red robin. "But sometimes so does staying where you are." She fidgeted and fluffed her feathers fearfully. "The cost for one of you, if you stay, will be your life."

"Is there no other way out of Fairyland?" the Wild Boy asked the red robin. "Tell the truth," he warned.

"Your mother and aunt have secret ways," said the red robin. "I don't know of them. The one way I know is the path on the Stepping Bones."

"Then," said the Wild Boy, "we must risk it."

"We must," agreed the Storm Girl. "What is the Opening Spell, Coriel?"

"Oh, no one knows the whole of that, my little jackdaws," said the red robin. "That sly old raven Auberon stole the Opening Spell many moons ago, and hid the fragments of it around the wood."

The Wild Boy was stumped, and so was the Storm Girl. It might take them a long time to find and collect all the parts of the Opening Spell. The Storm Girl didn't even know where to begin, but the Wild Boy knew that they had to, or else their deathly fate would creep up on them before they even knew it.

9

Royals and Ravens

Tempest stared in awe around the Royal Presence Chamber. The grandness of it felt overwhelming. The enormous windows, the golden chandeliers, the painted ceiling, the red ruched fabric flowing across every wall, the magnificent coat of arms with a lion and unicorn, plus lines of courtiers and servants, dressed in powdered wigs and rich, embroidered fabrics. She tried to count how many courtiers there were, but gave up after a while. Their number was far too great.

Most overwhelming of all was the King of England. George the First. A pallid man in a brown wig, wearing a cape trimmed with ermine over a velvet suit jacket with buttons made from glinting diamonds. The King's outfit was completed with lace ruffles, silk stockings and large polished gold buckles that sprouted from his shoes like priceless carbuncles. He sat poised with interest on the many cushions of his great throne.

"Lord and Lady Hawthorn are here at your request, Your Majesty," Mehmet said, indicating the Hawthorns and giving a nodding bow to the King.

"Your Majesty," Lady Hawthorn said, dropping into a deep curtsy.

"Your Majesty." Lord Hawthorn performed a grovelling bow.

Kwesi threw Tempest a warning look, then gave a curt bow too.

Thomas did not bow, but hunched into himself and stared at King George.

Tempest curtsied as best she could. She didn't know what else to do. She realized with shock that she was meeting the most powerful man in England. A man Prosper and Marino had spoken of to her with awe and fear.

"Which of these two children is the sorcerer's new apprentice, Mehmet?" the King asked. He had a very strong accent that sounded different to everyone else's. Tempest remembered Marino telling her once how the King was originally from Hanover in Germany.

His Majesty put a hand beneath his curly wig and scratched an itch on his neck.

Suddenly, in Tempest's mind, he was transformed into a dog with a tick.

"They are both the Royal Sorcerer's new apprentices, Your Majesty," Mehmet replied.

"Where do they come from, Hawthorn? And why do you look such a mess?" The King removed his hand from beneath his wig, which had gone slightly wonky on his head.

"They come from the Greenwood Forest, Majesty," Lord Hawthorn said, inching towards the King. "I've just returned from there." He waved his green silk-covered limbs like an insect, beckoning Tempest and Thomas to join him. "That's where I found them both: a Wild Boy and a Storm Girl. Together they've power and ability beyond their years."

Tempest was shocked. She'd barely discovered her magic, yet Lord Hawthorn was claiming she and Thomas had more potential and ability than they knew of. Could he be right? But how? She didn't feel powerful in that way at all.

"*None of this makes sense,*" she whispered to Thomas.

"*No, it doesn't,*" Thomas growled.

"What was that?" the King demanded. "What did they say?"

"The boy speaks no known language, Your Majesty," Lord Hawthorn said, "but the girl can communicate with him in some mysterious tongue, as well as speaking English."

"A linguist, eh?" the King said. "Sprichst du Deutsch?" he asked, in German.

Tempest stared blankly at him.

"I've yet to comprehend the origins of their language, Majesty," Lord Hawthorn continued smoothly. "But I've concluded it must be some sort of Fairy tongue. The Greenwood Forest is rumoured to be full of Fairy doorways. They're said to open fleetingly and be invisible to the human eye. I've not, as you know, studied much Fairy magic, but these children and their connection to Fairyland interests me."

Tempest thought about all the stories Prosper and Marino had told her about the Greenwood. They'd never mentioned Fairy doorways, or suggested that the other language she spoke might be connected to Fairyland. A niggling feeling deep down in her belly told her that Lord Hawthorn might be right. If that were so, she had no idea what it could mean…

"Let's see some magic from them then, Hawthorn," the King said impatiently. "Amuse me."

"As you wish, Majesty." Lord Hawthorn reached into his pocket and pulled out Thomas's Talisman, whispering his Control Spell as he crushed the stone in his fist.

"Bind and tie, make him cower. Hold his will within my power."

Thomas ground his teeth and scrunched up his brow, trying to fight against the magic.

"Boy," Lord Hawthorn said, "when I hand you this Talisman, you will shape-shift."

"Thomas," Lady Hawthorn added, "transform for the King."

Thomas's eyes flashed wide. He took his Talisman without looking at it. He was too busy gaping at Lady Hawthorn.

Tempest wondered what the matter was. Then she realized – Lady Hawthorn knew his name!

"How did you know he's called Thomas?" she demanded.

"I…" Lady Hawthorn said.

The King watched, intrigued.

"So he's called Thomas!" Lord Hawthorn interrupted. "Good news. A name always works better when casting the Command Spell, Majesty."

Tempest felt a flash of guilt for confirming Thomas's name, even though Lady Hawthorn had said it first.

Lord Hawthorn spoke in his spell-casting voice:

"Thomas, do your thing, perform your transformation for the King."

Thomas's eyes glazed over, as if he had no choice. He whispered a spell to himself:

"Tail, snout, pelt, paws. Wings, fins, teeth, claws. Shake me,

change me, magic truth. Make me into a Wild Wolf."

In the flickering candlelight, his body changed, in a reversal of the moment Tempest had first seen him. Thomas became the wolf.

He growled at the King. But his paws could not grasp his Talisman and he dropped it. Immediately, he returned to his own form. A boy once more, weary looking and with tears streaming down his face.

"Wunderbar! A marvellous display!" the King said.

"He seems to respond well to his name, Majesty." Lord Hawthorn muttered another spell. Thomas's Hag Stone Talisman flew to his outstretched hand and he put it back in his pocket. "He'll be easy to control now."

Tempest wondered uneasily what on earth was happening.

"I'll have the girl create a small rainstorm for your entertainment, Your Majesty," Lord Hawthorn said, reaching into his pocket for Tempest's Talisman.

"I don't think we want rainstorms in the Presence Chamber," the King grumbled. "Small or otherwise. Can she do anything else?"

"She can speak with her pet bird, Majesty," Lord Hawthorn said.

"In the same magical language she uses with Thomas, Your Majesty," Lady Hawthorn added.

Rage churned inside Tempest. How did Lady Hawthorn

know so much about both her and Thomas when the woman had never met either of them before?

Meanwhile, Coriel flew from Tempest's hood and circled around Lord Hawthorn's head. "*I am not a pet, you…you ragged old spleenwort!*" the little bird twittered.

"What!" the King said. "What's she saying?"

"She says she's not a pet, Your Majesty," Tempest snapped, as Coriel landed back on her arm. "I don't own her. She's a free soul. She comes and goes as she pleases. She chooses to stay with me as an equal because we're friends. I treat her with kindness, fairness and respect." She said the last part of this in a hard way. She wanted to add: *Unlike you people*. But she knew that would get her in trouble, so instead she said, "Your Majesty, I want to entreat you to free me and my friends so that we might return to—"

"Enough!" the King said angrily. "No more talk! And NO MORE TRICKS!" He put a hand to his temple. He seemed to be losing interest in the conversation. "All this twittering is giving me quite the headache," he grumbled. "Amusing as these new apprentices are, Hawthorn, I summoned you to say something else. I'm having a Royal Ball in three days, on the next full moon. A spectacular Masquerade. Everyone will dress up. And you, as Royal Sorcerer, will arrange a fabulous magic show."

Lord Hawthorn baulked at this.

"Perhaps, Your Majesty," Lady Hawthorn suggested, "the new apprentices could perform at the ball?"

"A splendid idea!" the King said. "But they'd better do something sensational. In the meantime, I want to hear no more about them."

"As you wish, Majesty." Lord Hawthorn inclined his head in a lowly manner. Tempest was shocked to see this side of him; he seemed so subservient suddenly. "Will that be all?"

"For tonight."

The King dismissed everyone with a flick of his hand. He stood, creating a wave of further bows and curtsies that ended with the opening of another set of doors at the far end of the room. Ignoring this fuss, the King descended the red-carpeted steps from his throne and quickly marched out. The guards and the rows of courtiers scrambled to follow him. Unlike the other servants, Mehmet glanced back at Kwesi, Tempest and Thomas. He smiled sympathetically, before he followed the King out too. Through the closing doors, Tempest glimpsed everyone jostling to get close to the monarch's retreating back.

Soon only Lord and Lady Hawthorn and the three apprentices remained, standing in the centre of the Presence Chamber. Lord Hawthorn looked deflated.

Tempest thought of how people like him could seem

large in one context and small in another. It made her remember the tales Prosper had told of how Fairies could make themselves little and big. Sometimes thumb-sized to sit on a mushroom, sometimes child-sized to converse with a fox, and sometimes adult-sized to negotiate with human beings.

It wasn't a real story, Marino had explained at the end, just a metaphor for how people's stature changed depending on who they were talking to.

Tempest knew now what they meant. Just because you behaved grand and important in one setting, like Lord Hawthorn, didn't mean you got to be grand and important everywhere.

"Dearest," Lord Hawthorn said in a tired voice, "take my three apprentices to their dormitory. I'll see the two new ones in my study in the morning to prepare a *magic show* for this *Masquerade*." The last few words were said with some disgust.

"Yes, beloved," Lady Hawthorn said. "Auberon, come with me. Help me watch over these three."

The white raven gave a loud "*CRAAWW!*" and landed ominously on Lady Hawthorn's shoulder, its beady red eyes staring at them.

"Good." Lord Hawthorn turned on his heels and marched off through the main doors and down the stairs.

"Auberon," Thomas said softly, speaking the raven's name in English. "*Auberon*," he repeated, in their own language.

Tempest tried to think why that name sounded so familiar, and why the phrase *Lord High Commander of Birds* kept circling round in her head, but she was too tired. This had been the strangest day she'd experienced since Prosper and Marino pulled her from the river. She missed them dearly, and wished they were here to explain what in the Greenwood was going on.

"I'll take you by the servants' passageways," Lady Hawthorn said, "since you'll have to learn that route soon enough for yourselves." She pressed a piece of panelling, which opened to reveal a stone staircase hidden behind the wall.

As they followed her through the secret doorway, Tempest glanced over her shoulder at Kwesi, who seemed to already know the passageways, and then at Thomas, who looked nervous and scared in these new surroundings. She reached out and touched his arm reassuringly, and a spark of strong static leaped between them that made her jump.

She still didn't understand the bond between herself and Thomas, but it was beginning to seem stronger with the passing of time. Somehow, at the centre of it, was this mystery surrounding the Fairies, and her missing memories of her past.

Tempest brushed those thoughts aside. Right now she had more pressing problems: how to snatch their Talismans back from Lord Hawthorn and get home to Prosper and Marino and the safety of Ferry Keeper's Cottage.

Lady Hawthorn was whispering to Auberon. Tempest caught snatches – quiet commands that sounded like they were in the same speech she used with Coriel. The same language spoken by Thomas.

Tempest was surprised to realize Lady Hawthorn might know that private language too, especially as Lord Hawthorn had said he did not. She watched with suspicion as the white raven launched itself from its mistress's shoulder and flapped along the passage. She'd have to watch what she said in its presence and, more importantly, she needed to guard herself around Lady Hawthorn; there was more to that nefarious woman than met the eye.

10

An Apprentice's Tale

Tempest, Thomas, Kwesi and Coriel followed Lady Hawthorn and Auberon along the dark stone passageways and up hidden staircases that ran like rabbit warrens behind the walls of Kensington Palace.

Coriel scrabbled, terrified, in Tempest's hood as Auberon flitted ahead in the shadows, gliding past various doors of different shapes and sizes.

"*Should we try one?*" Thomas asked. "*Make a surprise escape…*"

"*Not a good idea,*" Kwesi whispered. Thanks to his cleverness and magical abilities, his fluency and understanding of their language seemed to be growing stronger and stronger each time he heard Thomas speak it.

"He's right, little fulmar," Coriel twittered. *"We don't know the palace well enough."*

"*CRAAAAAAR!*" cried Auberon, swooping angrily at them, white feathers flying.

Thomas ducked as Auberon wheeled back up into the gloom of the ceiling.

"That was a warning," Lady Hawthorn said. "He understands everything, and reports back to me, so you can stop your whispering, the lot of you."

Kwesi looked fearful, Thomas shocked.

Tempest's heart fluttered. She peered, startled, at the ragged white raven, gliding above them. Her suspicions had been right. Lady Hawthorn could communicate with Auberon, just as Tempest could with Coriel. Did that mean there was some link between herself and this severe lady? At first sight, in the courtyard, she had seemed vaguely familiar. So had her raven…

"HEADS UP!"

"WATCH OUT!"

"COMING THROUGH!"

Various voices called from the dark.

"MIND YOUR BACKS! KING'S SERVANTS!"

A gaggle of maids came running – one with a warming pan, one with a gold bedpan, one with a candle, another with a steaming cup of what smelled like hot chocolate, with the King's Royal Crest embossed on it.

"OUT OF MY WAY!" Lady Hawthorn screamed at the servants. It was so loud it even made Thomas jump. Tempest felt Coriel claw nervously at her back.

"So sorry, Milady," the servants mumbled, pressing themselves against the sides of the passage to avoid brushing against Lady Hawthorn's voluminous dress.

Lady Hawthorn barged past everyone while Auberon screeched at the servants, and then at Kwesi, Tempest and Thomas to indicate they should follow.

At the top of another staircase, the passage became narrower and more crooked.

"These are the servants' quarters," Lady Hawthorn announced.

"We apprentices live and sleep here too," Kwesi whispered.

Tempest realized they must be in the roof of the palace.

At last they arrived at a narrow door with an A painted on its front in ominous blood red.

"Here we are," Lady Hawthorn said. "This is the room for the Royal Sorcerer's apprentices." She took a heavy iron key on a loop of string from her pocket, unlocked the door and pushed it open to reveal a horrible, poky room. Though it was nicer than being stuck in the cage on top of that dreadful carriage, Tempest thought.

She looked around the dormitory. The walls were bare plaster, and there were three narrow beds, each separated by a thin, yellow-stained linen curtain. A table and three plain chairs stood before a tiny fireplace. A small window was cut into the sloping ceiling that looked out into darkness.

"Noah, you will show them the ropes," Lady Hawthorn said, ushering them all into the room.

"Yes, Your Ladyship," Kwesi mumbled, resentfully.

"Someone will call for you in the morning," said Lady Hawthorn.

The last thing Tempest glimpsed through the gap was Auberon's beady red eyes watching her. The white raven loosed a horrible cawing laugh to accompany the clang of Lady Hawthorn's key in the lock, and Tempest realized they would not be escaping this place tonight.

"The apprentices' dormitory has been my prison for a long time," Kwesi said. "It's yours now too. I've tried to make it as nice as I can."

Thomas nervously paced the length of the room, whipping back the thin curtain round each bed. Of the three, two were empty, with a folded, moth-eaten looking blanket at their foot. The third bed was obviously Kwesi's. By his bedside was a little piece of board, about the size of a finger. Thomas gravitated towards it at once, and picked it up. "*Who's this?*" he asked, holding it up.

Tempest saw that there was a miniature portrait of a smiling woman drawn in pencil onto the tiny piece of wood.

"My mama," Kwesi said. "I made it when I first arrived here as a keepsake to remember her by. If I close my eyes, I can still recall her. She was beautiful, with the kindest eyes and a smile just like mine."

His eyes welled with tears. He took the trinket from Thomas and flipped it over. On the other side of the piece of wood was a drawing of a handsome man.

"Papa," Kwesi said. "At least, what I imagined him to look like from Mama's description of him. He was brave, clever and resourceful, like me, and his life was his own. Mama told me he built strong homes and alliances in our land. When I grow up I want to be just like him." Kwesi clenched the wooden miniature in his fist. "Do you know who profits from the Royal African Company – the company of slavers who destroyed my parents' village and took its people?" he asked. "Do you know who gave it their Royal seal of approval?"

"I don't," Tempest admitted.

"The Kings and Queens of England," Kwesi spat. "*This* King, in *this* palace. He and his Lords are responsible for my parents' deaths. For my people's enslavement. For transporting them far, far away from home, across the sea. Sugar and profit is all that matters to them. For the want of coin and a little sweetness, they have caused such pain and suffering."

Coriel flew to Kwesi's shoulder and nuzzled his ear.

Tempest did not know what to say. The more of Kwesi's story she heard, the more disgusted she became. "How did you end up here?" she asked. "In Kensington Palace, in the service of Lord Hawthorn?"

Kwesi took a deep breath. "Remember how I told you that the Captain of the slavers' ship considered me a good luck charm? He thought I was his property, and because of that my magic would keep him safe from harm. So he brought me back with him to England, from the Caribbean.

"At the Captain's house in London, one of his maids looked after me until I was big enough to care for myself. Then, when I was five or six, the Captain's wife made me her pageboy. African pageboys are quite the fashion with rich English ladies, you know."

Tempest shuddered.

"My magic continued to grow as I did," Kwesi said. "I discovered I could mend things that were broken and recover things that were lost. Though I could not heal my own pain, or find myself," he added thoughtfully.

"When I was strong enough I tried to use my magic to escape, but the maid caught me. She took my Talisman to the Captain, so no such thing would ever happen again."

"But how did you meet Lord Hawthorn?" Tempest asked.

"Lord Hawthorn and Lady Hawthorn were friends with the Captain and his wife," Kwesi replied. "They were dining with them one night, when Lady Hawthorn glimpsed some magic in me. The Captain showed them my Talisman and told them my story. Lord Hawthorn purchased me right away and brought me here to Kensington Palace to make me one of his apprentices. He taught me the basics of reading and writing, so I could help him with his spells. I learned quickly and devoured many more books than he or his wife were aware of. Mehmet helped me. He would sneak me stories from the King's library when the pair of them weren't looking. Thanks to Mehmet, I've read as much about life in England, and about magic, as I could in these last six years. Almost everything in the palace, with the exception of Lord Hawthorn's Grimoire, which he never lets that out of his sight.

"With all that knowledge, when a chance for freedom finally comes, I'll be able to seize it with both hands."

Thomas whistled in shock. "Six years," he whispered.

"I wasn't Lord Hawthorn's first apprentice." Kwesi picked stubbornly at a fingernail. "But I was a fighter and a survivor. The other boys and girls, Lord Hawthorn drained their power and they faded away. I'm warning you so you stay strong."

Tempest shuddered. "How can the Hawthorns do such things?"

"Publicly Lord Hawthorn claims to be a good man and teacher, and to some he may be," Kwesi said. "But to me, he is not. He is evil, and so is his wife. That is of little consequence here, though. The King of England has no issue with such villains. Evil has long been tolerated in this world. Many people are prepared to look the other way and ignore suffering if they feel the benefits to them outweigh the despair of others."

Tempest shifted uncomfortably on the bed. After hearing Kwesi's story, she could not help but agree with his sentiment.

Being Lord Hawthorn's apprentice was a deadly business, it seemed. They had to come up with a plan to get away from him and his horrible wife as soon as possible.

Thomas was obviously thinking the same thing. He jumped to his feet suddenly, and rushed to the window, forcing it open onto the wild rainstorm outside.

"Escape now?" he suggested. "Together?"

"Not that way!" Kwesi warned. "It's not possible!"

But Thomas had already set his foot on the sill and was preparing to climb out. Perhaps he didn't understand, or perhaps he chose to ignore Kwesi's warning. Either way, Tempest didn't have time to translate for him before he put his foot out the window and tried to step onto the roof.

He doubled up instantly, clutching his head and swaying dizzily, as he was thrown backwards into the room.

"*GRAAR!*" he cried. His face contorted in pain, he snatched up one of the chairs and threw it angrily at the wall.

BANG! The smack of the wood against the brick made Tempest jump.

The chair tumbled to the floor and lay on its side, one leg broken.

Thomas made a second leap at the window. This time he was repelled so violently that he hit the far wall and slid to the floor.

Tempest felt his torment as if it ran through her own body. She rushed over, dropping to her knees beside him. Kwesi followed, along with Coriel, who landed on Thomas's foot.

"*Thomas,*" Tempest whispered, putting a hand to his chest. "*Are you all right?*"

Thomas didn't answer. His face was grey and his eyes were screwed up in agony as he snatched ragged breaths.

"*Poor little rock dove!*" Coriel muttered.

"What's wrong with him?" Tempest asked.

"There's a Containment Spell around the window," Kwesi explained. "It creates a magical force field that extends over the roof and traps us in this room."

"Will he be all right?" Tempest said.

"I don't know." Kwesi put a hand tentatively on Thomas's forehead. "Even a few steps into that force field is enough to give you a terrible magical shock. If I had my Sunray Shell Talisman I'd cast a Healing Spell over him so he'd recover. But I don't, so we'll just have to hope."

Thomas shivered as a cold wind whipped around them. The window was still open, Tempest realized. She stood and nervously reached out to close it. Immediately the room felt a shade warmer, and that seemed to help.

Gradually, Thomas's breathing became steadier and the colour returned to his face. When he at last opened his eyes, Tempest explained to him what had happened.

"*We need to find another way out,*" Thomas said breathlessly when she'd finished.

"*We'll have to get our Talismans back first,*" Kwesi told him.

"*Kwesi's right, little pigeon,*" Coriel said. "*It's the only way you can overcome this savage prison.*"

"Is there a way we can steal back our Talismans?" Tempest said.

"Lord Hawthorn has them on him during the day, but he keeps them locked in his study at night," Kwesi replied. "Despite all my searching, I've never been able to find out where mine is hidden exactly."

"*Then we must break in and hunt for them!*" Thomas said.

Kwesi gave an exasperated laugh.

"What's funny about that?" Tempest asked.

"The study, the hallway and the grounds of the palace are all protected by magic, just like this room," he explained. "You'll see tomorrow. A scheme like that would be impossible to carry out."

This was too much for Tempest. Exasperation, tiredness, fear, hunger and despair all itched at her. Her brain was tangled with thoughts of escape. Her heart ached for her home, for Thomas, and for the pain and torment Kwesi had suffered.

Nevertheless, she was grateful the pair of them were here. Especially Kwesi. He was kind, brave and resourceful. He'd stuck by her and Thomas since the start and they were becoming fast friends. Most of all, Tempest felt sure that she could trust him and Thomas with her life. She vowed to help them both in any way she could.

"When Thomas and I have an idea of the lay of the land," she asked Kwesi, "then can we talk about escape?"

"If you like," Kwesi said. "But you must know what you're up against first. See it face to face. Good strategies are formed of facts. Rash plans, like your friend Thomas's, result in dangerous outcomes for us all."

"*Dangerous outcomes,*" Thomas groaned in reply, brushing his face. He was finally looking better. His belly rumbled loudly. "Is there any food?" he asked in English.

"Not tonight, I'm afraid," Kwesi replied. "Get some rest. Pick a bed and make yourself at home."

"Get some rest," Thomas repeated softly, in English. "Pick a bed."

Tempest pondered trying to sleep as Thomas threw himself down on the straw mattress beside Kwesi's.

"*Am I supposed to sleep under it, or on it?*" he asked.

"*In it,*" she replied.

Thomas made a stubborn face and ignored her advice. Instead he rolled to the floor and under the bed, pulling down the blanket and handfuls of mattress straw and tucking it in around him to make a nest.

Tempest took the last mattress, which was furthest from the door and had a little more privacy. "So Lady Hawthorn is magical too," she said to Kwesi as she made her bed. "She knew Thomas's name without anyone telling her, and she was whispering secrets to Auberon."

"I've always had my suspicions," Kwesi agreed. "But she's hidden it well in the past. Strange how that was the first time she's ever given herself away so blatantly. Auberon is not so good at disguising his powers. Sometimes I swear he has black feathers, then I rub my eyes and see they're white." He yawned and sat down on his bed. "Nothing in Kensington Palace is as it seems. The courtiers all have secrets and the Royal Court is a theatre of lies."

Tempest shivered. Things were going to be scarier and harder here than she'd imagined. There was one solution: they needed to escape as soon as possible.

Her head ached with tiredness thinking about it. She pulled the curtain round her bed, undressed to her petticoat, and hung her red cloak and the rest of her clothes over the end of the bed.

The last thing she did before lying down was to take out the little wooden boat with its painted figures and placed it on her bedside table.

Coriel perched by her head, as she always did, and that made Tempest feel a little safer as she dived under the covers.

Tempest settled her head on the straw pillow and stared at the little wooden figures in their boat. They looked like they were rowing across the tabletop. She wondered if she should make up a story about them to cheer herself up. It was what Marino or Prosper would've done.

But she couldn't think of anything, not at that moment. So she turned over instead, and called out in the dark: "*Night, Thomas.*"

Thomas didn't answer. A soft pining noise floated up from the floor. He must've already been asleep.

"Night, Kwesi," Tempest added.

"Night," Kwesi replied.

"Night, Coriel."

"Night-night, little sanderling," Coriel chirruped softly, in her ear.

Tempest shut her eyes and tried to fall asleep, but she could not, so she opened them again and gazed up at the ceiling, making plans for tomorrow.

First, she had to focus on her magic...she knew that she must learn enough to steal their Talismans back and use this power over Lord Hawthorn. Then she must escape somehow from this place that Kwesi had called a theatre of lies. Magic was at the bottom of everything, she knew that for certain now. And it seemed magic was their only way to survive. These uneasy thoughts filled Tempest's mind, until, at last, she dropped off to sleep.

Solstice Fragments

The midsummer solstice was dry that year, the leaves in the Greenwood crisp and veiny as old hands, and the pearlwort and chickweed around the pool ragged and drooping. The Wild Boy and the Storm Girl and the red robin set off to try and collect the parts of the Opening Spell that the Queen's sister's black raven had hidden many moons ago around the Greenwood. A spell that would create a magical doorway to England and take them away from their mother and the dreadful Curse.

"We'll ask the beasts in the forest to help us," said the Wild Boy.

They followed the path past the palace and stopped in a shady copse where birds filled the trees.

The Wild Boy cast his Transformation Spell and they

became two chaffinches. The red robin followed as they flew up into the trees to join the sparrows, greenfinches, warblers and bramblings in the branches.

"How do we find the parts of the Opening Spell?" trilled the Wild Boy.

"That opens the doorway on the Stepping Bones?" chirruped the Storm Girl.

The other birds shook their beaks. "We only know of the sky, clouds, wind and sun," they chorused. "But we remember hearing one line of that spell long ago. The first line. It is: **Open sky**."

"Thank you," sang the Wild Boy and the Storm Girl together. Then the two little chaffinches spread their wings and swooped from the tree. As their feet hit the ground, they returned to their human forms.

They scurried onwards, the Storm Girl picking a few rogue feathers from her hair.

Finally they arrived at a damp and stony part of the forest, where adders, toads and frogs congregated in a pile of mossy stones and rocks. Grasshoppers sang in the nearby shrubbery.

The Wild Boy and the Storm Girl crouched among the rocks and the Wild Boy cast his Transformation Spell. When they tumbled into the form of two tiny toads, the red robin flapped off in disgust and did not return.

The other creatures gathered round them, sniffling and snuffling at their dry, warty skin.

A beetle, green as the brightest emerald, flew by and the Storm Girl stuck out her long tongue and caught it, gulping it down her gullet.

"Yuck!" she coughed, realizing what she'd done.

The Wild Boy croaked with laughter, and the grasshoppers who had come to join the others nervously jumped back a few paces.

"We need to learn the parts of the Opening Spell," the Wild Boy told the assembled creatures. "So we can leave Fairyland and go to England."

"GURP! GURP!" said the frogs and toads. "We only know of the rocks and stones and the dark damp earth."

"TSSSSSS! TSSSSSS!" said the adders. "We only know of the trees and leaves, grasses and brown bark."

"BRIPP! BRIPP!" said the grasshoppers. "We remember the second line of a spell. We heard it once, in the mists of time, way back when. It is: **Open stone**."

"Thank you," the Wild Boy and the Storm Girl told the grasshoppers, who leaped about in delight.

The Storm Girl and the Wild Boy joined them, shaking their warty bodies until they were human again. Though the Storm Girl still had a few warts on her palms. She rubbed them until they disappeared.

Nearby a natural spring trickled over a pile of rocks, rushing to form a pool filled with water lilies and green weed.

The Storm Girl put her hand in the water and the Wild Boy muttered his Transformation Spell.

Soon they were silver minnows, flitting in the pool. The water felt warm and pleasant near the surface, but as they plunged deeper and the sun disappeared, the Storm Girl felt an icy shiver down her spine.

"We need the parts of the Opening Spell to create a doorway on the Stepping Bones," the Wild Boy called to a school of rainbow trout.

"We know nothing of doorways," cried the trout, circling the Wild Boy and the Storm Girl. "We only know of watery things, currents and tides, tadpoles and mayflies," they continued, their words bubbling from their mouths. "But we do recall one small fragment of a spell. Barely a whisper, buried deep in the mud at the bottom of the pool. It is: **Open waters.**"

"Thank you!" said the Storm Girl and her words formed two big bubbles that floated upwards and burst at the top of the pool.

"Good luck, little minnows," said the trout and they tickled the Wild Boy's and the Storm Girl's scales with their fins, until both of them cried with laughter and swam upwards.

The two minnows leaped from the water, shaking the cold drops away and falling to the dry ground in their own bodies once more. Their tails were the last thing to transform, so that for a moment they looked like beached mermaids. The Wild Boy was exhausted from the many magics he'd performed, but at last he managed to get the final part of his Transformation Spell to work, and then they had legs again.

He was worn out and breathing heavily by this point. "You try the Opening Spell," he said to the Storm Girl. "I haven't the energy for it." And she did:

"Open sky.

Open stone.

Open waters..."

"That can't be the whole thing," she exclaimed when she'd finished. "It doesn't seem enough. There must be more."

The Wild Boy shrugged. He was so tired and frustrated that he threw out his arms and whooped and hollered and hurled himself through the trees. The Storm Girl followed.

Finally they came to a rocky cave, where the wolves gathered.

The Wild Boy had just enough power left to cast a last Transformation Spell. He and the Storm Girl both became wolves.

The Wild Boy turned to the leader of the pack. "We are looking for the last part of the Opening Spell," he barked. "That was hidden by the old raven."

"We only know of wolfish things," yelped the wolf pack leader. "Running and hunting, sleeping and scratching."

"I know one line of the spell," snapped the oldest, greyest wolf. "It was found by the first howling wolf who walked through these woods. It is: **Open bone**."

"Thank yoOOOoooooooooO!" bayed the Storm Girl in gratitude.

"That is not the end of the spell," snarled the oldest wolf. "There's more."

"Where's the rest then?" growled the Wild Boy.

But the oldest wolf shook his mane and slunk away, and the rest of the pack did not know the last part of the Opening Spell either.

The Wild Boy and Storm Girl ran from the wolves and howled in despair until they were human again, though they still had shaggy tails that drooped for a long time before they disappeared.

The two Fairy children were so shattered from their magic that they headed home for a rest.

As they walked, the Wild Boy wondered if they'd ever find the ending of the spell.

When they arrived at the Heart of the Forest, the red

robin flew from a branch to greet them.

"How did it go, my little hoopoes?" she asked. "Did you find the Opening Spell?"

The Wild Boy shook his black curls sadly.

"The last part is missing," explained the Storm Girl.

"Well, don't get your feathers in a froth about it," said the red robin. "While you were gone, I remembered something; I saw Auberon sneaking about with the last part of the Opening Spell long ago. I think I know where he hid it."

"Oh, thank you, Coriel!" cried the Wild Boy, kissing the little bird on the head.

"If I tell you, my little bitterns, you must promise me one thing." The little robin's black eyes danced anxiously about. "Take me with you to England. If I stay and you're gone, the Queen's sister will find out I was the one who told you about the enchantment she cast over the Curse, and that I was the one who helped you find the Opening Spell and escape Fairyland. She'll see to it I fall from the Queen's favour and am banished to the Dead Lands." The little bird shivered.

"We promise to take you with us," said the Wild Boy and the Storm Girl together.

"So," said the Storm Girl, as the red robin flew nervously over to land on her arm. "Where is the last part of the Opening Spell?"

"In another big old tree called the Tree of Life that's far off in East Greenwood, my little sedge warblers," whispered the red robin. "When I was a small chick, younger than you are now, I saw Auberon hiding the last words of the Opening Spell there."

"Then," said the Wild Boy, with as much bravery as he could muster, "that is where we must go. To the Tree of Life."

11

Breakfast Bidding

Tempest dreamed of her mother again. She was calling to her, but a wide river kept them apart. Tempest got into *Nixie*. Thomas was there, and Coriel, and Kwesi, Prosper and Marino too, and they all rowed towards Tempest's mother.

But no matter how far or how fast they rowed, Tempest could not get any closer. She could not see her mother's face, nor catch her lost words in the blustery wind of the river.

She woke, leaned out of bed on the wrong side and hit her head on a wall that wouldn't have been there at home in Ferry Keeper's Cottage.

"Ouch!" she moaned loudly.

"You're awake, my little kittiwake!" Coriel cried, fluttering around her head. *"Cat's ears and goat's beards! What a time of it we had yesterday!"*

Tempest rubbed her crown and stared at the yellowed linen curtain drawn around her bed.

All at once, everything came flooding back to her. Thomas's capture. Her spell casting, and passing out. Lord Hawthorn and his magical cage. Her arrival at the palace. The meeting with the King. Lady Hawthorn and Auberon escorting her, Thomas and Kwesi to the apprentices' dormitory…

She pushed aside the painful memories along with her itchy blanket, and found a hand poking through the gap in the curtain. The hand swept the curtain aside to reveal a skinny girl with pale arms who stepped through the gap and began gathering up Tempest's clothes. She had a freckled face framed by kinks of red hair and was dressed in a grey smock, with an iron key like Lady Hawthorn's hung on a string around her neck.

"Give me those, you thief!" Tempest snapped, snatching at her stockings and dress as the girl tried to take them.

"Shan't," the girl replied, holding the things away from her.

A tug of war ensued, with Tempest cursing the girl and the girl cursing her.

"What's going on?" Kwesi called from further off.

"This criminal is trying to steal my things!" Tempest shouted.

Kwesi's laugh floated through the curtain. "That's Molly. She's Lady Hawthorn's maid."

"I brought you fresh clothes," Molly said, indicating a pile of things on the bed that Tempest hadn't even noticed. "Lady Hawthorn's commanded that you can't wear your old stuff in court. I was going to wash it for you. But maybe I'll burn it instead."

"Not my cloak!" Tempest plucked the red cloak from Molly and hugged it anxiously. "I've always had that. And not my clothes either. My adopted fathers gave them to me."

"All right. Keep them." Molly handed her back the rest of her stuff. "I'm sorry about the burning thing, miss. It was a joke."

"I'm sorry as well," Tempest said. "I didn't mean to get angry with you. It's just, I don't want to be here, and I've no idea who I can trust and who I can't. And most of all, I want to go home." She trailed off, her eyes smarting. She felt like she might burst into tears at any moment.

Molly's face softened. "You can trust me, miss." She put a hand on Tempest's arm. "And Kwesi." She glanced at the curtain in the direction his voice had come from. "He's a good sort. He'll tell you the truth of what goes on here, and I'll help you where I can – bring you good food and warm clothing, when my mistress isn't looking, like I do for Kwesi. But I can't let you out." She clutched the key round her neck. "Lady Hawthorn would kill me if I did that. She trusts me with her key only for a short time. I have to give it back to her as soon as I leave this room, and report on anything strange I see. I'll stay mum about anything I hear from you, but I'm not a very good liar. And you'd best be careful. The Hawthorns have magical spies everywhere in the palace. They know everything that happens here."

"Thanks for the warning." Tempest brushed her wet cheeks. "I suppose palaces and prisons are more similar than I realized."

"You might be right about that, miss," Molly said. "I'll go and fetch some breakfast." She left the room, locking the door behind her.

Tempest examined the pile of fresh clothes that Molly had left behind. They were nice things. A folded shift, freshly pressed, woollen knee stockings, stays and a petticoat, plus a simple embroidered dress that went over those. They smelled clean and crisp.

It took an age to struggle into the many layers of new clothing. When Tempest was done, she found she couldn't raise her arms above her head any more. The stays and petticoat restricted her movement. She supposed that was why the women courtiers in the Presence Chamber last night held themselves so straight and rigid, like peg dollies.

Lastly, she put on her own red cloak and felt a little more like her old self.

After she'd finished dressing, she grabbed the three painted figures in their little wooden boat from her bedside. She didn't want to leave them behind in case someone else took them, like they had her Talisman.

As she put the little boat and figures in her pocket, Tempest thought of Prosper and Marino in Ferry Keeper's Cottage. She missed them so. They were probably searching for her right now, along the river.

She swept the linen curtain aside and looked around for Thomas. His curtain was pulled back and his bed unslept in. Then she remembered he'd gone to sleep under it. She glanced downwards.

There he was, curled on the floorboards, his black hair poking from beneath his blanket. He'd snoozed through her ruck with Molly, but somehow her staring woke him.

He crawled to his feet and yawned widely. There were new clothes for him too, piled on the end of his mattress, but Thomas ignored them. Instead he skulked over to the table in his undershirt.

"*Aren't you cold?*" Tempest asked.

Thomas shook his head.

Molly soon returned with a tray. There were three slices of bread, a butter knife and a plate of cold congealed animal fat known as dripping. Molly placed everything briskly down on the table by the bare fireplace and left again, locking the door behind her.

Kwesi spread dripping on each slice of bread. "Eat something," he said. "You'll need the energy to face the Hawthorns in your first magic lesson. That's always a long day."

"Why? What happens?" Tempest asked.

"They'll have you cast your best spells," Kwesi replied, "but they'll have some mischiefs up their sleeves also. Tests and surprises to see what new tricks you can pull out of the bag for the King's masked ball."

None of that sounded pleasant. Tempest wasn't even sure she could remember how to cast her one spell. She didn't feel hungry either, but she sat at the table and ate her share of the food anyway, for sustenance.

"Maybe this lesson will be an opportunity for me to discover a way out of here," she said hopefully.

Kwesi gave a short mirthless laugh. "Oh, there'll be no chance of that!"

"Break-fast?" Thomas screwed up his nose and stared warily at his unappetizing slice of bread and dripping.

"That's right." Tempest offered him her chair, since the third one was broken, but Thomas crouched on the floor instead. He looked ready to leap away at any time, as if nervous about eating in front of anyone.

Tempest saved a few breadcrumbs for Coriel. The little robin hopped from her shoulder onto her hand and pecked at them, making Thomas laugh. Soon he forgot his nerves and stood by the table, stuffing all the bread and dripping into his mouth in one go.

"Do you think Thomas and I are Magicborn?" Tempest asked Kwesi, wanting to talk before anyone came for them. "Or could our abilities be connected to the Fairies, as Lord Hawthorn suggested?"

"I don't know any more about being Magicborn than I told you in the hut," Kwesi replied. "Or anything about the Fairies. The palace hasn't any books on them. But maybe today you'll find out," he added, reassuringly.

"Fairies," Thomas repeated. "*Are they the same as Fair Folk?*"

Tempest nodded. "*What do you think, Coriel?*" she asked the red robin.

"*Who can say, my little willow warbler,*" Coriel trilled. "*We'll worry about that later. Right now, escape's more important. Kwesi's right: pay attention to everything you learn today, my puffin. You need to find a way to recover your Talisman, and then we must try and cast another of those amazing spells, like the one you did by the riverbank – something that will help us get home.*"

Even if she did get her Talisman back, Tempest wondered how she'd do such magic again. She'd no idea how she'd managed it the first time. She could remember none of the words she'd said by the riverside. Not only that, but the spell had quite knocked her out. She would have to overcome such unpredictable difficulties if she wanted to use her powers to escape the palace.

A bell above the fireplace began to ring, distracting her from her thoughts and making Thomas jump. Tempest glanced up at it. It was attached to nothing. She watched in shock as a stick of charcoal that dangled on a long piece of string beside the bell, rose of its own accord and wrote on the wall:

THE NEW APPRENTICES ARE TO BE
BROUGHT TO THE STUDY RIGHT AWAY.
BY COMMAND OF LORD AND
LADY HAWTHORN.

"*I don't want to go!*" Thomas shouted, leaping from his seat in distress. "*I don't want to be that wicked sorcerer's apprentice!*"

Tempest was scared too. She didn't want to risk her life and Thomas's casting spells for Lord and Lady Hawthorn. She wasn't even sure she could perform for them. But she had no choice. Despite what Kwesi had said, she still hoped the lesson would present an opportunity – a chance to learn something new that would aid in their escape... It was a devil's bargain, to be sure, but one she realized she once again had to make.

"I'm here for your breakfast things!" Molly's voice called from outside the door. They heard her turn the key in the lock. Molly stepped into the room and left the door ajar for them when she saw the writing on the wall.

Kwesi stood and beckoned the others to follow.

"*Remember my promise*, Thomas," Tempest said, with resolve. "*I'll get us out of here. And I won't let anything bad happen to you.*"

Thomas nodded and took her arm.

Tempest put her other hand in her pocket. She could feel the three painted figures in their little wooden ferry boat nestled there, and somehow it gave her hope. This time, when they met, she vowed she would be ready for any magical tricks the Royal Sorcerer and his scheming wife intended to play.

Autumn Seeds

Death caps and slippery jacks and black snowdrops blossomed along the path the Wild Boy and the Storm Girl walked that autumn in the Greenwood. They were heading for the eastern side of the Forest, in search of the last part of the Opening Spell.

In the distance, they could see the leafy canopy of the Tree of Life, poking above the other branches, thinned of leaves. Only the great old oak in the palace, known as the Heart of the Forest, was more magnificent. When they reached the Tree of Life's trunk, the Wild Boy decided he didn't feel like turning them into squirrels, after all the other spells he'd cast that day. So he and the Storm Girl swung into the tree's branches instead, and clambered along its limbs.

The red robin flew about their heads, offering advice. It seemed she didn't really know where the black raven had hidden the last part of the Opening Spell exactly, only that it was somewhere in the tree.

The Wild Boy and the Storm Girl climbed higher and higher. But by the time they reached the top they'd failed to find any hint of the spell. Still, there was a good view. They could see all the bare branches of the Greenwood waving around them. To the Wild Boy it felt like being in a boat on a stormy river.

As they sat high in the tree's crown, a man dressed all in green, with a beard and hair of ivy leaves, appeared on the ground far below and called out to them.

"What are you doing up there, so far from the palace, my children? Don't you know that climbing in the Tree of Life is dangerous! If you're not careful you could fall to your death. Didn't you warn them, red robin?"

"Oh, I did, my ivy-bearded friend," said the little bird. "I warned them many times of the dangers of all this."

The Storm Girl ignored this outburst. "We're looking for the last part of an Opening Spell to create a doorway to England," she called down to the man in green. "It was hidden somewhere in this tree by a black raven named Auberon."

"I know nothing of that," admitted the man. "I only know of seedlings, stars and the stories of the universe. But

if a part of this spell of yours was secreted in the Tree of Life long ago, then the branches will have grown around that fragment and the knowledge will have become one with the tree itself. If you eat a fruit of the tree, a crab apple, it will give you the answer you are looking for. Search for the ripest one. Make sure you stick to the lowest branches. It's safer there. Not so far to fall!" The man made a move to leave.

"Wait!" cried the Storm Girl. "You haven't told us who you are."

The man stopped. "Why, I am just as I seem to be," he replied. "I am the light and the dark. The wholeness, and the flower growing through the crack in that wholeness. I was a suitor of your mother's once, long ago. I am the Green Man."

"You called us your children. Are you our father?" asked the Wild Boy.

"I am the father of everything," said the Green Man. "But yours most especially, my Wild Boy and Storm Girl."

The Green Man's words sounded like a riddle. The Storm Girl wanted to know what he meant, but this time he had really stepped away from the tree. As his footsteps faded, he fell from her mind. "What were we doing again?" she asked.

"I don't quite remember, my song thrushes," twittered the red robin.

"Searching for a crab apple that contains the last part of the Opening Spell, I think," replied the Wild Boy, rubbing his eyes woozily.

"That's right," said the Storm Girl.

And so the hunt for a ripe crab apple began.

The Wild Boy was the first to find one.

A hard little red ball on a stalk.

He picked it off the tree and bit into it.

The first bite tasted sour.

The second sharp.

The third bite was juicy and sweet, although he swallowed a fair few pips.

Then the final words of the Opening Spell came unbidden into his head:

"Seed of hope held in my hand, become the doorway to England."

The Wild Boy knew at once that those words had been embedded in the Tree of Life's seeds, and that he would need a few more of them to make the spell work. He winkled a handful of the little black pips from the core with his fingers and put them in his pocket.

"Finally we have the whole spell," he said, relieved.

With all its different parts, it seemed a complicated magic, more complicated than any they'd done before. But the Wild Boy was sure that, when the time came to cast the spell, the pair of them would be ready.

"Remember, little redstarts," said the red robin. "The Opening Spell will only work properly on the Stepping Bones. And there's something else I should warn you of," she added. "I was loath to say it until now, because I never thought you'd get this far. But there's something bad that happens to you when you journey to England."

"What's that?" asked the Wild Boy.

"You'll lose all memory of Fairyland," said the red robin. "And everyone you knew here. And you'll never be able to return."

"Why not?" asked the Storm Girl, shocked.

"Because, my little godwit, along with everything else, you will have forgotten the way home. Everyone who leaves does. Apart from the Queen and her sister, but they've secret ways to come and go, as I said before. Ways that mean they are immune to the forgetting."

"But why cast such a spell over the Kingdom?" asked the Storm Girl.

"For the same reason the Queen broke the old Bone Bridge and made the Stepping Bones in the first place, my little redshanks," said the red robin. "To protect the Fair Isle from outsiders. So no one who leaves can remember where Fairyland is hidden, or lead others to it. There is one chink in the Opening Spell, however. One pinprick of hope."

"What's that?" asked the Wild Boy, already thinking how he could use this knowledge to their advantage.

"Though you'll forget everything else when you leave," said the red robin, "you'll remember how to speak the Fairy tongue, but only if you've someone else to speak it with."

"That's all right then," said the Storm Girl, "because we'll have each other."

"Do people in England not speak Fairy?" the Wild Boy asked the red robin.

The red robin shook her feathers. "They speak English, my little turtle dove."

The Wild Boy thought about this. Their scheme was sounding more dangerous with each morsel of knowledge they learned. He hadn't realized if they left their home, both he and the Storm Girl would forget Fairyland and how to return. But maybe that was for the best, given what they'd discovered about the Curse. Anyway, they had no choice.

All the creatures in the woods knew of their plan now. Their mother was bound to find out about it sooner or later. Then, the Wild Boy realized, she would cast fresh spells to try and stop them. They had to leave at once, before that happened, or else one of them would not survive past their thirteenth Naming Day.

12

Magic Lessons

Lord Hawthorn's study appeared to be in some lonely, unpopulated corner of Kensington Palace, far away from both the Royal apartments and the servants' quarters.

While Tempest and Thomas trailed after Kwesi along silent, unfamiliar passageways, Coriel stayed hidden in Tempest's hair. Through a large window Tempest glimpsed a distant paddock, where a groom was exercising a horse on a rope. The horse trotted in never-ending circles, while the groom reined the animal in, tightening his grip on its tether, never letting go. Tempest thought of Lord Hawthorn and the power he wielded over them.

"Be careful in the Hawthorns' study," Kwesi warned,

as they descended a narrow staircase to the lower floors. "Take your time spell casting. Don't let them push you to do things that are beyond your ability. Or else you might faint, or fade away. And beware of the rug. Don't step on it. It has dangerous magi—"

"*CRAAAAAAR!*"

Auberon swooped, claws flashing. Kwesi cringed and threw a hand across his face.

Tempest realized with shock that the raven had been following them all this time, listening to every word they'd said. She wasn't sure what danger Kwesi had been about to alert them to, but it was too late – Auberon's warning was clear and Kwesi fell silent.

At the bottom of the servants' staircase, a secret door opened into a long hallway filled with monumental paintings of stern-looking men standing in dark landscapes. Their eyes seemed to follow the apprentices as they passed.

"These portraits are not to be trusted," Kwesi whispered, glancing around to make sure Auberon was out of earshot. "They spy for the Hawthorns. Even the paintings in the King's Gallery are loyal to them."

Tempest wondered how a portrait could spy. Paintings weren't alive. More magic, she supposed.

"This is where I leave you," Kwesi said. They had arrived at a set of polished double doors. "You two must face the

Hawthorns alone. Try to last as long as you can."

"And you'll be waiting here for us?" Tempest asked.

Kwesi shook his head. "I've had an idea that might get you out of trouble," he said. "I'm going to go and get help."

Tempest wondered what he meant. Who could Kwesi possibly find who was strong enough to take on the Hawthorns and their spying raven? She was about to ask, but he turned on his heels and ran off down the passage.

"*Who's he gone for, little fulmars?*" Coriel twittered nervously.

"*Not a clue,*" Thomas said. He glanced up at Auberon, who was still circling above, watching and listening. The white raven gave another loud cry that sounded like a cross between a warning and a laugh.

Tempest raised her hand to knock on the study doors, but before she could, they flew open of their own accord, revealing the study beyond.

At the far end of the room, Lord Hawthorn was sitting behind a large mahogany desk. His Grimoire was perched in front of him, along with Tempest and Thomas's Talismans. Lady Hawthorn stood nearby, in a bay window that was twice as tall and wide as she was, even in her voluminous red dress and high beribboned wig. She and the window were both framed by heavy velvet curtains, embroidered with colourful golden birds.

"ENTER!" Lord Hawthorn commanded.

Tempest and Thomas stepped cautiously into the room. Auberon sailed past them, gliding over to land on Lady Hawthorn's shoulder. The doors slammed loudly behind them, making Thomas tense and Tempest jump.

Tempest sniffed. The space had an air of malodorous magic. It wasn't just the morbid stench of Lord Hawthorn. It was something else...strong chemicals mixed with dead things. She didn't understand it at first, then she noticed the shelves and her toes curled in her shoes.

Strange dead creatures floated in cloudy sealed glass jars. Stuffed fish and lizards with more eyes and teeth than any beast had the right to possess grinned from glass cases. Dead butterflies, moths and beetles were pinned to boards on the wall, their wings fluttering ever so slightly in some non-existent breeze. Ram and goat and deer skulls with spiked and curled horns hung from the ceiling on strings. They spun slowly in the air, so that the shadows in their eye sockets made it look like they were watching everything.

Lady Hawthorn touched her brooch and called:

"Come closer, precious little lambs. Hurry to our caring hands."

She turned to her husband. "How do you think they are enjoying their stay in the palace, dearest?"

A big blue rug filled the floor ahead of Tempest and

Thomas, covered in woven waves that seemed to swell and shift. *Was this the danger Kwesi had been trying to warn them of?* Tempest wondered. But Thomas had already stepped onto the rug and she found she could do nothing but follow, as Lord Hawthorn spoke in his sing-song voice:

"Here they come, the Wild Boy and the Ferry Keepers' daughter. Looks like they've got themselves in deep water."

Auberon smirked.

Tempest tried to reply, but suddenly she was sinking into the woven waves.

Thomas writhed beside her, but it made no difference – they were both being gradually submerged.

"Help me!" Tempest screamed.

Coriel shot out of her hood and flapped wildly around her head. "*Kick, my little dunnock!*" she trilled. "*Swim for your life!*"

Tempest was flooded with memories of the Almost Drowning. Sweat poured down her back. She felt sick. This was dark magic and there was no Prosper or Marino to save her.

Auberon snickered as he watched from Lady Hawthorn's shoulder. Lord Hawthorn tittered too. Tempest could still just glimpse them bobbing far away, high above her. She was flailing in an ocean and they were on land.

Thomas splashed wildly. Tempest took his arm and tried to pull him towards the floorboards on the shoreline. But she could not. The waves of the rug were getting choppier the more they flailed around. Soon they'd be submerged entirely!

Suddenly, Lord Hawthorn tossed them their Talismans.

"Show me what you can do!" he called. "Use your magic to escape."

Thomas caught his Talisman and hooked it round his neck. Tempest fumbled hers in her wet, sweaty hands, almost dropping it. Her head was barely above the level of the floor. She felt herself sinking. She clasped her Talisman, her mother's gift, and suddenly words came to her, and she spoke them:

"To the warp and weft and waves I see. Heed my request and please help me."

She felt herself rising from the rug; Thomas too.

"Well done, my little warblers!" Coriel cried, landing on Tempest's wet shoulder. *"You're doing it!"*

The little red robin was right. In a moment Tempest and Thomas both collapsed on the floor, breathing heavily.

"Get up!" Lady Hawthorn commanded.

At once, they struggled to their feet and looked around.

The rug was behind them, and they were standing in front of Lord Hawthorn's desk.

"An impressive elemental invocation," Lord Hawthorn said.

"They have hidden talents, my beloved," Lady Hawthorn said. "That they only demonstrate when put to the test."

"I hope you don't mind?" Lord Hawthorn opened the Grimoire on the desk. "I like to note down any new magic I encounter for my records."

He flicked through its pages and Tempest glimpsed scribbled notes and fragments of phrases. There were amazing secrets hidden in that book. Spells gleaned from past apprentices. If she could get hold if it, she felt sure she'd be able to use it against the Hawthorns, but Kwesi had said Lord Hawthorn never let it out of his sight.

"Ah, here we are." Lord Hawthorn had found a blank page and began noting down Tempest's spell. "What was it again?" he asked. "*To the warp and weft*..."

Tempest didn't answer. Suddenly she felt very sweaty and ill. Lights danced at the corners of her eyes. Her head was spinning, as it had the last time she'd cast a spell. She remembered what Kwesi had said: *Take your time spell casting. Don't let them push you to do things that are beyond your ability. Or else you might faint, or fade away.* She glanced at Thomas. He seemed fine.

"For the rest of this lesson," Lord Hawthorn said, "we

shall practise entertaining spells for the King's upcoming Masquerade."

"No tricks, mind," Lady Hawthorn warned. "My husband is a powerful sorcerer. He has more magic in his little finger than you apprentices have in your whole bodies. Don't you, my love?"

"Thank you, my dear." Lord Hawthorn smiled winsomely at his wife.

His yellow teeth and her cloying endearments made Tempest nauseous. She shivered.

Thomas ground his jaw and said nothing.

"At the masked ball you will both be required to produce something spectacular," Lord Hawthorn said. "Thomas, you will be casting a transformation spell. Tempest, you will be casting a weather spell."

"*He wants us to practise our spells for the King's ball,*" Tempest explained to Thomas, nervously. She wasn't sure how much he understood.

Despite what Lord Hawthorn had said about "an impressive elemental invocation", Tempest had no idea how she'd escaped the rug. It had been an instinctive response to danger. She was tired now and a cold hollow emptiness had enveloped her. She was afraid she might pass out again if she did too much. She looked at Thomas, apprehensively.

"*I don't know how to do anything new,*" she admitted.

"I don't either," Thomas added. *"I only remember the wolf spell."*

"Don't worry, little teals," Coriel whispered, hopping from Tempest's hood. *"Just do your best. I'm sure you'll shine like summer snowflakes."*

Thomas eyed the rug with trepidation. *"What do you think will happen to us if we can't do something new?"*

"Thomas first," Lord Hawthorn interrupted. "I want you to turn yourself into a newt or a snake."

Lady Hawthorn folded her arms. Auberon hopped about on her shoulder. They both watched mercilessly as Thomas shifted from foot to foot and looked about.

Then Lord Hawthorn remembered that Thomas couldn't speak English.

"Tell him what I said," he snapped testily at Tempest.

"He understands you just fine," Tempest shot back. "He's a fast learner."

She instantly felt guilty. She'd given away another of their advantages in her anger. Although Auberon had probably noticed as much and had told the Hawthorns already.

"A newt or a snake," Thomas said, mimicking Lord Hawthorn. *"Or a wolf..."*

Quickly, he cast his Transformation Spell:

"Tail, snout, pelt, paws. Wings, fins, teeth, claws. Shake me, change me, magic truth. Make me into a Wild Wolf."

He leaped onto Hawthorn's writing desk in his wolf form and kicked over the inkstand, snatching at the Grimoire with his teeth.

Lord Hawthorn wrestled the magic book away from him and snapped it shut.

"ENOUGH!" he hollered. "I said a newt, or a snake."

He spoke a spell of his own:

"Cease, desist, resist no more. Sling this creature to the floor."

Thomas was thrown to the ground and became a boy once more. He was panting hard. Sweat dripped from his brow at the effort of doing so much magic.

Lord Hawthorn muttered more words and Thomas's Talisman flew from his hand into Lord Hawthorn's fist. "Do as I command, boy," he shouted, squeezing Thomas's Talisman. "Or you will face dire consequences."

Thomas squirmed on the floor, trying to free himself from the magic as Lord Hawthorn whispered his Control Spell to the Talisman:

"Bind and tie. Make him cower..."

Thomas whined. He clenched his fists and gritted his teeth hard to stifle the noise in his throat. Tempest could feel Lord Hawthorn's energy bearing down on him. Thomas fought hard, trying to resist it, but he was losing the battle.

Tempest gripped her Bone Cloud Talisman tight, feeling

the raw buzz of it, its edges against her fingers. She both wanted to run and to protect Thomas. Wanted to cast a spell to make all this end, but the magic wouldn't come.

"STOP!" she yelled, finally. "Just stop it!"

And, with a self-satisfied smirk, Lord Hawthorn did.

Thomas flopped breathlessly onto the floor. He screwed up his eyes and Tempest saw a tear trickle down the side of his face.

"Now," Lord Hawthorn said, turning ominously to Tempest. "It's your turn."

13

Three Princesses

Tempest grasped her Bone Cloud Talisman tightly and stared angrily at Lord Hawthorn. Coriel hid in her hair and, at her side, Thomas crawled shakily to his feet.

Tempest's skin felt itchy, her bones tired and her body sick and spent. What magic could she possibly conjure up for this horrible man and his vile wife?

She would rather be rid of them. Cast a thunderous snowstorm that filled their study and that they could not escape. Batter their self-belief and superiority with hail and rain and wild weather, until they were as cold and miserable and lost as she was.

But she could do none of that. She couldn't even

remember how she'd raised the water at the river, nor rescued herself and Thomas from the rug. There was nothing in her mind, or her heart that she could use to help herself.

"Here is what I want to see from you for the King's Masquerade Ball, Tempest," Lord Hawthorn said. "I want you to create a light rainstorm that falls from the ceiling in a gentle pitter patter of drops."

"Good thinking, beloved," Lady Hawthorn chimed in. "That is bound to impress the King."

Tempest had no idea what they were talking about. How could she make rain fall from the ceiling? There was no power left in her. The only thing she felt was a rush of anger at how the Hawthorns had mistreated them. That and her nerves swirling at the thought of doing more magic that might make her faint.

"Go ahead." Lord Hawthorn pointed up at the ceiling. "Make it rain."

"It's a small spell," Lady Hawthorn cajoled. "Perfectly within your capabilities."

Tempest pushed her nerves down into her stomach and stared upwards, at the ceiling dotted with the hanging animal skulls, twisting on their strings.

She pressed her Bone Cloud Talisman in her palm and felt the soft hum emanating from its centre. She tried to concentrate, remember the words of the spell she'd said by the river. It was something like: *Tide rise. Clouds gather…* She would have to change it to make it rain instead. Then a variation came to her from somewhere:

"***Drizzle. Mizzle. Showers gather. Clouds come. Rain patter.***"

As she said the words, she sensed a small tingle of power pool inside her, like the start of a sneeze. She let that magic roll in and felt a flood of relief that it was returning.

A moment later, she was shocked to see a few soft raindrops fall from the ceiling. They pattered onto the carpet, like a light summer shower.

"A passable effort," Lord Hawthorn said. "You'll have to do better than that for the real masked ball. Now add in some sunshine, to create a rainbow."

Tempest's heart sank. She was wilting already. She had no idea how to add an extra element to her spell.

Luckily, at that moment, the lesson was interrupted by a trio of girlish voices from the hallway.

"YOO-HOO!" they called.

It was so distracting that the power Tempest had mustered melted away as if it had never been.

Tempest's raindrops petered out as the doors to the room tumbled open and three young girls burst in, in a tidal wave of tulle and embroidery.

Kwesi followed in their wake.

"SURPRISE!" the three girls exclaimed loudly.

"Princess Anne! Princess Amelia! Princess Caroline!" Lady Hawthorn cried, giving an awkward curtsy to each of them in turn. Tempest tried to remember which name went with which. "What are you doing here, Your Royal Highnesses?"

"We've come to see the new apprentices," the oldest Princess, Anne, said. She had flaxen hair, a straight back and snub nose, and possessed, Tempest thought, a pale, fragile quality.

"Your Highnesses." Lord Hawthorn gave the three Princesses an oily bow. "What an exquisite delight to have the pleasure of your esteemed company in my humble study!"

"Don't fawn, Hawthorn," Princess Amelia, the second oldest Princess, admonished. She had a mess of strawberry blonde curls, and a haughty, no-nonsense demeanour. "We only want to see the apprentices."

"Fop wants to see the apprentices too!" Princess Caroline added. She had wavy dark locks and pink cheeks. Despite Caroline's slightly childish manner, Tempest guessed she and the youngest Princess were roughly the same age. Caroline was holding a little brown, black and white dog in her arms. "Don't they look marvellous, Fop?" she asked, kissing its floppy ears.

Kwesi stepped forward. "The Princesses wanted me to ·ing them here right away, Your Lordship, when they heard about the new members of your household. I'm afraid I couldn't stop them." He gave Tempest the slightest wink and mouthed the word: *Reinforcements*.

So this had been Kwesi's plan! Tempest felt relieved at his sudden arrival. Kwesi had endured the indignities of his low standing in the palace for so long, she realized that he'd learned to use some of them to his advantage. She watched the Princesses nervously. She didn't know what to expect of them. Thomas watched too. He seemed uncomfortable in their presence.

"New apprentices, greet the Princesses," Lord Hawthorn commanded in a pompous tone.

Tempest tried a curtsy and Thomas did his best to bow. Fop growled at them and barked at Coriel, who flew to the top of Thomas's head in alarm.

Auberon gave a cawing laugh from Lady Hawthorn's shoulder. He didn't seem at all scared of the dog.

"How are the preparations for the apprentices' show at Grandpapa's masked ball going?" Princess Caroline asked.

"What progress have you made that we can report back to Grandpapa?" Princess Anne said.

"What tricks will the apprentices be doing?" Princess Amelia added.

"Your Royal Highnesses…" Lord Hawthorn replied. "I must say, it is rather early to—"

"Your Highnesses, I don't think these questions are appropriate." Lady Hawthorn fiddled with the brooch at her breast.

Tempest wondered if it was Lady Hawthorn's Talisman. Then she realized with a jolt that she still had *her* Bone Cloud Talisman in her hand. Lord Hawthorn hadn't noticed! Quickly, she tried to hide it in the pocket of her cloak, but Lady Hawthorn had seen what she was doing.

"I'll take that, if you don't mind." Lady Hawthorn snatched the Talisman from Tempest. Tempest could've sworn it had been too far away for her to reach, but somehow she had it. Lady Hawthorn closed her fist around the Talisman, extinguishing a small slice of Tempest's hope. Then, in the blink of an eye, she was back at her husband's side, and talking to the Princesses. "Your Highnesses, don't you have lessons in your quarters? Music with Mr Handel? Then mathematics with Doctor Arbuthnot?" She began singing to them in a melodious voice:

"Knowledge is important. Especially for the King's granddaughters. Perhaps you should think about returning to your quarters?"

Tempest could see Lady Hawthorn was casting a spell. *Please let the Princesses stay,* she thought desperately as she stuffed her hands into her pockets for some sort of comfort and found the carved ferry boat. She gripped it tight until her fingers tingled. *Let Lady Hawthorn not persuade them to go away,* she whispered softly to herself.

"Lessons have been cancelled for today," Princess Caroline said suddenly. Somehow she had shrugged off Lady Hawthorn's spell.

Lady Hawthorn looked perturbed, her eyes widened in shock.

Tempest wondered for a second if her wish had somehow made enough magic to protect the Princesses. But she discounted that idea at once. She didn't know how, and anyway it wasn't possible without her Bone Cloud Talisman.

Perhaps, somehow, the Princesses' *royalty* had shielded them from Lady Hawthorn's enchantment? That seemed more likely.

"We asked Grandpapa to cancel our classes at breakfast this morning," Princess Anne said.

"And since it's so nice out," Princess Amelia added, "we've decided to invite the new apprentices to see the palace gardens."

"Right now, Your Highnesses?" Lord Hawthorn asked in despair. "We are in the middle of putting them through their paces..."

"Yes, right now," Princess Amelia replied.

"I'm afraid they told me as much, Your Lordship, on the way up here," Kwesi explained. "They were very insistent."

Tempest was glad that, for some reason, Lady Hawthorn's spell hadn't worked. She could see that, otherwise, the Hawthorns were no match for the three Princesses. It seemed the Royal Sorcerer and his wife were obliged to do as their Highnesses bid. Perhaps she could use that to her benefit, just as Kwesi had with his plan to rescue them.

"Fine," Lord Hawthorn relented. "But my wife and I will accompany you on your walk."

"Oh no, you will not!" Princess Caroline said.

"Why not?" Lady Hawthorn asked, shocked.

"You are far too boring," Princess Anne exclaimed.

"You'd spoil our fun," Princess Amelia said.

"*RUFF!*" added Fop the dog. Princess Caroline put her hand over his muzzle.

Lord Hawthorn sighed. "As you wish, Your Highnesses." He turned to Thomas and Tempest. "Apprentices, go into the gardens with Their Royal Highnesses. I will stay here and use this time to talk with my wife. Noah, you will stay too." He glared angrily at Kwesi. "It's time you practised your magic for the Masquerade."

"A Growing Spell would be a good fit for him, beloved," Lady Hawthorn suggested. "Perhaps he might sprout a sapling tree in the middle of the floor? It would make a nice counterpoint to Tempest's rainstorm, and a fine accompaniment for Thomas's transformation?"

Kwesi scrunched his brow furiously at being made to stay behind to perform such tricks.

"Good idea, dearest," Lord Hawthorn said.

But Princess Caroline interrupted. "Noah will not be practising his magic with you today," she commanded. "He will come with us to the gardens."

"We decree it," Princess Anne added.

By this point Lord Hawthorn had turned so red he looked just about fit to burst.

"AM I THE ROYAL SORCERER, OR AM I NOT?" he bellowed.

"Calm yourself, dearest." His wife put a soothing hand on his back. "Auberon," she said, flicking the white raven from her shoulder. "Go with the apprentices and keep an eye on them. Make sure they don't cause any trouble with Their Highnesses.

"You may be going outside," Lady Hawthorn told Tempest and Thomas. "But don't think that means you can get away from my all-seeing eye." She smiled at Auberon, who had swooped out into the hall.

Tempest shivered and crossed to the doorway, glancing at the raven and then at the rug that had almost killed them and the rest of the magical objects in the room, which had all seemed alive in one way or another.

At least now she knew what she and Thomas and Kwesi

faced. Not just the Hawthorns, but the enchanted obstacles as well. They'd have to get past them all, if they were to recover their Talismans and escape the palace.

She'd no idea how they'd manage it, but perhaps Kwesi had some thoughts. He'd made her realize they could use the hierarchy of the Royal Court to their advantage in their battle against the Hawthorns. And until they got their Talismans back and could use their magic again, that might be the only tool they had.

WINTER BONES

In the Greenwood, in the Fairy Queen's palace, at the base of the great old oak tree called the Heart of the Forest, on the winter solstice before their eleventh year, the Wild Boy opened his eyes at the thirteenth stroke of midnight in the bower room he shared with his sister. He shook the Storm Girl awake and roused the red robin, who was roosting on a branch that made up part of the ceiling.

Earlier that night, they had dressed in their warmest clothes, then gone to bed, pulling their blankets over them so no one would see, and so they wouldn't have to waste time dressing in the middle of the night when they woke, and could get on with the running away.

The Storm Girl rubbed her face. The red robin plucked sleepily at her feathers.

"Ready to go?" the Wild Boy asked them both.

The Storm Girl pressed her lips together. "I'm not so sure any more."

"Listen to your sister, my little siskin," said the red robin. "If your mother finds us while we're crossing the Stepping Bones, or saying the Opening Spell, then you'll be severely punished. Not to mention watched so you'll never be able to run away again."

"Then we must not be caught," said the Wild Boy. "I still think it's a risk worth taking, if it means we are able to escape the Curse and gain our freedom."

They snuck from the palace, through the Throne Room where they'd been given their Talismans on their first Naming Day, past the trees where the roosting birds had told them the first part of the spell, past the spring among the rocks, where the grassphoppers had told them the second part, and the mirrored pool, where the moon lay beneath the water like a puddle of spilled milk, with stars scattered around it like a pinch of salt. There, the rainbow trout, who had told them the third part of the spell, circled about as if they were swimming in the sky. A long way off, under the real moon, the Wild Boy heard his friends, the wolves, howling.

Finally they were far enough from the hidden bower where the Queen slept beneath the Heart of the Forest, that they could begin to run. They darted through the Greenwood, past snow-covered trees, until they reached the riverbank.

There, the Stepping Bones made a white and slippery T-shape in the dark river. Each rock gleamed, like a broken chunk of fallen moon.

The Storm Girl stared at the fast-flowing magical current, breaking around the stones. All they had to do was make it to the top of the T and cast the Opening Spell on the last Stepping Bone. Then they would be free of their mother and the Curse for ever.

But the Storm Girl couldn't do it. Even after everything she'd learned and everything her mother hadn't been. She knew she would miss her. And she was frightened to step into the unknown.

"Come on." The Wild Boy offered her his hand.

But she didn't take it. "The past, our fate..." she said. "It's all too heavy."

"We can outrun them," said the Wild Boy. "But only if we leave now, together."

"All right," said the Storm Girl. She turned away from the shore and took a deep gulp, swallowing a small shudder of longing deep down into her belly. Finally she took her brother's hand.

They leaped as one onto the Stepping Bones. Roiling tongues of water licked at their feet.

With each step, the Wild Boy felt they might fall into the bottomless depths and sink to the Dead Lands, or wash downstream to the sea and oblivion. A kind of giddiness overtook him. He could practically smell the freedom he'd wished for rising from the waters. His shoulders straightened. He felt taller, stronger, ready to face a new world and be free! He couldn't wait. His mind was so full of what lay ahead that he lost his footing on the Stepping Bones.

The Storm Girl clutched his arm tight and dragged him to his feet.

"Careful, my courageous cormorants!" warned the red robin, flapping between them. "The stones are slippery!"

The Wild Boy looked down and saw he'd cut his leg. It was a small graze, but red blood flowed from it, the colour of the Storm Girl's cloak.

They reached the cross at the top of the T, where the route from the shore forked in two. That crossroads of rocks, in the middle of the river, marked a line that sewed Fairyland and England together. Or a point that cut the two realms apart.

The Wild Boy took a crab-apple seed from his pocket, grasped it in his hand, and began to cast the Opening Spell. The Storm Girl joined him.

"Open sky, open stone, open waters, open bone.
Seed of hope held in my hand, become the doorway
to England."

The Wild Boy tossed the apple seed into the river, and a tree of silver threads appeared above the water. The Storm Girl watched, mouth agape, as one slice of magic, thin as a single shining thread of a spiderweb, tore the sky slowly in two, ripping it softly like a piece of cloth. The rip hovered a few feet from the ground, just above the height of the Storm Girl's head, then split wider into a gap opening in the air.

Finally the hole was wide enough and square enough that it resembled an open doorway. The space on the other side looked practically the same as where they were. They could see a fast-flowing river and a riverbank with trees, and a few wattle-and-daub buildings in the distance, little cottages with thatched roofs.

The one other difference was that it was daytime in England, and everything was as bright as a diamond. The sun shone on the waters, which were not black like those in Fairyland, but blue and green and shimmering with silver reflections.

Something more: there were no Stepping Bones over there. If they leaped through, they'd fall into the rapid flowing river.

The red robin flew straight into the crack and hovered in the bright blue air on the far side, bobbing and weaving about above the streaming waters and working her wings like a hummingbird.

"Quick, my little redshanks!" she called. "We don't have much time. The spell opens the gap for such a short while."

The Wild Boy and the Storm Girl both hesitated. Neither of them were strong swimmers. But the thought of the Curse and the pact they'd made to leave drove them onwards. Of the two, the Storm Girl was the stronger. "I'll go first," she told the Wild Boy.

"STOP!" came a yell from behind them.

They both hesitated.

The Storm Girl knew that voice. It was their mother.

"Hurry, my little goosanders!" called the red robin, darting about in the doorway. "Don't look back!"

The doorway was closing, the silver threads of magic sewing the sides of the door back together.

The Storm Girl couldn't help but take one last glance over her shoulder at the Fair Isle and the Greenwood and the world she was about to leave behind.

That's when the Queen emerged from the edge of the forest, her feet hovering a few inches off the ground. Her eyes flashed black and her silver hair blew behind her as she floated across the Stepping Bones towards them.

Light pulsed from her like she was aflame. The stag antlers, bird wings and briar twigs in her crown sprouted curling thorns. She caught the Storm Girl in her gaze like a fish on a hook. The Storm Girl thrashed, trying to break free, but her mother's eyes were bright stars, holding her in their grip. The Queen muttered a Control Spell:

"Bind and tie my precious flower, hold her will within my power."

The Storm Girl felt her thoughts fog with confusion. "I don't think..." she said in a flat monotone voice.

The Wild Boy could see the spell was working, making the Storm Girl change her mind about leaving. He didn't know what to do. He couldn't go without her. His plan was crumbling.

If they didn't leave now, they'd be trapped and beholden to the Curse. At least he could save his sister.

He struggled free of his mother's gaze and pushed the Storm Girl through the gap. She blinked and gave a surprised scream as she tumbled backwards and hit the river on the far side of the doorway, in the dazzling daylight of England, with an almighty

SPLASH!

"Swim!" called the red robin, swooping around the Storm Girl as she flailed in the rushing currents. "Swim my little duckling! Swim like your life depends on it!"

The Storm Girl gargled and bobbed about, snatching

breaths, just managing to keep her head above the writhing surface of the water.

The Wild Boy steeled himself to dive through the doorway and join her, but before he could, his mother was suddenly at his side.

She grabbed his arm and held him with a force so strong he thought the bone might break.

"You're not going!" she hissed.

"Help me!" screamed the Storm Girl, through the last gap of the closing doorway.

A final slice of light leaked through, as the silver threads closed, sewing the two halves of the dark night back together.

Then England and the daytime and the other shore and the other river, and the Storm Girl and the red robin were gone. It was night once more, and a flame in the Wild Boy's heart went out.

His sister and his bird-friend were gone. Stranded in another world. At least they were safe. He'd saved his mother from having to make a deadly choice between them, and his sister from having to face their fate. But there was still a price to pay: now that she'd crossed over, the Storm Girl would forget him and their life here.

And he would be forever lonely, until the day he faced the Curse alone.

The Wild Boy stood beside his mother, the Fairy Queen, on the humped Stepping Bones, looking back across the Tambling River to the Greenwood and the Fairy Kingdom.

Here, in just over two years' time, he would die so that his mother might live and rule for another hundred-and-thirty-three years. Then he wept for all he had lost, and the terrible fate he knew was yet to come.

14

Walled Garden

On that last day of winter, the gardens of Kensington Palace looked impressive. Tempest and Thomas and Coriel and Kwesi followed the three Princesses along an avenue of trees. Tempest's head ached with weariness from the spell she'd managed to cast in Lord Hawthorn's study. She'd surprised herself by performing that magic, and the drain of it was making her feel shaky, but Coriel's presence in her hood was a comfort. That and the fresh air. She watched as Fop ran along the pathway, its floppy ears flapping. The little dog stopped to bark at every wren, daffodil and squirrel.

Auberon flitted between various branches, and spied

goggle-eyed on the apprentices, cocking his head to try and listen to their conversation. The Princesses seemed delighted by their newly acquired companions, but Tempest could only think of how she could get herself and her friends out of their company so they could have time to scheme and regroup.

Tulips, crocuses and snowdrops edged the pathways, along with tall budding bushes Kwesi said were called camellias. The sight of those buds made a flower of hope bloom in Tempest's heart. After hiding away through the coldest months, the good things in life were aching to return, if you were prepared to look hard enough for them.

"Thank you for bringing the reinforcements," she whispered to Kwesi.

"I said I would, didn't I?" Kwesi smiled at her and Coriel, who was peeping over Tempest's shoulder. "Can't have my new fellow apprentices drowning in the rug during their first magic lesson."

Tempest shivered, thinking of the rug. It was as if Lord Hawthorn had known of the Almost Drowning and had decided to use it against her, but how could that be?

"Look!" Princess Amelia cried. The three Princesses had stopped by an elaborate glasshouse filled with orange trees "The Orangery!"

"The last English Queen, Queen Anne, had it built," Princess Anne explained.

"She planted the orange trees," Princess Caroline added.

Tempest tried to imagine a Queen in a crown with a spade planting orange trees, but she could not. She realized that the monarch probably had not actually planted them herself, merely ordered someone else to.

They crossed a large patio, chequered like a giant chessboard and spotted with great stone statues of Kings and Queens. They passed fountains and wiggly hedges in squiggly shapes, and pointed trees, like green witches' hats, being trimmed by gardeners with big hedge clippers. There were kitchen beds, where children picked winter herbs for the palace chefs to cook with. And nursery gardens, filled with cloches, tended by yet more gardeners. Tempest guessed there were at least thirty or forty servants dotted around in total. If that was how many it took to look after the King's winter garden, she couldn't imagine the number of staff in the palace, not to mention the stables. There'd have to be…well, hundreds.

The Princesses and Fop seemed free to wander wherever they liked. As did whoever wandered with them. Fop barked and the girls giggled as Thomas cartwheeled across the grass. Coriel zigzagged along behind him.

"Are the Princesses allowed to leave the grounds?" Tempest

asked Kwesi. She was still of a mind that perhaps Their Royal Highnesses might be useful for finding a way out.

"They're kept prisoner here, like us," Kwesi said.

"Who are their parents?" Tempest asked, thinking of Prosper and Marino and how much she missed them.

"Their father is another George; the Prince of Wales," Kwesi said. "Their mother is the Princess of Wales, Caroline. The Waleses live elsewhere. They quarrelled with the King over the death of their baby son. The King had their daughters – his granddaughters – brought here as his wards in revenge."

"How horrible," Tempest said.

"Oh, don't feel sorry for the Princesses," Kwesi replied. "They have everything their hearts desire. Music, art, archery, fencing, games, great minds to entertain them, plus every kind of food and cake under the sun. I wish I had such gifts," he said, bitterly. "Even Amelia's dog was a present from her mother. All I've got to remember my mama by is the Sunray Shell Talisman, and Lord Hawthorn has that."

Tempest put a hand on his shoulder to comfort him.

"Isn't it funny how alike Thomas and Tempest are?" Princess Caroline said loudly to her sisters, interrupting Tempest and Kwesi. "They even have the same eyes. One green, one blue."

"One green, one blue," Thomas repeated in English.

"Are they related, do you think?" Princess Anne asked.

"Could be," Princess Amelia said, peering at Thomas.

"*Tell her not to stare!*" Thomas requested.

"He says please don't stare at him, Your Highness," Tempest told Amelia. She wished she'd been brave enough to say that on her own behalf.

"And they speak the same odd foreign language!" Princess Amelia exclaimed.

"It's not German or French," Princess Caroline said. "We'd understand those."

"It doesn't sound like any tongue we've heard in court," Princess Anne said. "What language do you think it is?"

"Our language," Thomas replied in English. "Unique to us."

"They're both multi-lingual!" Princess Caroline said. "Like us! Wie aufregend!" she said, in German.

"Comme, c'est excitant!" Princess Amelia added in French.

Fop barked delightedly at her feet.

"And what about the little robin?" Princess Anne asked.

"She understands English and their language, Your Highnesses," Kwesi explained.

"Though she can only speak in our language herself," Tempest added.

"Well, then she is quite the wonder!" Princess Caroline said.

"*She is!*" Thomas grinned at Coriel, and the fact he'd managed to understand the Princess's chatter.

"Will the little robin land on my arm, do you think?" Princess Amelia asked Tempest.

Coriel shifted on Tempest's shoulder. "*Should I, my moorhen?*" she queried.

"*We need them to be on our side,*" Tempest admitted. "*So yes.*"

"*All right, little linnet.*" Coriel flitted onto Princess Amelia's arm, crooked her head and gave the Princess a loud tweet. "*How's that for a trick, you sneezewort?*"

"What did she say?" Princess Amelia asked.

"She said she's honoured to meet you, Your Highness," Tempest replied.

"*CRAAWW!*" Auberon cried dismissively from a nearby treetop. He was still spying, Tempest realized.

"Let's keep moving," she whispered to Kwesi, staring around at the gardens. They were yet to find a viable way out. "Please might you show us some more of the beautiful gardens, Your Highnesses?" she asked the Princesses.

"Of course," Princess Amelia said.

"We'd be delighted to," Princess Anne added. "This way. Follow us."

The three Princesses set off round the edge of the gardens which were surrounded by a high wall, bare of trees a vines. It looked unclimbable, but no wall was insurmountable, Tempest told herself.

Suddenly the Princesses cheered. Tempest saw that Thomas had scaled a tree beside two corner walls. He was swinging high in the canopy, his woollen stockings bright in the sunlight and his fur coat rucked around his shoulders as he clambered among the fresh spring leaves.

The Princesses skipped around the tree's trunk like they were playing ring-a-ring o' roses. Fop cavorted around their feet, barking as Auberon flapped threateningly towards Thomas, snapping his beak.

"*Quickly,*" Tempest told Coriel, seeing how much trouble Thomas was about to be in. "*Distract that raven! And the Princesses and the dog, while you're at it!*"

"*Right you are, my turtle dove,*" Coriel sang. She swooped up from Tempest's shoulder and dive-bombed Auberon, sideswiping him with her wings. "*Take that, you white-feathered fool!*" Then she went for Fop, peppering the pup with pecks from her beak. "*You too! Have at it, you overindulged floor-mop!*"

Fop growled and snapped at Coriel. Auberon swooped angrily at the robin, but the little dog tried to bite him too. Soon the irritated pup was leaping in the air and chasing both birds across the garden.

Coriel drew the mutt and the raven off into the ubbery, leading them a merry dance. Fop was wild with the chase, while Auberon became so distracted trying to fend off the dive-bombing robin and the maniacal little dog that he didn't have time to register anything else.

"Look!" Princess Amelia cried, drifting away from the tree trunk to join the chase. "A bird-and-dog fight!"

"How exciting!" Princess Anne said, stepping after her sister to watch Auberon, Coriel and Fop.

"Who will win, do you think?" Princess Caroline called, trailing them both. "The raven, the robin, or my precious hound?"

"*Hurry!*" Thomas whispered loudly from the tree, when they were all gone. "*I've spotted something you should see.*"

Tempest looked around for any other courtiers or servants who might be watching, but there was no one. She put her right hand on the trunk and felt the coarse wrinkles of the bark against her skin. Something about it reminded her of the Greenwood. Her legs were itching to climb. She glanced at Kwesi. "Are you coming?"

He nodded. "But we'd best be quick."

Tempest hiked up her skirt and tucked the trailing end into the sash at her waist, then she climbed into the tree with Kwesi following her. As they clambered towards Thomas in the topmost branches, Tempest looked around. Below them, the Princesses, their little dog and the birds scooted off, chasing through the archway beneath th clocktower. Beyond the palace walls were fields and hamlets and the outskirts of London and, far off, the thin blue curving thread of a river.

"The Thames," Kwesi said, when he saw her looking at it.

Tempest was reminded of her own dear river a long, long way off.

"*I think there might be a way out over here!*" Thomas pointed down through the branches at the corner of the perimeter wall, which stood a foot or two away from the tree.

He was right, there was a way.

"Careful," Kwesi warned. "The wall has a Containment Spell on it like the one across the window in the apprentices' dormitory. It'll hurt you badly if you try to step over it."

"*It doesn't feel as strong as that other spell,*" Thomas said.

"One way to be sure." Tempest held his arm for support and leaned out from the branch, reaching tentatively to brush her fingertips along the top of the wall.

The magic bit hard, stinging like an angry wasp. Tempest's eyes smarted with tears. She pulled her fingers back and sucked them. There'd be no escaping that way without disarming the spell first.

Suddenly she heard Coriel's twitter. She was returning across the garden.

"*Where are the Princesses?*" Tempest called to the little robin as she alighted on a nearby branch.

"*I lost them by the clocktower, my little linnet,*" Coriel sang.

"*And Auberon?*" Thomas asked.

"*Gone for the Hawthorns,*" Coriel chirruped.

"We'd best get down before anyone arrives," Kwesi warned.

They had reached the lowest branches of the tree and were almost at the ground when Auberon appeared with Lady Hawthorn, followed by three servants, the three Princesses, a worried-looking Mehmet, and a bounding, barking Fop.

"I know *exactly* what you've been up to," Lady Hawthorn cried, staring up into the tree at them. "You'll find no escape route over the enchanted walls. And even if you did, Lord Hawthorn could track you down with the aid of your Talismans. Now get down at once! It's time to go back inside." She waved to the three servants, who grabbed the legs of one apprentice each.

Tempest's assailant was a burly man and, before she could fight against him, he yanked her unceremoniously from the branch and she tumbled to the ground.

"Be gentle with them, Your Ladyship," beseeched Mehmet.

Lady Hawthorn waved him away. "This is none of your concern. Get back to your duties for the King."

Tempest sat up, winded. The servant holding her dragged her to her feet. Thomas and Kwesi were being wrestled to their feet too. Then, when they were all safely standing, Lady Hawthorn, with Auberon on her shoulder, led the party back towards the palace.

Tempest glanced over her shoulder to see Mehmet disappearing into the distance, and the three Princesses and Fop gambolling in the grass. The Princesses seemed to have completely lost interest in the plight of the apprentices. Behind them was the corner tree; its highest branches sagged over the wall. Tempest knew with surety that was their way out, but only if they could disarm the spell first. For that they would need not just to recover their Talismans, but all their strength and magic too.

Lost Boy

"You will be punished for helping the Storm Girl escape, you silly boy," said the Fairy Queen. Her silver hair fluttered about her shoulders as she marched the Wild Boy along the riverbank away from the Stepping Bones. "See how dangerous the water is. You may be wild, but the river is wilder. Your sister will see that on the other side. In England."

"Go and get her then," said the Wild Boy. "If you're so worried about her."

"I shan't," said his mother as they walked through the Greenwood. "She's a strong swimmer. Coriel will guide her to the far riverbank and safety." She paused and looked at him. "But then what, I wonder?"

"She'll be in a better place," said the Wild Boy. "A place called England."

"Ah, glorious England!" The Fairy Queen laughed. "You think life's perfect there?"

The Wild Boy wasn't sure how to answer that.

"Not perfect," he said. "Just different. Less...difficult."

"Your sister will be fending for herself in England," the Fairy Queen told him. "Alone, except for that foolish bird. That will be difficult enough. But she will also forget everything she's ever known. Her family and friends and her free, idyllic, cosseted life here. That will be the penalty she suffers for disobeying me. The affliction she carries."

The Wild Boy bit his lip to stop himself replying. "Free" and "idyllic" were not words he would use to describe their life in the palace, or on the Fair Isle. But then he supposed words were not set things. They could be bent to any purpose, just like spells could.

He didn't know which was worse: staying to face your fate, or leaving and forgetting your past and that your deadly fate ever existed. He'd been the one who'd planned their running away. The one who'd persuaded the Storm Girl and the red robin to go. And he was the one left behind. He'd never be able to escape Fairyland. Not with his mother watching.

"Perhaps England will be the making of my sister," he suggested.

"Either way," his mother replied, "in two years' time, on

the thirteenth anniversary of your Naming Day, when the payment of the one-hundred-and-thirty-three-year Curse is due, you will be the one to suffer." She lifted the Talisman around the Wild Boy's neck and held it in her hand. "You won't escape me. You carry a part of me with you, in your bones. In your essence and your soul. As does she. And if you run, as she did, I will fetch her back to take your place."

She dropped the Talisman. It hit the Wild Boy's chest with a THUMP! that made his heart jump.

The weight of her words hit him too. He'd thought he'd succeeded in setting his sister free, but he was wrong. The Queen could bring the Storm Girl back whenever she wanted to, it seemed, and him too if he ever left.

If that was the case, then everything he'd done had been for nothing. His sister's fate and his own had been sealed long ago by the Curse. It was a death sentence he hadn't asked for and had no power to change. And that was hardly fair, was it?

There was one thing left he could try. It was probably a futile petition, but at this point he had nothing left to lose; perhaps his mother might show him clemency.

"Your sister altered the Curse, mother," he told her. "She was supposed to be the one to suffer the consequences of it, but she changed the wording so that it would be my sister or me. Then she cast a spell over you, so you would never learn, or believe, the truth of what was done that day."

"Nonsense," said the Queen. "It has always been you or your twin sister named in the Curse."

"How can it always have been us?" the Wild Boy asked. "The Curse has been around from before we were born."

"No." His mother shook her head. "I will hear no argument from you regarding this matter," she advised. "And let that be an end to it."

Then the Wild Boy realized the red robin had been right about his mother all along. His aunt's spell was strong over her, and she was truly averse to logic. It was impossible for him to argue against his fate. Escaping with his sister had been his only real option, he realized with dismay, and now that too was gone.

"Come on," his mother said. "Enough of your dawdling. Let's go home."

As the Wild Boy trailed at his mother's side, he touched the wolf's tooth the Storm Girl had given him. It was the sole gift he had from her. He'd sewn it to the neck of his fur coat as a button, as she'd suggested.

They crossed the clearing and skirted the pool and the spring and took the path that led deeper into the woods. Up ahead the Wild Boy saw the Heart of the Forest growing through the roof of the palace. His home and his prison.

Silently, he swore an oath that, one day, never mind the consequences, he would cast the Opening Spell again. He would step through the doorway, swim the river, and search all of England to find his sister and the red robin, before leading them both far, far away. There they'd hide somewhere their mother could never find them and in that way they would escape the Curse for ever and win their safety and their freedom.

Eleven more lonely months passed in the Greenwood and every day the Wild Boy regretted the fact that he hadn't made it through the doorway with his twin. He often wondered what the Storm Girl and the red robin were up to. A part of him hoped his mother would never find them. That way the Storm Girl would've truly escaped the Curse. Although that would mean she was lost to him too, and he didn't want that.

Every so often during the autumn he would return to the Tree of Life to look for a fresh apple with a seed he might use in an Opening Spell. But the Tree of Life was always bare. No more apples grew on it. It was as if someone had cast a spell to make it wither. Then one day the Wild Boy found he had forgotten the words of the Opening Spell too. He guessed all of this was his mother's doing, or his aunt's, but he could never prove it.

The Wild Boy's twelfth Naming Day came and went, and he knew that in less than a year, the end would be upon him. For a time after that he was unable to do anything and he lost himself in a deep well of sadness.

Another spring and summer drifted into another autumn, then winter.

On the winter solstice, three months before the first day of spring and the Wild Boy's thirteenth Naming Day, black snow fell and coated the bare silver trees of the Greenwood. The Wild Boy opened his palm and let a single snowflake fall into his hand and melt away. The sharp feel of it on his palm woke him from his despair, and he walked through the forest alone.

It was a cold day and he put his hands in the pockets of his thick fur coat to keep them warm. In his left-hand pocket, sewn from leaves and rabbit fur, he found a hole that had been growing for some time and was large enough to fit his hand through.

There, he discovered an old apple seed from the Tree of Life nestled in the coat's moss-padded lining.

The Wild Boy pulled the seed out and examined it hopefully. As he did so, he remembered the words to the Opening Spell.

He looked about. There was no one in the forest around him. None of the Queen's spies.

Quickly, he made a plan. He would go to England disguised as a wolf, so nobody from Fairyland would be able to recognize him there, if they came looking.

Then, when he finally found somewhere safe to hide, and humans who might protect him, he'd return to his true form and ask them for their help to find his sister and the red robin.

It was a good plan and he acted on it at once, bounding briskly through the Greenwood, past the pool and fountain, down to the riverbank and the Stepping Bones.

He decided not to leap across them all this time, for fear of being swept away by the rising tide. He wasn't as strong a swimmer as his sister, but he hoped the Opening Spell would work even if you stood on the first Stepping Bone. The important thing, he felt, was to be close to the flow of the river and to have the seed in your hand. That mattered the most, and the believing.

The Wild Boy stood on the Stepping Bone nearest the shore. He held the apple seed and said the Opening Spell, just as he had with his sister two years ago, near this same spot, on this same solstice night, and dropped the seed into the water.

At once, a tree of rippling silver threads grew from the shallows, rising into the sky before him. One silver thread that was thinner than the others tore the air in two, growi brighter and opening out like a rip. Gradually, the hole grew, until it had become a doorway facing away from the river that was large enough to climb through.

It was the middle of the day in Fairyland, but in England, on the other side of the gap, the sky was the deep dark of night, and sprinkled with a new moon and stars.

Beneath them the Wild Boy saw another Greenwood Forest. It was almost identical to the one on this side of the doorway, except that over there the trunks of the trees were brown instead of silver, and the snow on the ground was white instead of black.

The Wild Boy took a deep breath and readied himself to step through the doorway. But then he remembered the red robin's warning: once he was in England, he'd forget everything about his old life.

Everything!

That meant, on the other side of the doorway, he wouldn't just forget who he was, but he'd forget his sister too, and his friend the red robin. He wouldn't know they'd ever existed. Not only that, but they'd have forgotten him as well. Even if they met by accident, they wouldn't remember each other.

He vowed he'd climb through the doorway anyway. England was the sole chance he had of escaping the Curse. part of him was certain that fate would take a hand and lead him to his sister on the other side. And that, somehow, through the magic they both possessed, they'd overcome the Forgetting Spell that was thrown over them when they had passed through the doorway, and remember each other.

And so, with that one wish in his heart, the Wild Boy stepped through the doorway, to England, in search of his little winged friend and his long-lost sister.

15

Escape Plans

That evening, in their dormitory, Tempest, Thomas and Kwesi suffered a second meal of bread and dripping brought by Molly, who glanced over her shoulder into the hallway to check Auberon wasn't there listening or watching, and secretly passed Kwesi a folded piece of paper. "Mehmet sent this for you," she whispered, "as you requested. You can keep it for tonight, but he'll need it back first thing in the morning, as usual."

"Thanks." Kwesi held the paper behind his back, making sure it was hidden until Molly had left, locking the door behind her. Then he spread it out on the table.

It turned out to be a small, hand-drawn map of London.

The River Thames snaked through its centre, just as Tempest had seen earlier in their view from tree.

"Mehmet and Molly sneak this to me when they can," Kwesi explained. "It's from the King's library, so I can only ever keep it for a short while, in case he notices it's missing. I've been gradually memorizing every detail. That way, when I finally get out of here, I'll be able to navigate my way across the city. You too, if you're with me."

"Clever," Thomas said.

Tempest thought so too, but they'd still have to pass the magical barrier that surrounded the palace. She gobbled hungrily at her slice of greasy bread, and her stomach rumbled at the thought of the good food at home she was missing – the fish Prosper caught on the river and the vegetables Marino grew in the garden, roasted on the fire together until they were tinged with sweet charcoal, or stewed in a hearty broth full of flavour.

As they ate and Kwesi studied his map, he, Tempest, Thomas and Coriel discussed what they'd learned today and tried to use that knowledge to come up with a plan.

"The magic on the wall was very strong," Tempest told the others.

"I did warn you," Kwesi said. "It's probably strong enough to kill you."

"It's not worth trying anything without disarming it

my little bitterns," Coriel said.

"But if we could *disarm it,"* Thomas said. *"Then freedom would be within our grasp."*

"We'd need our Talismans to stop such a spell," Tempest said. "And so that Lord Hawthorn can't trace us with them," she added, remembering Lady Hawthorn's earlier threat. "To get those, we'd have to break into Lord Hawthorn's study, which we can't do without magic either."

It made Tempest's head ache to think about it. She finished her meal, and stood and paced the floor, shuffling her thoughts to try and come up with an answer to something that seemed utterly unsolvable.

The others watched expectantly, but she said nothing. Just kept pacing back and forth.

Something was banging against her thigh. Distracting her.

She put a hand in the pocket of her cloak and felt the three tiny painted figures in their little wooden ferry boat nestled there.

She pulled the carving out and turned it over in her hand. I[illegible]he one thing she had from home. The gift that
[illegible]rino had given her when they first suggested
[illegible]laughter. And to her it represented love as
[illegible]loud Talisman from her mother did.
[illegible]ures in their boat and felt the smallest

of hums tingle beneath her fingers. It was the same hum she'd felt when, without thinking, she had held the little boat in Lord Hawthorn's study. When her whispered wish had seemed to protect the Princesses from Lady Hawthorn's magic. She had dismissed any connection at the time, but the feeling was here again, and…

That was it!

Tempest waved the carved boat trinket at the others. "Look!" she cried, elated. "This is the answer. It was staring me in the face all along. The solution to our magic problem!"

"*What do you mean?*" Thomas asked.

"I mean," said Tempest, "that *THIS* can be my new Talisman."

She placed the boat down in the centre of the map, on the River Thames.

"How?" Kwesi said.

"It's like you told me in the hut, Kwesi, when we first met," said Tempest. "'A Talisman is crafted for its user by a sorcerer. It's made from an object gifted to them by someone they love, usually associated with their ancestors.' It doesn't matter that Lord Hawthorn took our old Birth Talismans, we are powerful sorcerers and we can make new Talismans from the things we have. All we need to do is find an object that represents love to us and it will focus our magic. Like this…

"This boat is from my guardians, Prosper and Marino, and it was given with love."

"Try it then," Kwesi suggested. "Do some magic with it."

"What should I try?" Tempest asked. She felt a little unsure of her idea now that it came to confirming it.

"Weather," Thomas said. "*Cast a Weather Spell.*"

Tempest took hold of the boat and felt its familiar shape. The three little figures in it had weathered such storms, like herself, Prosper and Marino. She touched the tiny carvings of her guardians and thought of how much she missed them.

To her surprise, the tingling hum from before reappeared, and she felt the magic welling up inside her. Strangely, with this new Ferry Boat Talisman, the buzz of magic felt stronger than with the Bone Cloud. Tempest was able to focus more easily. She spoke the words of the first spell she had done by the river, as they formed in her head:

"***Tide rise. Clouds gather…***"

She trailed off. She couldn't remember the rest. It had slipped away, like flotsam over rapids. A ragged tide of disap[illegible]t overwhelmed her.

[illegible]rong," she said sadly. "And you can't make [illegible] your own."

[illegible] her. "I think you're right. Keep going.

"*You almost succeeded, little reed warbler,*" Coriel twittered, flapping to her shoulder.

"*You can do it,*" Thomas reassured her. "*Forget everything you know. Be one with the power. Feel the magic flow like a river. Let it be a part of who you are.*"

Tempest clutched the boat once more. She felt the hum of it in her hands and thought of a rainy day when Marino had made pasties, and Prosper and he had taken Tempest out fishing in *Nixie*.

Suddenly, there in that dusty, stuffy dormitory, her brain was filled with the beautiful gurgling song of raindrops pattering on water. The same Rain Spell that had come to her in Lord Hawthorn's study fell into her head again and she said it aloud:

"***Drizzle. Mizzle. Showers gather. Clouds come. Rain patter.***"

The Rain Spell was much stronger this time than it had been that morning. Thousands of raindrops spattered from all corners of the ceiling and plopped onto the floorboards, dripping down between them.

"*Gypsywort and yarrow-weed!*" Coriel cried. "*Well done, little chiffchaff!*"

"*It worked!*" Thomas cheered, leaping to his feet.

"So it did!" Kwesi hooted, clapping his hands.

"I did it, didn't I?" Tempest said, a little taken aback. The rain was still pounding joyful down on her head, dripping though her damp hair. Quickly, she spoke a Weather Calming Spell to stop it:

"Clouds split. Rains break. Weather calm. Storm abate."

Immediately the patter of drops silenced and the rain stopped.

Tempest breathed a great sigh of relief. For the first time in two days, she allowed herself a small smile. She'd solved a problem and performed the strongest, clearest magic she'd yet managed, with a new Talisman and the loving memory of Prosper and Marino. She rather felt as if she was becoming her own person at last, so much so, that the storm of worry that had hung about her lately seemed to recede a little.

"We need to find you each a new Talisman. To focus *your* magic," she told the others, as they brushed the drops and damp from their hair and faces.

"*I have this.*" Thomas showed her the wolf's tooth, sewn to his fur hood. "*I don't remember who gave it to me, but I'm sure it's from someone I love.*"

He grasped the tooth in his hand and said his Transformation Spell:

"Tail, snout, pelt, paws. Wings, fins, teeth, claws. Shake me, change me, magic truth. Make me into a Wild Wolf."

Thomas changed into a wolf and back in the blink of an eye. The transformation was so quick and clean that for a second afterwards he was still panting.

"*Well done, Thomas!*" Tempest cried. She felt filled with sheer delight. "Now it's your turn, Kwesi."

"I don't have anything from my family," Kwesi said sadly.

"That's not true. You have this." Tempest ran to his bedside and snatched up the wooden board with the miniature portrait of his mother and father on either side.

"It wasn't given to me by Mama," Kwesi said. "It's just drawings I made."

"I don't think it's that important where the object comes from," Tempest said, holding it out to him. "It's the emotion it evokes. Your drawings do that, Kwesi. It's a memory of your mama and a vision of your papa, done with love."

Kwesi took the piece of wood with his mama's and papa's images on and held it in his hand, closing his fist around it. "I can feel my power gathering," he said.

"Try some magic," Tempest suggested.

"How about a Healing Spell?" Kwesi stepped over to the broken chair in the corner.

As Tempest and Thomas watched, Kwesi kneeled and put his hand on the chair and whispered some words to it.

"**Fix, repair, heal, restore. Return to how you were before.**"

The snapped leg of the chair straightened and grew back into the seat.

"I did it!" Kwesi cried, elated.

He stood the chair by the table. He was radiating with joy at being able to perform magic without Lord Hawthorn's supervision. "I want to try something else," he said. "A Growing Spell. The one I'm supposed to perform at the Masquerade."

He kneeled and touched the damp floorboards with his hand: "**Wood**," he murmured, "**remember your seed, brown and dun. Grow like a sapling and seek the sun**."

He took his hand away.

A tiny searching shoot burst from the floorboards, grew to the height of his ankle and unfurled two green leaves.

Kwesi smiled at the beauty of it.

Coriel twittered with happiness.

Thomas laughed in amazement.

And Tempest's heart swelled with joy.

That bright shoot, growing from the middle of the dusty floor, represented one thing to all of them in the apprentices' dormitory that night: hope.

"Now that we have our new Talismans," Tempest said. "And your map, Kwesi, we can finally make a proper escape plan. It'll be hard, but with magic this strong I think we stand a good chance."

"What would be the first step?" Thomas asked.

"Open the door lock somehow," Tempest suggested.

"*How, my little puffin?*" Coriel said. "*We don't know the words Lord Hawthorn uses to unlock his magical locks.*"

"I could use the Growing Spell to warp the wood in the door," Kwesi suggested. "That should pop the lock, which will break the enchantment on it. Then it will open."

"Then we'd need to get down the corridor without Auberon noticing," Tempest said.

"Plus," Kwesi added, "we need to make sure we don't meet any servants in the passageway who could alert the Hawthorns."

"If only we knew Lord Hawthorn's Invisibility Spell," Thomas said. "The one he used to hide us and his magical cage, when he brought us from the river."

"Well, we don't," Tempest said. "So we'll have to make do with what we do know. I can create a Fog Spell to hide us. What about your Transformation Spell, Thomas? Could you use that to disguise us as mice?"

"I don't think I can recall mice," Thomas said. "But I can probably do wolves again for everyone."

"I can add a small Concealment Charm," Kwesi said. "Lord Hawthorn made me learn it. It's not as good as his Invisibility Spell, but it is something."

"We'll have to hope all of that will be sufficient until we're safely in the garden. Then we can break the Containment Spell and climb over the wall," Tempest said.

"You're forgetting one thing," Thomas added, in English. He had become so fluent he could conduct whole conversations in English. "We still need to steal our Birth Talismans from wherever Lord Hawthorn hides them in his study at night."

"Thomas's right," Kwesi said. "If we leave our Birth Talismans behind, Lord Hawthorn will use them to track us down and recapture us, just as Lady Hawthorn suggested. In which case, we may as well not escape at all."

Tempest shivered. She really didn't want to return to Lord Hawthorn's study, not after what had happened there this morning, but she could see Kwesi and Thomas were correct. If they wanted to avoid being recaptured, it was a risk they'd have to take. She hoped they'd be able to overcome whatever fearsome magical protections the evil Lord and his cunning wife had set over the place and get out with their Birth Talismans and themselves still intact.

"We should wait until midnight," Kwesi said. "It'll be safer that way, with no one about. And we can't take the map. Mehmet and Molly would be implicated if it's found to be missing. We'll have to leave it, and rely on my memory instead."

"Good idea." Thomas stood and snapped the long piece of string and charcoal from the wall.

"What are you doing?" Tempest asked.

"We'll need this string to make necklaces for our new Talismans," he explained. "If we're wolves, we won't be able to hold them, so we'll have to wear them round our necks."

"So we have a plan then," Kwesi said. "I hope it works."

Tempest hoped so too. She couldn't help but feel that they had forgotten some vital detail that would throw things off course. They would just have to ford that stream when they came to it, she told herself. Everything was set. All they had to do now was wait for midnight.

"What will you do if we get out of here?" Tempest asked Thomas as he snapped the string in three and handed a piece to each of them.

"Come with you back to the Greenwood," Thomas said, pulling the wolf's tooth from his jacket and tying his piece of string around it. "We have more to discover still."

"How about you, Kwesi?" Tempest tied one end of her string to the stern of her little boat and the other to the bow, before hanging it round her neck. "What'll you do?"

"Maybe you could come to the Greenwood too?" Thomas suggested.

"Or to Tambling Village?" Tempest said. "I'm sure Prosper and Marino would be happy to look after both of you, until you've grown enough to take care of yourselves."

"Thanks for the offer." Kwesi threaded his string around his wooden picture. "But I'm not sure I can accept. The truth is, I want to find my own community. I belong with them. With my knowledge and magic, and their connections,

I think we can build a resistance that will help free the rest of our people."

"Where will you look?" Thomas asked.

"I've heard there are African traders down by the docks," Kwesi said. "Sailing folk who might help me get on my feet. I could earn my living selling small magics while I do. It's dangerous out there, though. There are vicious street gangs who kidnap Black people and sell us back into slavery. No one's ever completely safe, not really. Not even those who came to England of their own accord. But at least once I'm out of this prison, my magic and my life will be my own, and I'll finally be free."

He took a deep breath, as if revelling in that feeling right now.

Tempest joined him, wondering if there was any other way she could help.

A thought struck her.

"My fathers know some African traders in London, who live down by the docks. Their names are Adofo and Yaba Fremah. Adofo trades peat and charcoal. He and his wife visit Tambling occasionally. They're very friendly and resourceful. Maybe they can help you with your plan?"

"Maybe they can," Kwesi said.

They talked some more until, at last, darkness fell. Then Kwesi extinguished their candle and everyone retired to bed, still dressed so they wouldn't have to waste time putting clothes on when they woke at midnight.

Tempest laid her head on the pillow and closed her eyes to try and get some sleep. She tried to think of the nice things they'd talked about that evening, as well as the details of their escape plan… But in the dark of her dreams all she saw was a murderous white raven, screaming in anger and diving at them from the roof of the hallway. And no matter how far or how fast she ran in her dreamscape, she couldn't seem to escape Auberon's razor-sharp claws.

16

MIDNIGHT RAID

Tempest was woken by Coriel standing on the end of her nose, pecking at it with her beak. "*Twelve o'clock, and all's well, my little grey heron!*" Coriel whispered, as the last few chimes of the hour drifted into the room from the clocktower.

Tempest brushed the little bird aside, then checked she was still wearing her new Ferry Boat Talisman round her neck. It hummed ever so slightly. She rose quickly and quietly from her bed and drew back the curtain around it.

Kwesi and Thomas were up already, wearing their own new Talismans, and struggling into their coats and boots. Kwesi hid the map of London under his mattress, where

Molly would find it, along with a note thanking her and Mehmet. Tempest's hands trembled. As she buttoned her red cloak and tied her shoelaces, her mind drifted to the immense task that lay ahead. Magic and theft were two things she had never fully imagined herself doing, but now her very survival depended on both.

When everyone was ready, Kwesi touched the door beside the lock and whispered:

"Wood buckle. Swell and sprout. Open the door and let us out."

The door grew knots, squashing the lock until it buckled and cracked. Kwesi took his hand away. His spell was done. The lock was broken. He flexed his fingers together and rubbed his palms. "I can't believe it worked!" he cried. His eyes were wide with shock.

Now it was Tempest's turn.

She felt the hum of the Ferry Boat Talisman against her chest. Storm clouds tingled in her belly at the thought of trying another, much harder Weather Spell. But the magic had worked for her earlier, as it had for the others. She just needed to perform with confidence. She steeled herself and, clutching the Talisman, said the spell she'd been planning.

"Smog. Haze. Gloom slather. Murk come. Mist gather."

A thick fog emanated from the air around her, wafting

everywhere until she could barely see the far end of the room. The fog seeped under the door, like someone was pulling a blanket through a gap.

Then Thomas said his Transformation Spell to turn them into wolves, adjusting it to account for the fact that there were three of them.

"Tail, snout, pelt, paws. Wings, fins, teeth, claws. Shake us, change us, magic truths. Make us into Wild Wolves."

It was a funny feeling, Tempest discovered, to find herself changing shape so quickly. Hair sprouted from her skin and through her clothes until she was completely hidden by her new pelt. Her fingers fused into paws. Her nose grew into a snout, her teeth becoming long and yellow. By the time the spell was done, she felt an overwhelming urge to howl with joy, but she managed to keep herself silent for the sake of their mission.

Finally, to make doubly sure they were hidden in the fog, Kwesi whispered a small concealment charm in his new wolfy voice:

"Conceal, hide, keep us from sight, let us not be seen tonight."

Slowly and quietly, they pushed the door open with their snouts and peered out.

With their sharp wolf vision, they could make out a white shape in the fog, sitting on the nearest window ledge, wide awake and watching. From the smell of it, Tempest knew what it was…

"*Auberon!*" Thomas growled quietly. "*He's awake!*"

"*Leave him to me,*" Coriel twittered. She jumped from Tempest's back and flew down the passage towards the white raven, snapping her beak.

"*CRAAW!*" Auberon cried, and leaped, startled, from his perch, soaring into the air.

Coriel circled him, trilling, "*Come and get me, you mangy old sack of feathers!*" Then she led him off down the corridor.

Tempest stared anxiously after Coriel and Auberon as they disappeared into the fog. She wondered at the courage of the little robin, who was braver than a wolf pack! She hoped Coriel would be all right alone, facing off against the cunning raven. Who knew what that beastly creature would do if he caught her?

"*Quiiiiiick!*" Thomas howled. "*We'd best get moooooving while they're gone.*"

The three wolves padded quietly along the empty passageways, towards the far and lonely corner of the palace where Lord Hawthorn's study was located, and the fog trailed with them as if they were dragging it along by their teeth.

Even with their disguises, the darkness and Kwesi's Concealment Charm thrown over them like a magica' blanket, Tempest didn't feel safe. The three wolves had just reached the monumental hall of watchful portraits, which were luckily hidden in the fog, when Coriel fluttered down, landed on Tempest's head and whispered in her pointed, furry ears, "*I'm back, little wolf cub.*"

"*Where did you go?*" Tempest growled. "*I was worried sick.*"

"*I'm such a birdbrain! It took me a while to find you hidden in this grey murk,*" Coriel whispered, "*until I remembered you were wolves, not children!*"

Tempest gave a yapping laugh.

"*Quiet!*" Thomas snapped, his ears pricking up in alarm.

Kwesi shot them both a look and gave a loud sniff.

They'd reached the door of Lord Hawthorn's study.

As quick as he could, Thomas turned them back into their own forms. Then Kwesi carefully put his hand on the door and whispered his newly found, powerful Growing Spell into the keyhole of the lock and the knots of wood.

A moment passed. The magic petered out.

"What's wrong?" Tempest asked urgently.

"This door's enchantment is harder," Kwesi said. "It has more locking magic in it."

"Maybe if we worked together?" Thomas suggested. "Spoke the spell in English, in unison?"

The three of them quietly sang Kwesi's Growing Spell at the door.

The magic in the lock tried to fight them, but, eventually, they were stronger.

At last the wood warped, cracking the lock. The door swung open and they stepped into the study, pushing it almost closed behind them. Tempest's fog didn't follow them through the slim gap; instead it stayed where it was, hanging in the hallway like a natural barrier. Without their wolf shapes and the mizzle cloaking them, Tempest felt suddenly a lot more exposed.

"*Keep a lookout, Coriel,*" she told the little bird.

"*Right you are, my puffin!*" Coriel fluttered down to the door handle and poked her head through the narrow crack in the door.

"Search everywhere," Tempest told the others. "Leave no stone or skull unturned, no drawer unchecked. We must find our Birth Talismans."

"Remember," Kwesi warned, as the three of them snuck further into the room, "no matter what happens, don't step on the rug!"

Thomas and Tempest followed him cautiously round the edge of it to reach the rows of vitrines and cabinets and Lord Hawthorn's desk beyond.

Thomas began by looking behind the embroidered curtains and then started pulling out desk drawers. Tempes rifled nervously through the boxes on the lower shelve the cabinets. Kwesi checked for secret safes behind the rows of pictures. But their Birth Talismans weren't hidden in any of those places.

Tempest and Thomas tried feeling along the higher ledges of the vitrines, between the pickled creatures. It was a bit icky. Tempest didn't mind insects or living things, but these were dead and floating, magnified in their glass containers. She steeled herself and reached behind a jar with an eye in it, searching the dark unseeable corner of the shelf with just her fingertips.

Suddenly, the dead eyeball whirled around to face her, making her jump. Tempest stifled a scream and whipped her hand away, but her fingers caught and pulled the jar forwards.

It wobbled on the edge of the shelf for a second, the floating eyeball inside rolling worriedly.

Then it fell…

…smashing on the polished floor with a loud *CRASH!*

The eyeball tumbled out and bounced under a cabinet, as the rest of the glass jars began to jiggle against each other with a horrible *tinking* rhythm.

A lump stuck in Tempest's throat. Hairs rose on the back of her neck. The pickled creatures were waking up.

Their bulging faces boggled as they slammed themselves to the sides of their water-filled jar-prisons.

"*What have you done?*" Thomas whispered as the stuffed fish, lizards, rats and bats on plinths awoke, opened their glass eyes, and started croaking and growling and crawling towards them.

Then the moths, butterflies and beetles pinned to boards on the walls broke loose from their frames and fluttered around, their dead wings disintegrating with each beat.

The golden birds embroidered on the curtains began to squawk, and the animal skulls that hung from the ceiling bit through their strings and fell to the floor, where they leaped about, snapping at the apprentices' ankles.

"OUCH!" Thomas cried, as he was bitten by a yellow horned goat's skull with a jaw full of cracked molars. He covered his mouth to muffle his cry.

Kwesi thrashed his arms about frantically and stumbled backwards, trying to fight off a wave of moths.

Tempest grabbed his hand and pulled him towards her to stop him from stepping on the rug.

"Thanks," he cried over the noise of aggrieved, snapping sheep's skulls.

Finally, the few portraits in the study awoke and the figures in them began screaming at the tops of their voices: "INTRUDERS! ALERT!"

"*Loosestrife and teasels!*" Coriel squawked angrily across the room. "*What a racket! Silence those dead beasts and painted toffs before someone hears! Thank heavens we're so far from the centre of everything here!"*

"A spell!" Tempest hopped on her toes, batting away a mangy stuffed bat. "We need a Quietening Spell!"

"Let me try one." Kwesi brushed more flailing moths from his face and spoke:

"**Paintings, beasts, we've had enough! Quieten down and please shut up!**"

The cries and roars and squawks continued. If anything, Kwesi's spell made the enchanted creatures even angrier.

Kwesi pressed his lips together. "We need to try something else, before the Royal Sorcerer arrives!" he cried.

"I've got nothing," Thomas said through gritted teeth.

"Me neither," Tempest began. But then she remembered: Royalty trumped sorcery in the palace – she knew that from observing Lord Hawthorn interacting with the King, and the Princesses. If she turned herself into a Princess, the magical creatures would have to listen to her. She thought about it and decided she looked most like the haughty Caroline.

"Can you disguise me as Princess Caroline?" she asked Thomas. "I've had an idea."

"I'll try," Thomas said. He chanted a new version of his Transformation Spell:

"*Crown and sceptre, magic sublime. Turn Tempest into Princess Caroline.*"

As he spoke the words, Tempest felt the spell working. Her face and body were changing shape once again. She glanced over at a full-length mirror leaning against the wall. The resemblance was uncanny. She'd become Princess Caroline. She even had on the outfit the Princess had been wearing that afternoon. There was just one thing missing.

"*Fop!*" she told Thomas. "*I won't be convincing without the dog!*"

Thomas nodded. He pointed at Coriel, fluttering anxiously by the door, and said:

"Wet snout, muddy paws, floppy ears, tail up! Change this bird into a pup."

In a whirl of growth, Coriel's wings became front legs and paws, her beak became a snout with a soft dark nose, her body grew, her feathers sprouted into brown fur, and she gained a fluffy tail.

Soon Coriel looked absolutely identical to Princess Caroline's little hound. The one difference was, where Fop had a white fur bib on his chest, Coriel's bib was red like the little robin's apron she wore as a bird.

"*My new coat and paws are quite becoming!*" Coriel growled. "*I'm almost as handsome as you were as wolves.*"

"*Quiet, Coriel...I mean, Fop,*" Tempest reprimanded her friend in the most Royal voice she could muster. The little dog ran to her side, floppy ears flapping.

Tempest turned warily to the screeching dead creatures and clapped her hands in the loudest, most pompous, Princess-y manner she could muster. The noise carried the length and breadth of Lord Hawthorn's study.

"Enchanted creatures of the palace!" Tempest announced in a self-important tone. "I am Princess Caroline." The lie felt a little heavy on her tongue, but Coriel jumped up into her arms and gave Tempest's face a rough doggy lick, which helped banish her nerves.

"My grandpapa is none other than King George the First, ruler of England," Tempest continued. "His power far exceeds the Royal Sorcerer's. I decree that you will stop your clamouring at once and be quiet!" She wondered, nervously, if this was quite enough, and added in quickly as a last thought, "By Royal Command, you magical beasts must do as *I* say!"

17

Mirror Door

The magical creatures of Lord Hawthorn's study fidgeted and stared at one another, considering Tempest's command.

Tempest clutched the little doggy Coriel to her chest and waited. She was still disguised in the form of Princess Caroline, her heart thumping after her improvised Royal decree. She hoped it would be enough to end the study creature's attack.

Thomas and Kwesi stood beside her, holding their breath to see what would happen.

A long moment passed.

Finally, as if by an unspoken agreement, each of the

floating specimens in their jars, the stuffed fish, lizards, rats and bats settled back in place and did not resume their chatter.

Soon the butterflies, moths and beetles dropped to the floor too.

Then the animal skulls stopped snapping.

And the portraits in their frames froze where they stood.

At last, everything was still. Relief washed through Tempest. Her plan had worked!

Kwesi leaned on the wall and let out a huge sigh.

"For a moment there, I thought we were done for," he admitted. "But you did it!"

"Well done!" Thomas cheered softly.

"*Who knew the dead held Royalty in such high regard,*" Coriel growled, licking her nose with a long pink tongue before jumping down from Tempest's arms and padding back to her lookout spot by the door.

Still, they needed to find their Birth Talismans without further delay.

"We didn't check the desk properly," Tempest said. She'd noticed the image of a ring of thorns, like the Talisman Lord Hawthorn wore round his own neck, on a desk panel whose edges didn't quite meet flush with the sides.

"This bit looks odd. Perhaps..." She pressed the carving with one finger.

Click!

The panel sprang aside on hidden hinges exposing a secret drawer with a tiny keyhole.

A shiver rolled up Tempest's spine. "This has to be it!" she said, hopping from foot to foot. Thomas and Kwesi peered over her shoulder.

"I'll try my Growing Spell to break it open." Kwesi dried his palms on his shirt and cupped both hands around the lock.

"*Someone's coming, little spaniels!*" Coriel warned from her spot in the doorway.

"We need to hide at once!" Thomas said.

Coriel kicked the door closed with her back paw and scurried across the room, taking care to avoid the rug.

Kwesi and Thomas rushed behind the embroidered curtains in the bay window; Coriel joined them.

Tempest stood where she was, surveying the horrifying mess. The broken jars and open drawers, the dead insects, the skewed paintings, the scattered animal skulls. Her heart sank. It wouldn't matter where they hid, the chaos would tell whoever set foot in this room that they were here.

She had to do something quickly. Kwesi's Healing Spell sprang to mind. Perhaps she could use it to repair the room. *Could you use someone else's magic like that and tweak it?* she wondered. There was one way to find out.

Tempest pressed her hand to the Ferry Boat Talisman on her chest and quickly recited a version of Kwesi's spell, with alterations she'd just thought of.

"Fix, repair, heal, restore. Return the room to how it was before."

She finished speaking and felt an immense surge of power radiating from her, channelled through the Ferry Boat Talisman.

The animal skulls jumped up in the air and re-hung themselves from their strings. The butterflies, moths and beetles fused themselves back together and fluttered from the floor back into their cases. The glass jars re-formed and their dead creatures plopped back into them as they flew to their shelves in the vitrines. The portraits righted themselves, the painted figures scrambling to reassume their original poses. The stuffed fish and lizards leaped and scuttled back to their plinths. Even the door lock returned to how it had been before the three apprentices had entered the study.

Finally, everything was in place, bar Tempest.

"Quick!" Kwesi whispered.

"Hurry!" Thomas called.

"*Get moving, little beagle!*" Coriel growled.

The door lock clicked.

Fatigue and fear fought inside Tempest. Quickly, she vaulted the rug and dived behind the curtains, squishing in beside Kwesi and Thomas. As the door creaked slowly open, Coriel leaped nervously into her arms. Tempest hugged the little dog's furry body tight against her chest and flattened herself against the wall, while Kwesi quickly refreshed his concealment charm to strengthen their hiding place.

"Camouflage, conceal, secrete away. Hide us now, in every way."

As he finished, the door smacked hard against the wall. A flickering candle held by a frightening figure in a white nightgown embroidered with ribbons, with thorns and brambles growing through her ragged wild hair, appeared. A ghostly bird with a scythe-like beak was sitting on her shoulder. Auberon!

Auberon flapped his wings in agitation as the wild figure, her brambly hair writhing like a fistful of angry snakes, stepped into the room.

"*Hawthorn!*" Coriel whispered, stiffening in Tempest's arms and curling back her lip to reveal her dog-teeth.

It was Lady Hawthorn. But she was a Fairy, Tempest realized, with a horrifying and uncomfortable jolt that shot through her like a lightning bolt. The idea seemed so shocking and alien, and yet also so familiar, Tempest wondered how she had not realized it before. Beside her, Kwesi flinched and Thomas hunched uncomfortably into himself. They had both obviously come to the same conclusion.

Each of them tried to keep as still as possible as Auberon and Lady Hawthorn looked beadily about Lord Hawthorn's study.

"*You said they came this way,*" Lady Hawthorn snapped.

"*I can't see them, Milady,*" Auberon cawed. "*And nothing's out of place. I don't think they're here.*"

"*Why didn't you follow them properly?*"

"*Coriel distracted me.*"

"*Never mind,*" Lady Hawthorn said. "*We must speak with my sister at once. We've put off seeing her long enough.*"

Tempest was confused. What sister? Who was she talking about?

"*For once your husband's stupid greed for magic has paid off,*" Auberon replied. "*She's sure to reward us when she hears we've found her children. But will she believe us?*"

"*There's one way to make her,*" Lady Hawthorn said ominously.

She stepped across the room, towards where they were hiding.

Tempest clasped Coriel tighter in her arms and shrank further back against the wall, trying to make herself as small as possible. Beside her, Thomas and Kwesi did the same. The three of them held their breaths. Tempest hoped the dark and Kwesi's spell would be enough to keep them concealed.

The Fairy and her raven were a few feet away from their hiding place. Tempest could just see a sliver of the approaching pair through the crack in the closed curtains. Kwesi pursed his lips to stifle a gasp. Thomas's eyes bulged; his face was contorted in fear. This was it, Tempest thought with heavy dread. They were about to be discovered.

But instead, Lady Hawthorn turned to the desk. She put her candle down on it, leaned forward, and pressed the hidden button on the thorn symbol.

Click!

The false panel sprang aside. Lady Hawthorn took a key from her pocket, unlocked the secret drawer and pulled it open. Auberon hopped down from her shoulder and perched on the inkstand, peering into it.

"There they are!" Lady Hawthorn reached into the drawer, but her back was to them so Tempest could not make out what it was she'd taken.

"*She'll believe us when she sees these.*" Lady Hawthorn held her prize aloft.

Thomas gasped. Coriel scrabbled in Tempest's arms. Kwesi gripped her shoulder. And with a racing heart, Tempest saw her Bone Cloud Talisman and Thomas's Hag Stone dangling from the Fairy's fingers.

Lady Hawthorn relocked the hidden drawer and reset the panel over it, then put Thomas and Tempest's Talisman away in a hidden pocket of her dress. "*Help me prepare the Opening Spell, Auberon,*" she commanded.

"*As you wish, Milady.*"

Auberon flapped from the desk over to the frame of the full-length mirror and perched on top of it. Lady Hawthorn walked over to the mirror too. She put one hand on the brooch at her breast and the other on the mirror, and spoke these words:

"***Open sky, open stone, open waters, open bone.***

Magic Mirror in my hand, become the door to Fairyland."

As Lady Hawthorn finished speaking, a thin spiderweb of silver threads grew from her hand, emanating through the mirror. The strands writhed like the thorn bush on her head, weaving through the glass with a sound like cracking ice.

Behind the curtain, Tempest wrung her hands together as she watched Lady Hawthorn's magic expanding. She recognized the Opening Spell and the silver doorway. Something about them seemed awfully familiar. She wanted to get closer, to see better, but Kwesi's fingers dug into her shoulder, warning her to keep still. Coriel scrabbled anxiously in her arms and, beside her, Thomas nervously ground his jaw.

Lady Hawthorn's spell was almost done. The glass himmered like the surface of a lake as the clouds of silver threads split open. Soon both the mirrored room and Lady Hawthorn and Auberon's reflections disappeared, replaced by a clearing, where a spring ran over rocks down into a deep, clear pool.

"I know that place," Thomas whispered quietly under the soft hum of magic. "It's the Greenwood."

He was right, Tempest realized. It was the Greenwood that sat over the river from Prosper and Marino's home – but not the same Greenwood she knew. This was another Greenwood. A mirror version, with silver trees and black frosts. This was a Greenwood in another world. A Greenwood in the world of Fairyland. The mirror had become a magical doorway to it. Tempest gasped silently to herself.

Lady Hawthorn reached a hand through the glass, which warped and bent with magic. She took a deep breath, then stepped through the mirror. Its surface rippled behind her.

A single white ribbon from her nightgown floated down and landed beside the carpet. Auberon watched it fall.

"*I hate this part,*" Auberon muttered. Then he launched himself from the top of the frame, flapping through the doorway after his mistress. The wave he made was so violent that shining droplets of pure magic flew from the mirror and splattered on the study floor.

Tempest shielded her eyes against the dying glassy brightness of the sparks.

When she looked up, she saw Lady Hawthorn, with Auberon on her shoulder once more, standing in the shallows of the pool on the far side of the mirror.

A strange alteration had occurred in both of them. Auberon's feathers had turned from white to black and Lady Hawthorn's writhing bramble-bush of hair was sprouting with hawthorn flowers.

Tempest watched as Lady Hawthorn carefully stepped from the pool and across the clearing, heading towards a distant building nestled in the trees.

"Is it safe to come out?" Kwesi asked.

"What do you reckon, Tempest?" Thomas said.

"I hope so," Tempest replied softly.

"*I don't think they can hear us from all the way away in those woods, little terriers,*" Coriel growled. "*And not on the other side of that Magic Mirror.*"

The four of them emerged silently from their hiding place and peered at the glass.

Coriel jumped down from Tempest's arms and sniffed at the Magic Mirror with her wet nose.

Now that Lady Hawthorn had stepped away from it, the doorway embedded in the Magic Mirror was shrinking, the iris of its pulsing silver threads closing slowly. Tempest peered through the diminishing gap.

"I think we should follow," she told the others.

"We might have to fight her on the other side," Thomas said.

"*And Auberon,*" Coriel added.

"An angry raven and a Fairy who travel between worlds." Kwesi shivered. "Who knows what powers they hold."

"We must," Tempest said. "Lady Hawthorn has our Birth Talismans. She can track us wherever we go with those, remember?" She stared nervously at the Magic Mirror. Its doorway had closed a few more inches in the time they'd been dithering, but it was still big enough for them to dive through if they hurried.

"*The doorway will shut after we're through it, my little whippets,*" Coriel barked. "*Then we'll be stuck. Better you keep to the plan and climb over the palace wall to freedom.*"

Tempest shook her head. "No, we must go through the looking glass. We have to take that risk. If we don't get our Talismans back, Lady Hawthorn will use them against us. Perhaps," she suggested, hopefully, "we can open the door again from the far side."

"We might not be able to find a way to do that once it's shut," Thomas said.

"What if someone stays here," Kwesi said, "and casts a Holding Spell to keep the doorway open until you get back?"

He was volunteering to remain behind, Tempest realized.

"Are you sure?" she asked.

"It could be the more dangerous task," Thomas added.

Kwesi nodded. "It'll take some chanting. And the spell won't last for ever. An hour at most. You'd best be no longer than that."

The Magic Mirror's doorway had closed some more while they'd been speaking. Soon it would be sealed off completely. Kwesi pointed at the shrinking hole and spoke a Holding Spell to keep it open.

"Wedge, chock, door stop. Till my friends return, your closing's blocked."

The shrinking shimmered to a standstill. The remaining hole pulsed slowly. It was about ten inches in diameter, barely wide enough to squeeze through. But that was what they'd have to do.

It was now or never.

Good luck," Kwesi told them.

"And you." Thomas hugged him.

Tempest kissed Kwesi's brown cheek. "See you when we return," she said.

"*If we return!*" Coriel growled.

"*Ready?*" Thomas asked her nervously.

"*As I'll ever be.*" Tempest's voice came out shaky. Coriel jumped into her arms, and she held the little puppy against her chest. She was still Princess Caroline, she remembered suddenly, and there was no time to fix that now. It would have to wait until later.

She took Thomas's hand, and, together, the pair of them squeezed through the narrow hole in the Magic Mirror that was all that remained of the enchanted doorway into Fairyland.

18

FAIRYLAND

T*hud.*

Thud.

Thud.

Tempest's heartbeat echoed in her chest. As they tumbled through the doorway, time seemed to ricochet about them. She felt herself floating…

Up.

Up.

Up.

Finally, she scrambled from the black pool of water, with Thomas and Coriel at her side.

They were in Fairyland.

Tempest was weary and spent. Her bones and head ached from the spells she'd cast in Lord Hawthorn's study. She was scared and excited to be somewhere new that seemed so different and yet so familiar.

Coriel flapped awkwardly to her shoulder. She was no longer a puppy but a red robin. Tempest looked down at her hands and realized they were no longer Princess Caroline's but her own. Her deception had been washed away by the Magic Mirror; she had shed the disguise spell and was herself once more.

It looked to be about one in the afternoon in Fairyland. A bright sun, a sliver past the midpoint in the sky, was melting the last of the black winter frost, readying the damp ground for the first flowers of spring. Lady Hawthorn and Auberon were nowhere to be seen.

"Fly off and find them, Coriel," Tempest said.

"All right, little dove," Coriel replied. She stuttered a little. Having just got used to being a dog, she seemed to have forgotten how to take off. But then she leaped from Tempest's shoulder, spread her wings, and was off.

Tempest and Thomas clambered to their feet and took one last glance back through the Magic Mirror into England. Between the wavering silver threads, Tempest could just glimpse a ghostly image on the far side of the doorway. It was Kwesi, standing in the study with his arms full of magic, holding open a sliver of the mirror's doorway. He seemed far off and blurred, like she was watching him through the wrong end of a telescope. Tempest hoped he would be able to keep the doorway open until they got back, but they'd best hurry.

Her red cloak felt soaked and heavy from the crossing. She glanced at Thomas – his fur coat was slick with water and magic too. The single yellow Wolf's Tooth Talisman glinted round his neck. She had given him that, Tempest remembered suddenly. As a gift. She'd found it in a hole in a tree years ago, before she had last left Fairyland.

At this thought, her mind bloomed open like a spring blossom and memories tumbled out...

Memories of their Naming Day. It had taken place on this Fair Isle, in this Greenwood, in the Fairy Palace. A day short of thirteen years ago. All the Fairies, including Lady Hawthorn and Auberon, had been at that ceremony. Their mother, the Queen, had named and blessed each of them with water from a flower, and given them both their Birth Talismans: Tempest her Bone Cloud and Thomas his Hag Stone.

Then the Fairies had cheered and thrown dried petals, and everyone had danced the winter into spring.

Tempest remembered who she was now: a Fairy Princess. And Thomas, her twin brother, was a Fairy Prince.

She wondered how she could've forgotten such a magnificent heritage. And how Thomas could have

forgotten too. How was it that in England they hadn't recognized each other, when they'd spent every day of the first ten years of their life as brother and sister. And how was it neither of them had recognized their Fairy Aunt and old magic teacher, Lady Hawthorn, or her friend and confidante, Auberon Raven?

It must've been a strong forgetting-magic that had descended on them when they'd first left, to make them lose sight of their past. But now that Tempest had her memories back, she recalled everything. So much so that she had to stop for a moment and take a deep breath and put her thoughts and feelings to one side, so she could concentrate on the present. This was the first time she'd seen Fairyland in two years, and yet it seemed like a lifetime since she'd last been here.

"We're home," she whispered to Thomas when she finally regained her breath.

"My soul aches to be seeing it with you again," said Thomas with a faint smile. He looked tired. The glut of transformation magic he'd performed in Kensington Palace must have been starting to wear on him. Or perhaps, Tempest guessed, he was feeling the same niggling doubt she had in the back of her mind, that was telling her they shouldn't be here.

Suddenly Coriel returned. "Lady Hawthorn and Auberon went this way, my little Storm Girl and Wild Boy," she twittered, fluttering above their heads. "You can catch them if you run." Her red belly and brown wings flashed between silver tree trunks, as she guided them along a path from the pool, through the trees.

"I don't recall why we ever left this place, my Storm Sister," said Thomas as they ran.

"Neither do I, my Wild Brother," said Tempest.

And it was true. She could not.

If they were Prince and Princess, why should they be sneaking through a magic portal into the Greenwood, like unwelcome guests, to the palace of the Fairy Queen? Yet Tempest had some terrible feeling that they needed to keep hidden, because there was one memory missing, like a hole burned in parchment, that would not quite come yet. The one thing Tempest knew for sure was it had something to do with what Lady Hawthorn and Auberon had been discussing in the study, and that it was very bad.

Then, with a stinging jolt, she remembered what it was.

The Curse.

Written in the hidden bower. On the trunk of the Heart of the Forest.

It meant that on their thirteenth Naming Day, their mother would sacrifice a single twin so that she might live to rule for another hundred-and-thirty-three years.

That was why Tempest and Thomas had left Fairyland in the first place!

Tempest felt an acrid bile rise in her throat. So this was the truth of her past: their mother had barely cared for them. She had only given them their Talismans to keep them in her power and make sure she could find them when the time came. Anxiety cut through Tempest, twisting her running feet, until she felt as if she might keel over like an old dead tree. It was a horrible realization. And there was more, Tempest recalled. The thirteenth Naming Day was due to happen tomorrow. She and Thomas had stumbled home at the very moment they were most in danger.

They had reached the edge of a clearing. On its far side stood a grand palace with a tree growing through its roof, surrounded by a forest. Lady Hawthorn and Auberon were barely a few steps from the palace entrance.

Tempest and Thomas had to confront their aunt and stop her telling their mother where they were, and they had to get their Talismans back from her somehow, but they couldn't do either of those things in the open without risking being seen. Better to stay hidden. They scooted behind a crumbling wall at the edge of the clearing and crept towards their aunt as quickly and stealthily as they could.

What they really needed was a plan, but there wasn't time to think. Lady Hawthorn was already knocking on the palace door. Auberon, who'd been flapping a few feet behind her, landed on her shoulder.

The door was opened by a small creature with bark-grey skin and large spines like those of a hedgehog. His name was Hoglet, Tempest remembered suddenly.

Behind Hoglet was a palatial hall, filled with tree-columns and windows that looked onto a sea of waving branches. The arched ceiling of the hall was sewn from a canopy of leaves.

"Your Ladyship," said Hoglet, in a deep voice for one so small. "We weren't expecting you."

"I must see the Queen at once," said Lady Hawthorn.

"As you wish, Milady." Hoglet held the door open for her and Auberon. "She's in the Throne Room."

Auberon hissed at Hoglet as he and Lady Hawthorn brushed past. Hoglet tutted and closed the door behind them.

Coriel flew with Tempest and Thomas, who ran along behind the ruined wall to reach the palace. Fragments of root and tree trunk twisted through the building's brickwork, and branches bowed down from its roof.

"I remember this place," said Tempest. "And this tree. This is the Heart of the Forest."

"I remember it too," replied Thomas. "We can climb through its branches. They make up the palace's roof beams. That'll see us past Hoglet and the rest of the palace guards, and safely inside. We'll need to secretly retrieve our Birth

Talismans as quickly as possible, before Lady Hawthorn presents them to the Queen, otherwise our mother might use the Talismans against us."

It was a long climb through the Heart of the Forest, but each hand- and foothold felt familiar. Tempest glanced at her brother. He was the best climber. Though their mother had tried to forbid it, they'd climbed this tree together many times. These were precious recollections she'd entirely forgotten, along with the other memories she'd lost of Thomas, her twin, during her time in England.

They climbed further and finally found themselves in the oldest limbs of the tree that made up the roof of the Throne Room.

Beneath them, in a green bower, Lady Hawthorn and Auberon were approaching a pale lady wearing a crown of thorny roses and spiked brambles, who was sitting on a throne of twisted tree boughs. Beside her was a small table made of living tree branches.

"The Fairy Queen," twittered Coriel.

"Mother," said Thomas, grim-faced.

Tempest's heart stuck in her throat. A shiver rippled up her spine, like a pebble dropped in water, as she examined the Fairy Queen's brittle face.

The Queen's eyes were cloudy and black and without feeling. Light pulsed from her body as if she was aflame;

stag antlers, feathered bird-wings and briar twigs sprouted through her straight silver hair and wove together to make a crown that perched just above the points of her elfin ears.

So this was her mother. A mother who she'd long thought lost. A figure she'd imagined with love and longing. Searched for all this time.

For Tempest to see her in the flesh after so long, when she'd only just recovered her lost memories, felt strange. She wanted to cry out and climb down the tree into her mother's arms, but she knew if she did she would put them all in danger.

For this mother was not the one of her imagination. This mother was a dangerous Fairy. And she had sinister motives for wanting her children back in her grasp.

"Sister," said the Fairy Queen, as Lady Hawthorn crossed the Throne Room towards her.

"Your Majesty," replied Lady Hawthorn. "I have come to tell you that your twin offspring, Thomas the Wild Boy and Tempest the Storm Girl, are safe at Kensington Palace in England with me. They are to attend a grand masked ball tomorrow night, where they will perform magic in honour of the English King. But do not worry, no harm will befall them there. They're under my watchful eye until you come for them."

She produced the Bone Cloud and the Hag Stone and gave them to the Queen.

"I would've found my children without your help," said the Fairy Queen, running her fingers across the Talismans coldly.

Tempest remembered the words written on each Talisman. They were carved into her heart as deeply as they were in the bone:

From your mother

She'd wanted to be with her mother for so long. The desire had filled her every waking wish and night-time dream, but this was not how she'd imagined their reunion – hiding from a cold, hard stranger, who appeared to have no feelings for her. It was like jumping and expecting to land on a soft bed but smacking into a block of ice instead.

The Fairy Queen smiled and turned the Talismans over in her hand. "I could've traced the twins while they were still wearing these. But bringing them to me does make things easier." She threw the Talismans down carelessly on the side table.

Tempest was hurt to realize that she wasn't even that interested in them.

"And I'm delighted at your discovery, sister," continued the Queen. "Tomorrow evening, on the first day of spring, on the one-hundred-and-thirty-third anniversary of the

Curse and the twin's thirteenth Naming Day, I will come to collect them from this English King's masked ball. I shall gather the Fairy Court. We will bring my children home."

"How will you decide between them when the time comes?" asked the Queen's sister.

"They will do the choosing," said the Queen. "Whoever wins the Magical Duel on the Stepping Bones will be the sole survivor."

"It is a small price to pay so that you and Fairyland might flourish for another century and more," said the Queen's sister. "I pity those poor little lambs though. No one returns from the Dead Lands, but they will both suffer." She didn't sound as if she meant it.

"Better them than me," said the Queen. "I must survive. Fairyland needs me."

Thomas gave a soundless gasp. He took Tempest's hand and fidgeted uncomfortably with it. Tempest felt sick. *What sort of a person would make such a statement, or such a choice?*

She wanted to get a closer look at their mother's face. The Fairy Queen who'd condemned one of her own children to die so that she might live.

She inched out along the branch...but with a crack, it gave way! She would've fallen if Thomas hadn't yanked her back.

The crack had not been loud, but Auberon had heard it. His sharp beak snapped towards the noise.

"There's someone in the tree," he croaked, taking off from Lady Hawthorn's shoulder and swooping up into the branches of the Heart of the Forest.

Tempest cowered beside Thomas, but Auberon was already in her face, black feathers flapping, sharp beak screeching. "Your offspring are here, Your Majesty!" he screamed. "They must've followed us through the Magic Mirror from Kensington Palace."

"Shut up!" shouted Thomas, swiping at the bird. But the raven flapped and dodged away.

"Come now, that's not polite," cawed Auberon sneeringly. "The Queen's Guard demands you give yourself up to face your fate! Fairies, to me!" he screamed.

At his call, Hoglet and the Fairy guards crawled from the hidden corners of the Throne Room. Some of the Fairies had skin like tree bark. Some had green shoots for hair. Others wool-encrusted horns. A few had twiggy features, or furry legs and hooved feet.

Tempest looked at Thomas, aghast, as the Fairies leaped into action, propelling themselves into the tree branches and racing angrily towards them. What on earth and in Fairyland could they do to stop them?

19

Thorn Wall

Thomas and Tempest clung to the Heart of the Forest and stared in horror at the fast-approaching horde of Fairy guards. "Do something, my skylarks!" Coriel twittered from Tempest's shoulder. "Before it's too late!"

"Coriel, quick!" cried Tempest. "Get our Birth Talismans back!"

"Of course, little gadwall!" Coriel swept around the trunk of the tree and down into the Throne Room. Circling round behind the Queen and her sister, who were staring up at the ruckus in the roof, the robin swooped down to the side table and snatched up the two Talismans.

Swiftly, she glided back the way she had come, skimming

behind the unaware Queen and her sister, and flapping back to Tempest and Thomas to drop their Birth Talismans into their waiting palms.

The Fairy guards were scrambling towards them. There was scant chance to think, but a version of Kwesi's Growing Spell sprang like a green shoot into Tempest's mind.

She held the Bone Cloud in her hand and felt its hum, as well as that of the wooden Ferry Keeper Talisman around her neck. With the two Talismans working in unison, she felt a sudden surge of confidence. She'd not tried growing spells before, but things were desperate. She decided to try Kwesi's. She adjusted her casting as best she could:

"Heart of the Forest, silver and dun. May your branches grow and seek the sun."

A few new branches sprang up, blocking the Fairies' path. Tempest pushed the magic harder, making the tree's branches entwine together, but it took everything she had. Something was fighting against her. She had to stop before she passed out.

"Your turn, Thomas," she said urgently, "Make us birds, so we can fly."

Thomas clasped his Hag Stone in one hand and put the other to the Wolf's Tooth Talisman then he sang:

"Wings, feet, beaks, claws. Turn us into birds that soar."

Tempest felt a few feathers sprout in her hair, but the magic fizzled away to nothing as quickly as it had come.

Thomas sagged, spent. The spell had been right, but nothing was working. Tempest glanced down to see Lady Hawthorn muttering a Blocking Spell.

In desperation, Tempest plucked a heavy lump of broken branch from the tree and threw it at her.

The branch hit her aunt bang on the nose, stopping her spell-casting for a brief moment.

Meanwhile, the angry Fairies were snapping Tempest's freshly grown branches, pushing them aside as they climbed the tree to get to Tempest and Thomas.

"Time to try something else, little water rails," twittered Coriel.

Thomas took up the mantle once more, chanting the only other spell he could think of. It spilled out of him, full of tearing words:

"Spike, bristle, rip, torn, Heart of the Forest, make a wall of thorns."

The remaining tree limbs became a thorn wall, scratching at the Fairies who were climbing towards them twice as hard, barring their progress.

"Follow me, wily wrens," called Coriel, flapping above, trying to guide them through the thorny tangle. Tempest and Thomas followed her between the bristling branches,

climbing down the tree. But Auberon, who had avoided the thorn wall, was circling around them.

"CRAAR!" he called. "They're headed this way!"

Tempest and Thomas came to a dead end on the lowest limb, on the far side of the tree. Tempest glanced back. Most of the Fairies were still climbing upwards, to where they had been, but a few were following Auberon, leaping down towards them and closing in.

"Jump, my brave puffins!" cried Coriel.

Tempest's legs shook. She looked at the drop, her head spinning with recovered memories, the knowledge of the terrible secret, and the muddle of the many magics she'd cast. She swayed on her feet, woozily wondering if she could make it. The fall was a long way, but there was a bed of moss at the foot of the tree.

"You can do it, sister." Thomas squeezed her hand tight and they leaped from the branch together.

Thorns and briars tore at their cloaks.

They landed with a THUMP! on the soft pile of moss.

Thomas stood and yanked Tempest to her feet. They were outside the palace, in the hidden bower. Tempest glimpsed faint words carved into the gnarled trunk of the Heart of the Forest; the Curse that had caused all this. But there was no time to remind themselves of it – they had to run.

Tempest clasped Thomas's hand tight and they raced through the trees. Coriel swooped overhead through the patchwork of branches and sky, directing them towards the clearing and the pool. There the Magic Mirror's doorway would return them to the study and Kwesi waiting in Kensington Palace.

With relief, Tempest saw the bright white light, strong and silver-sharp as a spiderweb, flooding from the pool and spilling around the edges of everything. "Kwesi's managed to hold the doorway open! Over there!" she cried. "Keep running!"

They had almost reached it. She needed to concentrate on keeping her footing, but another part of her wanted to look back at their mother, wanted to see finally and properly who she'd been running from for so long. A mother who she hardly knew, who she had forgotten. She froze and Thomas almost barrelled into her.

"What're you doing?" he cried. "Don't stop. Don't look back!"

"We can't rest here, little lapwing," screeched Coriel overhead. "She is coming, with her Fairy hordes!"

But Tempest couldn't help it. She had to turn around, just like the last time, an uncontrollable yearning pulled her gaze back towards her mother.

The Queen glided towards them through the trees, her silver hair flying in her wake, sweeping ahead of her phalanx

of Fairies, Hoglet, and Auberon and Lady Hawthorn. The Queen was shrieking. Her living crown writhed angrily. Its briar branches burst into thorn and flower, before their petals died away and fell like autumn leaves.

Tempest stared at this strange vision. She and her mother locked eyes. The Queen's black pupils flashed bright, like angry collapsing stars. Tempest was filled with an overwhelming desire to sprint towards her and dive into her arms. Chittering insects sang warning songs from the trees. Moles and mice screeched worriedly from beneath ferns.

"You can't run for ever, my children," said the Queen. "And you can't hide."

The trees in the clearing crowded in towards them, weaving together thick and fast, cutting off the way to the Mirror Door. The Queen was using Tempest's Growing Spell against her.

"I'm coming for you both," she said. "I shall be there tomorrow, at the accursed hour on your last Naming Day, when the clock strikes thirteen. At that moment the Curse will make its final choice. One of you will live and one will die."

Her words echoed from every branch and leaf of every tree in the clearing, pounding a drumbeat in Tempest's blood, whirling like a hurricane in her head, crawling sharply across her skin and fizzling through her bones as fast as wildfire.

Still she couldn't tear her gaze away from her mother.

Then Coriel burst through the edge of the clearing, chased by Auberon. The little robin swooped away from him and flapped desperately around the Queen's head, pecking at her.

The Queen broke her gaze to thrash at Coriel, and it was enough to quash the spell.

Tempest felt like she was escaping a strong current. She took a step backwards, tripped over a tree root and slammed into the ground. The Bone Cloud Talisman tumbled from her grip and she scrabbled to pick it up, stood and blinked and brushed herself down.

Thomas was at her side. "Come on," he cried. "Let's go! We can still escape!" He yanked her onwards; his palm felt coarse and damp with sweat. Tempest gritted her teeth. Thomas pulled her away from the Fairies and their mother.

The silver doorway danced before them in the mirrored pool. Kwesi was still chanting on the other side, trying to hold open the way through to England, but with the Queen's arrival in the clearing, the hole between the two worlds had started to shrink.

Thomas leaped through first, pulling Tempest behind him. Coriel came last, barrelling into the water and through the doorway with a splash! They tumbled…

Down…

Down…

Down…

Past rainbow trout
and silver stars,
cobwebs,
and the milky moon.

And found themselves…

…back in Kensington Palace.

They collapsed onto the floor of Lord Hawthorn's study, dripping with water and magic from the mirror and gasping desperately for breath. The leap through the closing Mirror Door had taken everything out of them. But they had the Bone Cloud and the Hag Stone Talismans clasped in their hands. At least they had succeeded in that goal.

Tempest sat up and was relieved to see Kwesi's worried face.

"I held the Opening Spell for as long as I could," he said, wearily. "What happened?"

But there was no time to explain. The doorway into Fairyland wasn't quite fully shut.

Suddenly it reversed course and began opening again. In the widening gap, Tempest saw the Queen on the far side.

She was muttering words to pull the Mirror Door wider open. The Fairy horde, led by Lady Hawthorn and Auberon, rushed closer. Auberon's red eyes flashed and the thorn branches of Lady Hawthorn's hair snapped and crackled in anger. Hoglet and the Fairy phalanx behind them grinned, showing their needle-sharp teeth.

"*Speak a Closing Spell to shut the doorway, my little redstarts!*" cried Coriel. "*Do it now!*"

"*We don't know one, Coriel!*" Tempest shouted, scraping herself desperately off the floor. Her eyes stung with tears.

"I'm almost out of power," Kwesi screamed. His eyelids fluttered heavily. He looked faint.

"It's too late!" Thomas croaked.

"*CRAAARRR!*" Auberon cawed, bursting through the Mirror Door. His feathers changed from black to white as he dived at Thomas and Tempest.

Thomas ducked and swiped the angry raven from the air. Auberon writhed and squawked in his free hand, white feathers flying.

"*Get away, you foul creature!*" Thomas tossed Auberon back through the mirror.

Auberon tumbled through the glass, screeching and hit the Queen on the cheek.

Lady Hawthorn, Hoglet and the pack of Fairies gasped in shock.

"Quick, smash the glass!" Thomas snatched an object from a side table.

Kwesi and Tempest did the same. Together they threw whatever they could find, each hitting different spots on the Magic Mirror. There was an ominous *creaking* and then a…

CrIcK!

The mirror cracked like ice.

And…

KKKERRRAAAAASSSSHHHH!

Seven sharp silver shards slid down its surface and collapsed in a terrible cacophony of tinkling sounds on the floor.

At once the magical doorway and the raging Fairies disappeared. And all that was left was a long profound silence, like the aftermath of some terrible explosion or lightning storm.

"*Great horsetail!*" Coriel said. "*We did it! I didn't think we'd make it out of there alive! Your mother was furious! So was your aunt!*"

"*You remembered, Coriel,*" Tempest said, snatching a breath. She could recollect everything too, even after leaving Fairyland for a second time. Something had broken the Forgetting Spell. Maybe it was smashing the Magic Mirror?

"You finally recalled the Curse, my little marsh harrier!" Coriel shot back. *"And so did I! It's why we left that dreadful realm in the first place!"*

"*We remember,*" Thomas said. His eyes were wide and his breath was ragged with the exertion of the escape. "*It was our home. A paradise of sorts, with awful secrets underneath... But we got our Talismans.*"

"Look!" Kwesi interrupted.

Something was happening to the seven broken shards of mirror. They had turned translucent.

"*The Fairies are taking them back!*" Coriel squawked.

It was true. The shards of the Magic Mirror were fading away.

"We have to do something!" Tempest cried.

Kwesi snatched up a single shard of mirror and spoke a spell:

"Shard of Mirror, glass so sheer, stay here now, don't disappear."

Tempest and Thomas snatched at the six other shards, but they were too late. The broken pieces of the Magic Mirror vanished. Only the one in Kwesi's hand remained, thanks to his spell.

Quickly, he put it in his pocket. "Without that," he said, "there's no way those Fairies will get the Magic Mirror working again. We need to get my Sunray Shell Talisman back from wherever it's hidden inside that desk, and get out of here."

Kwesi and the others rushed over to the desk and began rattling the secret drawer once more, trying to open it.

"Stop that," said a voice in the doorway. It was Lord Hawthorn.

"I don't know what's going on, or how you got those back –" he nodded at the Talismans in Tempest and Thomas's hands – "but I intend to find out NOW."

The Lord muttered some words and the Bone Cloud and the Hag Stone flew from Tempest's and Thomas's grasps into his palm. Then he crushed them in his grip once more and Tempest felt a pounding in her temples so strong, she clutched her ears in anguish. Beside her Thomas fell to his knees. Kwesi stood behind the desk, frozen in fear.

"None of you are going anywhere," Lord Hawthorn announced. "Some terrible magic has occurred here. Caused by your having *stolen* these, I imagine." He flourished the Bone Cloud and Hag Stone.

He looked around, spotting Auberon's white raven feathers and Lady Hawthorn's ribbon on the floor, and the empty wooden frame that once held the mirror.

"Where is Auberon?" he asked. "Where is my mirror, and what have you done with my dearly beloved wife?"

"Nothing she didn't deserve," Tempest snapped. She

climbed, unsteadily, to her feet. Lord Hawthorn still had some power over her, but it was no longer enough to make her submit to his will.

"Tell me now!" Lord Hawthorn spat. Anger radiated off him, gleaming in his eyes as he spoke a spell:

"Unstop their words, the truth awaken. Make them tell me where my wife's been taken."

Tempest bit her lip and stayed quiet. Lord Hawthorn's threats no longer held any fear for her. Nor did the power of his spells, with her new Talisman to protect her. She felt the hum of the FerryBoat Talisman hidden round her neck. It had saved her from her mother's magic, and it would shield her from Lord Hawthorn's.

Kwesi and Thomas refused to speak too.

"I *shall* find out what has happened here," Lord Hawthorn raged. "Then you will all be punished for this insubordination!"

"Not if I have anything to do with it," Tempest said, raising her arms suddenly. She could feel the hum of power sputtering through her Ferry Boat Talisman. The magic flared and sparked like a steel striker on a wet flint, but Tempest hadn't the energy to pull it to her and it faded fast. Her head spun dizzily. She swayed, trying to catch her balance, but her body had other ideas. It tipped…

sideways.

And Lord Hawthorn's study and his mahogany desk and the animal skulls and the taxidermy lizards and the creatures in their cloudy jars leaped like the room was on fire, while the stuffed fish flapped their fins as if they were swimming.

Then she fell.

The last thing she glimpsed as her head hit the floorboards was Thomas slumped at her side, and Coriel flittering worriedly around Kwesi's head. Tempest hoped, woozily, that Kwesi could continue to withstand Lord Hawthorn alone...before, finally, the world collapsed around her.

20

Fate Awaits

Tempest did not dream of her mother. In fact, she did not dream of anything at all. She woke to find herself back in the attic prison of the apprentices' dormitory, the yellow linen curtain pulled around her bed. A feverish fatigue sat deep in her bones and weariness lay on her body like a shroud. Her skin shivered and burned and her blankets were wet with sweat.

Gradually, the events in Lord Hawthorn's study came flooding back to her. The spell-casting and the fight with the dead creatures when they first broke in. Lady Hawthorn and Auberon opening the Mirror Door. Kwesi holding the fort while she and Thomas went to Fairyland. Seeing their mother at last and hearing the revelations about their past. Lastly, the Fairy chase, and their bungled escape attempt and recapture by Lord Hawthorn.

With these memories swirling in her head, Tempest sat up, pulled back the curtain and looked about the room.

Worryingly, Kwesi was missing. But she could see the shape of her brother Thomas curled up in the next bed. At least he was no longer sleeping under it.

Thomas! Thomas was her brother! How could she have forgotten him for so long? She put her feet on the floor. Dizziness overwhelmed her for a second, but she soon recovered her sense of equilibrium. She hobbled across, pulled Thomas's curtain aside and sat down next to him.

"Brother," she said.

Thomas turned over and opened his eyes. "Sister," he replied, with a smile.

He held out his arms and they hugged properly.

Tempest was feeling all kinds of things, but she didn't say them out loud. She just let the warmth of his hug fill her up and burn away the pain of the missing years. They had each other and there didn't need to be any more words than that.

She let go and pulled back to look at him properly. She still couldn't quite believe it. Her brother! She needed time to take him in. But that was the one thing she didn't have. There was no doubt in her mind that their mother would come for them. Not out of love, as Tempest had once supposed, but out of a terrible necessity to appease the hundred-and-thirty-three-year-old Curse.

"It's a good thing we smashed the mirror," Thomas said. It was almost as if he could hear what she was thinking. "And that Kwesi kept that last shard," he continued. "Mother and the Fairies will have to find another way through tonight if they come."

"*When* they come," Tempest corrected, anxiously. "I don't think that will be enough to stop them."

"*Couldn't we negotiate with your mother?*" Coriel asked, landing on Thomas's bed. "*Petition her for clemency? You never did attempt that course, little doves.*"

"*I did,*" Thomas said. "I tried after you both left two years ago. I even explained to Mother how Lady Hawthorn had tricked her and changed the terms of the Curse, but she dismissed it out of hand." He dropped his head sadly.

This revelation made Tempest despair. Hearing Thomas's words and remembering what she'd witnessed on the far side of the mirror, she knew there was little they could do to turn the tide of their fate.

Her thoughts were interrupted by the rattle of a key. Tempest glanced over at the door and noticed the lock had been replaced by an even bigger and stronger one than before. No doubt it was charmed with twice as much magic.

Whoever was on the other side was having a little trouble getting it open.

The door swung to and Lord Hawthorn pushed Kwesi roughly into the room.

"Don't think your uncooperative insolence will go unpunished," Lord Hawthorn warned, as a worried-looking Molly brought in three green boxes printed with leaves and tied with green ribbons. She placed one at the foot of each bed, then left quickly, squeezing past Lord Hawthorn – who was still standing angrily in the doorway – with an apologetic smile.

"You are to start getting ready for the Masquerade at once," he said. "It begins at eight. I will come to collect you then. And you'd better be prepared to perform your spells for the King. After that, there'll be time enough to discuss what you've done with my wife."

He slammed the door shut angrily, locking it behind him.

Kwesi climbed to his feet and dusted himself down. "You're awake!" he said, happily. "And fine, thank goodness. I was so worried."

"We were worried about you too," Thomas said. "I'm glad you're all right. What time is it?"

"About six o'clock," Kwesi replied.

"In the evening!" Tempest was shocked. "Where did the day go?"

"You slept through most of it," Kwesi said.

"What has Lord Hawthorn been up to?" she asked.

"Questioning me about the disappearance of Lady Hawthorn." Kwesi sat down at the end of his bed. "When I refused to tell him anything, he tried to force me to explain how you got hold of your Talismans and what magic you were doing in his study. I told him nothing on that count either, so he returned to ranting about his wife. He really is upset about her disappearance. He doesn't seem to have realized she went of her own accord. Or that she and Auberon were Fairy spies, and you went to Fairyland after them."

"Thank you," Tempest said, sitting down beside him. "The less he knows about what went on, the more chance we have of surprising him the next time we're all together. That way we can get our Birth Talismans back and escape. Which reminds me, have you still got your map?"

"Molly took it back this morning, which is for the best. If Lord Hawthorn had discovered it, she and Mehmet would've been implicated in our escape attempt. But don't worry." He tapped his head. "I still have it stored. In here."

"What happened after Lord Hawthorn questioned you?" Thomas asked.

"He threatened that if the two of you weren't up and ready for this evening's performance soon, he'd use your Talismans against you."

"So he doesn't know we have new ones?" Thomas asked.

"No." Kwesi shook his head. "At the end of our fruitless discussion, Lord Hawthorn tried to punish me with spells from his Grimoire. But they were weaker than normal, and luckily I was wearing this to protect me." He pulled out his new Talisman from where it was hidden under his shirt. The portrait of his mama and papa on its string glinted between his fingers. "Without his wife," Kwesi continued, "Lord Hawthorn seems to have lost some of his magic."

"Could it be that Lady Hawthorn was lending her Fairy powers to him this whole time?" Thomas suggested.

"That's what I thought," Kwesi said. "Though I didn't let on to Lord Hawthorn it might be so."

"We don't know any of that for sure," Tempest said. "But I agree it would make sense. In which case, the diminishment of his magic and his lack of knowledge about our growing abilities or our new Talismans are very strong advantages we hold over him."

"There is one more." Kwesi felt under his mattress and produced the shard of Magic Mirror. "This. It might come in handy, when you're both back at full power."

"That may be some time," Tempest admitted. "I'm still feeling terrible."

"Me too," Thomas said. "But we need to recover. Our

mother is coming tonight to finish the Curse," he explained to Kwesi. "So we need a new plan."

"I don't know if I'm well enough to face her *and* Lord Hawthorn," Tempest said. "In fact," she said, wearily, "I don't know if I'm well enough to face either of them."

"I can help with that," Kwesi said. "After all the magic I did last night and facing Lord Hawthorn this afternoon, I suppose, by rights, I should feel as bad as you, but something about your friendship over the last few days has given me strength and hope. And I want to share that with you too." He took each of their hands and cast a Healing Spell:

"Fix, repair, heal, restore. Be hale and well, just like before."

As his words finished, Tempest felt energy seeping back into her bones. And, from the heartiness of his complexion, she saw Thomas was healing too.

"Thank you, Kwesi," she whispered, hugging him. "For *your* friendship and help."

"Thank you, Kwesi," Thomas joined in.

"*We still need a plan, little skylarks!*" Coriel chirruped. "*With all your chatter about this advantage, and that trick, none of you have come up with one.*"

That knocked some of the wind out of their sails.

Tempest thought about it for a moment. She had to admit the little bird was right. The others thought so too.

Thomas tugged his ears and Kwesi tapped his fingers on his knee as they tried to come up with a solution.

Finally, Tempest hit upon an idea. "When Lord Hawthorn hands us back our Birth Talismans to perform the show," she said, "we'll use the combined power of them and our new Talismans together to cast the greatest magic ever against him and everyone else in the ballroom."

"What kind of magic?" the others asked.

"Something bigger and better than anyone there could possibly imagine," Tempest said. "We'll grow a wood in the King's apartments."

"How will that help us?" Thomas asked.

Tempest paused, thinking. "Our wood will be so untamed and tangled," she announced, "that it'll create a great confusion and commotion among the courtiers and crowds! Just like the chaos we caused escaping Fairyland last night, Thomas, remember... Only the mayhem that we make tonight will be far bigger and better! Far wilder!"

"A mess like that will require all Lord Hawthorn's powers to set right," Thomas said with excitement.

"That'll be a far harder task for him in his weakened state," Kwesi added eagerly.

"He'll be so distracted unpicking our spells," Tempest finished, "he won't have a chance to throw any of his controlling sorcery at us."

"For such a plan to work, my little chaffinches," Coriel said, *"the three of you will need to use your best magic."*

Tempest nodded. "We must each play our part. You too, Coriel. I will make a storm."

"I will make tall trees sprout from the floor," Kwesi said.

"I will turn the guests into wild animals," Thomas said.

"I will dive-bomb that pignut, Lord Hawthorn, my brave sparrows," Coriel said, hopping onto Thomas's shoulder. *"I will make his every move difficult as he rushes around trying to put things right."*

"While all that's going on, we must keep hold of all our Talismans and slip from the ballroom unnoticed," Tempest said. "Out into the garden,"

"Break the Containment Spell," Kwesi continued.

"And escape over the wall to freedom!" Thomas finished.

"We can hide out in the streets of London to beat the clock," Tempest said. "You can guide us, Kwesi, using your memory map."

"What'll happen at the thirteenth stroke of midnight if Mother can't find us to offer us up to the Curse?" Thomas asked.

"Then she'll face the consequence herself," Coriel chirruped.

"Which is what?" Tempest asked.

"Banishment to the Dead Lands, my raven, which means certain death and the end of her centuries-long reign over Fairyland."

"So be it," Tempest said in a steely voice. *"Why should her life be worth more than ours?"*

"We're agreed on the new plan, then?" Thomas said.

Kwesi nodded.

Tempest did too. She still wasn't sure in the slightest they could win, but she didn't admit that to the others. She hoped desperately that they would succeed for all of their sakes, but they'd need total confidence in each other to complete the plan. If things went well, she'd soon be home with Prosper and Marino, and if they didn't the outcome would be too awful to contemplate.

By the time they finished talking, the sun was setting slowly over the garden. The chimes of the clocktower echoed out across the thin cold air above the palace.

"Seven o'clock," Thomas said, counting the bells. "We'd best start getting ready."

There was just enough light to put on their costumes. Then, they turned to the green boxes that Molly had left. Kwesi opened his first to find a cat mask, with whiskers and pointed ears. He tried it on, then pushed it back atop his head.

Tempest was about to open her box when she noticed a leaf-shaped card fixed to its side. Odd. Kwesi's box had

had nothing like that. Tempest opened the card and read the words inside it:

For my Wondrous Storm Girl on her thirteenth Naming Day.

A similar card was fixed to Thomas's box:

For my Marvellous Wild Boy on his thirteenth Naming Day.

Thomas tore the card and ribbon off and rummaged inside the box. He baulked.

"What is it?" Tempest asked.

Thomas revealed his mask. A long-snouted wolf, trimmed with fur. "Our mother made this," he said. "I'm sure of it."

"*It's Fairy mischief, my little rock doves,*" Coriel said. "*To frighten you. And so that she'll recognize you in the crowd. Who knows what else she has in store?*"

Tempest held her breath and took the lid off her box. Inside, nestled on a bed of moss, was a mask with a bright yellow streak of lightning and a dash of raindrops: the mask of a Storm Girl. "It's a bad omen," she said.

"Perhaps you can change them?" Kwesi suggested.

They tried. Thomas held a hand over each mask, and whispered Transformation Spells. But the masks wouldn't budge. They were fixed in shape with unbreakable magic.

Tempest put her storm mask on. At least that way she wouldn't have to look at it any more. The others followed suit. Thomas as the wolf and Kwesi as the cat.

"This doesn't change anything." Tempest clasped the Ferry Boat Talisman round her neck. She wasn't even sure where her sudden bravery was coming from. So often in the past, her fears had owned her. But not this time. Not this night. "We're taking matters into our own hands," Tempest told the others confidently. "We'll stick together and fight. No matter what happens at the Masquerade, we *will* escape."

The sun finally set as she spoke those words, and twilight shadows filled their faces with gloom. None of them said anything more. They just sat in the gathering darkness and waited. Soon the clock in the clocktower struck eight.

Then eight-thirty.

Then nine.

Lord Hawthorn was very late.

With each passing hour, the tension inside Tempest ratcheted higher, tightening like a spring. It scrunched up the courage she had tried to kindle with all her brave talk.

By ten o'clock, Lord Hawthorn had still not arrived. Tempest thought fearfully that, perhaps, he wasn't coming at all… What should they do then, she wondered. What could they do? If time ran out while they were still stuck in this little room, what would happen to them?

At the eleventh bell, Tempest realized midnight was only an hour away. She was certain their mother would arrive at that critical moment, and they'd have no choice. They'd have to cast their spells in the dying embers of winter.

The clock in the clocktower struck a quarter past eleven, the tolls echoing with the sound of heavy footsteps stomping along the passageway.

And finally, a key turned in the lock.

21

MASQUERADE

The door to the apprentices' dormitory swung open to reveal Lord Hawthorn. A mask depicting a rainbow trout covered his face, and his Grimoire was wedged under one arm. A magical globe-light floated eerily a few inches above his head like a great glowing soap bubble, illuminating his shimmering blue jacket that rippled with silver threads, bright as the sun on water.

"Apprentices," Lord Hawthorn murmured from behind his fish mask. He was holding their Birth Talismans in one hand and the door key in the other. "Your time has come. Remember, I have your Talismans, so don't try anything outside your performance, or else you'll be severely punished. Later we will talk once again about Auberon and my beloved missing wife."

He muttered something else and Tempest felt a shot of pain course through her. Kwesi and Thomas winced too. "Come along," Lord Hawthorn sang gleefully over their anguish and, with their minds abuzz, Tempest, Thomas, Kwesi and Coriel found themselves compelled to follow him and his bobbing light along the servants' corridor and down the north-west staircase.

Tempest reviewed the master plan in her head, checking the links as she would when she helped Marino with the darning, or Prosper to repair *Nixie*'s nets. The storm mask felt stiff and awkward on her face. It was a bad fit, and it made her think of the dangers yet to come.

She watched Lord Hawthorn through the mask's eyeholes, turning their Birth Talismans in his hand, grumbling to himself about his missing wife and Auberon. Tempest didn't quite catch the details, but she noticed that he was swaying and heavy-footed on the stairs, his ball of light weaving about above him. He was out of sorts. She hoped that would mean he'd be easier to trick when the time came.

"Extinguish!" Lord Hawthorn slurred from behind his fish mask as they stepped through a door and out into the palace gardens. At his command, the ball of light floating over them disappeared with a fizzling pop.

There was no longer a need for it, anyway. A full moon hung above the path and the budding branches of the trees glistened. A few prophetic snowdrops bloomed in the flower beds, softening the night air with the scent of spring, and distant music drifted from the brightly-lit windows of the King's grand state rooms, where they were headed.

Thomas walked in short anxious bursts along the path, his wolf's nose darting this way and that, while Kwesi glanced around nervously, his eyes flicking about beneath his cat mask. Tempest gritted her teeth, as she, Lord Hawthorn and the others approached the clocktower. The bell struck once more.

"*Half-past eleven,*" Coriel warned in her ear. "*Only thirty minutes before your mother the Fairy Queen arrives, my little Storm Girl.*"

"*I know,*" Tempest replied testily, quickening her step.

At the palace's main entrance, they made their way along the stone gallery. As they climbed the King's staircase, the raucous sound of the party drew closer. Tempest and Thomas had come this way before, on their first night here, two days past, when they were taken to the Presence Chamber to meet the King. Already that felt like a lifetime ago.

In honour of the Masquerade, a splendid Royal mural of the King's most interesting courtiers had been painted in the stairwell. Thomas, Tempest and Kwesi were included, but there was no time to stop and admire it, for Lord Hawthorn was moving too fast up the staircase and they had to hurry to keep pace.

The doors to the state rooms were flanked by two guards in red uniforms. Tempest looked around for Mehmet to announce their entrance as he had done before, but he wasn't there. Then again, it was a masked ball, she supposed. Guests were supposed to arrive incognito.

In a way she was relieved. Mehmet had been a good friend to Kwesi. She wouldn't want him to be caught up in whatever magic they conjured tonight.

They stepped past the large, polished doors into a magnificent gallery. Before them were giant chandeliers full of dripping wax candles that gave off glittering waves of light and wafted perfume-scented smoke through the gaily-decorated room. Nearby were the Royal Princesses, Caroline, Amelia and Anne wearing matching rabbit masks. All around them in the room was a menagerie of animal-masked, bewigged and beribboned guests, each wearing enough silk to keep a thousand silkworms spinning for a hundred years. Tempest heard the nearest group dropping the names of notable attendees – Walpole, Swift, Handel, Newton and Defoe – as they plucked greedily at golden tables laden with charred meats, fish, breads and jewelled pastries.

"If our Aunt could disguise herself as human, there's no telling whether she and the Queen are here already," Thomas, said staring nervously round.

"Or how many other Fairies are among the crowd," Coriel added.

"Especially with masks to disguise them, as well as magic," Kwesi agreed.

Tempest shivered. She didn't think her mother or Lady Hawthorn were there yet. She was certain she would've felt their presence. But the other Fairies would be impossible to spot in the crowds on a night like this. Though she still believed most of them would want to make an entrance, rather than have to sneak in incognito.

An orchestra of twenty-four green-coated, grasshopper-masked players accompanied a lady wearing a songbird mask and a ladybird-spotted dress, who was singing a beautiful aria.

The music dived and soared in filigree flights, drifting up to a ceiling peppered with painted stars, while the King, in a gold-flecked lion-skin coat and mask, led his guests in the refined dance of a minuet, all of them daintily stepping and gliding between gold columns and statues and the velvet-covered gaming tables.

Tempest's senses sang at the many marvels, but she told herself she wouldn't be diverted. They were here for a purpose. As soon as they got their Birth Talismans back, as soon as their act began, they would sow chaos at the party and then all three of them would escape this theatre of lies and their mother's Curse, once and for all. Tempest knew they'd need to start soon. Spring into action before the Fairy Queen arrived to whisk one of them back to Fairyland and their death. But it was already almost too late…

The clock on the grand mantelpiece chimed a quarter to midnight and Lord Hawthorn raised his hands. The orchestra and the singer trailed to a stop.

"Fellow Lords and Ladies," Lord Hawthorn announced, pulling off his fish mask and waving a hand to make it disappear. The hubbub of guests and dancers died away.

"For the last few days, I, as Royal Sorcerer, have been training two new apprentices. A Storm Girl and a Wild Boy, found wandering lost in the woods. Both have magical abilities beyond their years. Tonight, under the King's command, they and my other apprentice, Noah, will perform a mesmerizing show of magic for you. And so, without further ado…here they are! Apprentices, remove your masks!"

Kwesi, Thomas and Tempest took off their disguises and laid them to one side on a table.

"It's now or never," Tempest whispered as the crowd clapped in delighted anticipation. "*Remember the plan, Coriel.*"

"*Of course, my puffin,*" Coriel replied.

"Together we can beat the Curse and escape," Thomas said.

"Let's do it," Kwesi said.

Lord Hawthorn was still talking, handing each of them their Birth Talismans so they could perform with them.

"It will be a show the like of which you have never seen before," he waffled, as he gave Tempest her Bone Cloud Talisman.

Tempest hung the Bone Cloud around her neck so that it nestled next to the carved Ferry Boat against her chest. As Lord Hawthorn returned Thomas and Kwesi's Talismans, she felt the harmonizing hum of the two magical objects echo through her. Summoning all her power, she whispered a Weather Spell under her breath to try and catch Lord Hawthorn off guard.

"***Sun rise. Clouds gather. Skies open. Rains batter.***"

Magical clouds scudded across the ceiling, blocking the painted stars. Then it began to rain – just a soft pattering at first, as it had in the dormitory and Lord Hawthorn's study. The masked guests opened parasols over their heads; a rainbow appeared between the bright flaming chandeliers, and they gasped in awe.

Tempest strengthened her magic and the storm turned wild, throwing thunder, lightning and hail over the crowd. Soon there were puddles at their feet. Then the punchbowls on the table and the glasses in their hands overflowed, pouring a river of water over their outfits and making them holler and shout in consternation.

"Stop it!" Lord Hawthorn cried, swaying and flicking through his Grimoire for a suitably severe Punishment Spell.

But it was too late – Tempest had her two Talismans and all of her power.

Kwesi was starting his magic too. He kneeled to touch the floorboards and cast his Growing Spell.

"Wood that once was trees, remember your seeds, brown and dun. Grow like saplings and seek the sun."

Trees tore through the floor, their roots cracking the floorboards and knocking guests from their feet. The trunks and branches shot towards the ceiling and crashed through the roof, creating wide holes that showered the guests in falling debris.

The guests screamed and scrambled for the walls. Crab apples and acorns fell from the branches and peppered the ballroom floor. Grasses and wild flowers grew through the cracks in the floorboards, made muddy by Tempest's raging storm.

"ENOUGH!" cried the King, pulling off his lion mask and flinging it aside. "Stop this, Hawthorn!"

"Yes, Your Majesty!" Lord Hawthorn snapped to attention and began to cast his Control Spell:

"Bind and tie, make them cower. Hold their will within my power."

But he had none of his apprentices' Talismans and his magic was weak without his wife. He searched his Grimoire for something that would bind them to his command, but he was too slow.

Thomas was already saying a version of his transformation magic.

"Tail, snout, pelt, paws. Wings, fins, teeth, claws. Wild magic, growl and grow! Turn these folk into what their masks do show."

Hair and snouts and teeth and extra limbs began sprouting from the King's servants, the three Princesses and the rest of the costumed guests. Their scared screams trumpeted into tweets and roars as each one became the beast their mask depicted. Soon there were foxes and badgers and weasels and shrews jumping over the tables, knocking food and drink and statues and glasses and playing cards onto the muddy woodland floor. Some guests transformed into birds and flapped wildly about. Still more became frogs and tried to jump into the overflowing punchbowls. Or toads and adders, crawling and slithering into spilled carafes of water. Eventually, apart from the three apprentices, only the unmasked King and Lord Hawthorn remained human-shaped.

Lord Hawthorn was clutching his own Talisman, the

carved ring of thorns, and ranting passages from his Grimoire. His spell-casting was desperate as he tried to protect himself and the King with magic, while trying to reverse what Tempest, Thomas and Kwesi had enchanted. The Lord's power was split so many ways, Tempest was certain he had none left to stop them leaving.

"Let's go," she said to Thomas and Kwesi as Coriel landed on her shoulder.

They turned and ran as fast as they could for the exit, nestled between the distant trees.

But, no matter how far or how fast they went, the doorway never seemed to get any closer. The woodland that stretched between them and the door appeared endless.

Tempest glanced at Thomas and Kwesi. Was this Lord Hawthorn's doing? It couldn't be; his power was vastly weakened.

Her head spun with fatigue, her body sagged, losing energy. Surely, she thought, with sudden clarity looking around the room at the chaos, the three of them hadn't done this much magic by themselves?

Just then, the trees stopped growing, the storm stopped raging, the wild-animal guests stopped braying, and everything went silent.

A great breeze blew through the woodland in the gallery, extinguishing all the candles on the candelabras. Then, as if spotlighted by the full moon, which shone, unwaveringly, through a hole in the gallery roof, a tiny spiney hedgehog man appeared. Hoglet!

He began announcing the names of more guests in a great, booming voice.

"Her Grace, Lady Primrose Cowslip – Baroness of the Midge Marshes. Madam Angelica Hogsweed – First Lady of the Periwinkles. His Grace, Lord Mayfly-Peasmould – Earl of Walnut Husk. Her Grace, Lady Holly-Blue – Countess of Bedstraw. Sir Argus Firebrat – Knight of the Order of the Dung Beetle."

"What's happening?" Kwesi asked, as the long list of strange names continued.

"It's the Fairy Hordes," Tempest said. "They're finally here."

"There's so many of them," Thomas said, apprehensively.

"As many as on your first naming day, my little puffin," Coriel replied.

And Tempest shivered in agreement.

The Fairies slunk out from behind various trees. There were wraiths, boggarts, gnomes and elves in capes of blue and green. Squawking and crowing and cheering, they began whirling in a dazzling devilish dance around the woodland clearing in the centre of the room.

Tempest glanced worriedly at Thomas and Kwesi, then at the King of England's and Lord Hawthorn's maskless staring faces, which were goggling clueless and open-mouthed at the spectacular new arrivals.

"The Fairy Court!" Lord Hawthorn muttered, entranced. "I've always wanted to meet them."

The Fairies, with their skin of bark and their spines and green shooting hair, their rams' legs and furry feet and eyebrows, waltzed across the room. The bigger goblins and pixies wore carved masks attached to their own faces. The smaller hedge-creatures and sprites had their whole heads hidden beneath masks of leaves and grass.

The last two names to be announced by Hoglet were familiar to everyone. "Her Grace, Lady Hawthorn, Duchess of Stalactite and Stalagmite. His Grace, Sir Auberon Raven, Lord High Commander of Birds."

Lady Hawthorn wore a black raven mask. Her twiggy hair writhed like snakes. On her shoulder sat Auberon, regal in white feathers.

"Milady!" Lord Hawthorn cried, pitching himself at his wife as she appeared through the trees. "Oh my dear heart, where have you been?"

"I can't speak with you now, beloved," Lady Hawthorn said.

"What? Why, dearest?" Lord Hawthorn whined, trailing behind her.

"I have important duties to perform." Lady Hawthorn

joined the rest of the Fairies, who were dancing around the wooded grove, singing:

"At the chiming of the thirteenth hour,
At the plucking of the thirteenth flower,
On the hundred-and-thirty-third Naming Day...
By the Tambling River,
on the Stepping Bones,
Our Curse will be sated and two twins will become one alone."

The clock began to strike. By the time it had rung its thirteenth chime, the Fairies had separated and made two lines in the forest-glade of the gallery. Tempest, Thomas and Kwesi watched nervously. They took a few steps back, trying to inch away, but a lines of trees blocked their path.

Lady Hawthorn raised her arms and spoke to the crowd of humans, Fairies and forest creatures alike.

"Your Majesty, Your Royal Highnesses, Lords, Ladies, gentle-beasts, Royal Sorcerer, and apprentices, please welcome my sister. Warden of the Fair Isle. Duchess of Dust. Royal Lady of the Most Excellent Order of the Hedgerow. Protector of the Forests and the Wild Meadows. Knight of the Greenwood, the Natural World and the Seven Secret Kingdoms. Ruler of Fairyland. Empress of the Fairies. Her Exalted Majesty Queen Mab..."

The Fairy Queen stepped from the forest, her green silk dress ruffling like the leaves of a tree, her body surrounded by a halo of white light and her eyes sparkling like distant galaxies. Twigs, thorns, stag antlers, bird wings and briars sprouted through her silver hair like a crown. She wore no mask. One long red scratch ran down her cheek from where Thomas had thrown Auberon in her face.

"*My twins,*" she said, with a smile as cold and hard as cracked porcelain. "*Here you are.*"

22

Thirteenth Hour

Tempest's legs shook. She felt sick. Despite her life with Prosper and Marino, despite her discoveries and adventures, despite her learning, remembering and relearning, despite her friendships with Kwesi, Coriel and her brother, despite her magic and her plans to get away… her mother was finally here for her and Thomas.

The King of England stared in awe at the Fairy Queen. Lord Hawthorn gaped at her, wide-eyed. The servants and Princesses and courtiers who'd been magicked into beasts and birds shifted and fluttered in nervous silence. Coriel gave a startled squawk. Kwesi chewed his lip. Thomas bounced, terrified, from foot to foot.

Tempest gazed into her mother's eyes, deep as two shadow-filled wells.

"*Mother,*" she said at last. "*We've been expecting you.*"

"*Is that why you tried to run?*" the Queen asked.

Tempest didn't reply. This was a battle she had spent her life trying to avoid, but it was finally here, and there was nothing she could do about it.

"*There'll be no more running,*" the Queen continued. "*I told you what a waste of time that was. I'm afraid I cannot leave, and you cannot escape me. It would be easier if you came of your own accord, Tempest. You too, Thomas.*" She gave her son a withering look. "*The Curse is calling and there is a destiny to be fulfilled.*"

"*I don't believe in destiny,*" Thomas growled. "*Never did. Never will.*"

Tempest wondered if this was even true. She believed in it. That was why she'd run so far and so fast for so long.

"*You won't take us without a fight, Mother,*" she said, "*so it would be easier if you left.*"

She was shocked to discover how powerful her words sounded. They floated from her, warm and confident as summer rain, and Thomas, Kwesi and Coriel looked on admiringly.

"*That's the spirit!*" The Fairy Queen tilted her head like a hawk. "*That's the daughter I remember! Never afraid of anything. Not the mermaids in the river, nor the giants in the mountains.*

Always the tempestuous one. You have a wild and stormy nature, Tempest, like the name I gave you. Like me, even." She smiled. "*My dear little Storm Girl. We are more alike than you could ever imagine.*"

Hope rose in Tempest. This was what she had expected and wished for: her mother's acknowledgement of who she was. Perhaps there was the chance of a loving compromise between them?

The Fairy Queen turned to King George. "Your Majesty," she said in English. "I have come to take my children home. You will give them to me."

Then Tempest realized there would be no compromises.

"What will you trade for them, cousin?" the King asked, bewildered. "They are my property."

The Fairy Queen laughed and the feathered wings in her crown flapped. "You're mistaken, sir. We are not cousins. I do not trade. And they are not your property. They are my children, which makes them my property."

Tempest didn't think she was anyone's property. As far as she was concerned, everyone was put on this earth equal, but since no one was listening to her she didn't have a chance to say so.

"Madam!" The King coughed in annoyance. "Indisputably we're cousins. I am related to every Royal household in Europe."

"Didn't you hear me, you cloth-eared, leonine fool?" the Fairy Queen replied in Fairy. *"I'm of a far higher lineage than you. Of the seas, skies and earth!"*

The King looked confused. The Fairy Court's titters, like breaking mirrors, sent a shiver down Tempest's spine.

"Never mind," the Fairy Queen continued in English. "I will make an exception and trade, in this case."

She signalled to her sister. Lady Hawthorn brought forward a box covered in buds and leaves. As she opened it, a golden light poured forth, flickering across her face and Auberon's. Lady Hawthorn plucked a glittering laurel wreath from within and handed it to the Queen, who muttered a spell over it:

"For the King of England. To seal a bargain grand."

Tempest gasped at the Fairy Queen's blatant use of magic against the King.

"This is Queen Titania's crown from the days of old, Your Majesty," the Queen explained. "She was a great ruler of Fairyland. I present it to you in exchange for my children."

"That's not Titania's crown," Coriel whispered in Tempest's ear as the Fairy Queen placed the wreath on King George's head. *"It's fool's gold. And only a fool would take it!"*

Tempest thought of the magical bargain she'd made with Lord Hawthorn for twelve gold coins, the one that had got her into this mess in the first place. It seemed anyone could be tricked by a little glamour and enchantment if you gave them what they thought they wanted.

The King touched the laurel wreath as it balanced precariously on his wig. Coriel was right. Now it was out of the box and on his head, the Fairy crown didn't look half as lustrous. The colour was dull, the shape lumpen, yet the King seemed utterly beguiled by the gift, and by the Fairy Queen. He was in her power, and Tempest already knew what he was going to say.

"Exalted Highness," he replied. "You may take these children from my charge."

"Wait, Majesty," Lord Hawthorn interrupted. "These are my apprentices. I've not given *my* assent."

"And what do you desire?" the Fairy Queen asked, giving him the full beam of her attention.

"Nothing from that magic box, Exalted Highness." Lord Hawthorn glanced disdainfully at King George. He smiled winsomely at Lady Hawthorn, who stared neutrally back at him. "I merely ask that my dear wife is returned to me. I don't know what charm you have her under, but it must be very powerful."

"She's under no charm," the Fairy Queen said. "She is my beloved sister. She is to return with me to Fairyland to witness the new era of my rule. And there she will stay, until I give her permission to depart once more."

"Then I beg your leave to return to Fairyland with her," Lord Hawthorn said. "To witness the glory of the Fairy Kingdom myself would be most marvellous!" He shivered with delight. Tempest could already see his mind calculating how to use this new-found connection with the Fairy Queen to his advantage.

"As you wish," the Fairy Queen replied disdainfully.

"You mustn't, my dearest," Lady Hawthorn told her husband. "It would be far too dangerous for you!"

"Nonsense, my darling," Lord Hawthorn replied. "It's my bargain to make."

"And so you have. The deal has been done." The Queen handed the box to her sister and turned to Tempest and Thomas. "*As for you, my children, it is time for you to face the Curse.*"

"*NO!*" Thomas barked. "*We will not. I tried to tell you the truth, Mother, but you wouldn't listen.*"

"*Careful, my little rock dove!*" Coriel twittered, staring startled at the Queen.

"*I may not be the stormy one,*" Thomas continued, "*but I'm the wild one, and I'm warning you, I will not come quietly. Go! Or we shall set our magic on you.*"

"*Why do the pair of you insist on defying me?*" the Fairy Queen snapped. "*First there was the running away, then the arguing, and now you resort to these…these…*" She waved a hand dismissively. "*Empty threats!*"

"*They're not empty threats!*" Tempest warned. "*We will fight you.*"

"And I'll help them," Kwesi added, taking Tempest's hand and Thomas's.

"*Fine.*" The Fairy Queen pursed her lips angrily, as Thomas always did. "*If it's a fight you want, a fight you shall get. It does add a tinge of excitement to proceedings. The thrill of the chase. What is a hunt without a little skirmish at its conclusion?*"

They'd reached the end of their discussion, but Tempest felt herself gaining strength. This was not her mother, not really. Tempest's Ferry Boat Talisman, her gift from Prosper and Marino, thrummed against her chest more loudly than her mother's Bone Cloud Talisman. The two ferry keepers were better parents to her than this Fairy Queen had ever been. She needed to live so that she could see them again.

"*Fairies!*" the Queen called to her minions. "*Bring them to me!*"

"*Yes, Exalted Highness!*" the Fairies screamed, gnashing their pointed yellow teeth. Their sharp and twiggy hands grabbed at Tempest and Thomas.

Tempest was already casting her Fog Spell under her breath. Kwesi and Thomas joined her, and the words of their three spells, in two languages, mixed together into one big mess of magic:

"Fog rise. Tail **spark.** *Gloom fly.* **Fire** *snout. Murk pelt.* **Bright** *paws. Shake teeth. Rattle claws. Change us, magic art. Make us the creature of your heart."*

The three of them working together, and the magnifying power of their twin Talismans, made the enchantment bigger and bolder. Tempest's sharp words blended with the brightest of Kwesi's to become a blinding white fog, which made the Fairies shrink in horror, while Thomas's wild Transformation Spell added to the mix, sending a stormy animal energy soaring through each of them, covering their limbs with fur and lightning.

Tempest stared at her hands and feet. They were becoming footpads. Her cloak grew around her body into a crackling pelt. Soon she fell on to all fours. Her fingernails clawed. Her face lengthened. Her teeth got sharper, her nose became a snout, and she became a Storm Wolf.

She glanced at Thomas and Kwesi and saw they were Storm Wolves too.

Thomas howled a war cry and led the pack of three, lunging at the circle of Fairies, teeth snapping, fur flickering with thunder and lightning that arced away into the trees, starting electrical fires.

The Fairies screeched and dived for cover.

"*Get them!*" the Queen screamed.

The Fairy hordes turned and chased the pack, Auberon leading them on.

"*Be swift, my doves!*" Coriel called, swooping above.

The Storm Wolf pack skidded away from the Queen and her courtiers and scrambled down the length of the hall, between burning saplings shooting from the floor. They weaved past badgers, foxes, stoats and birds who'd once been human guests at the King's masquerade. Their shocked, furred and feathered faces peeked from nests of torn mantua dresses, hats and capes.

The three Storm Wolves leaped among the trees, heading for the exit, but the spell was dying. The pack had burned too bright. Tempest felt the lightning in her fur dissipating. Soon their pelts were plain grey and they trotted wearily, done in from the strength they had used to cast the spell.

"*This waaaaay!*" Thomas panted.

The pack hid beneath a table with a tree growing through it, but they were quickly found.

"*They're here!*" Auberon cawed shrilly. "*Thomas and Tempest and the Sorcerer's Apprentice are hiding here!*"

A thicket of sharp Fairy fingers snatched at them. Kwesi, Thomas and Tempest snapped their wolf-teeth, but it was no good – there were too many Fairies, they were going to be overpowered.

"*Quick!*" Kwesi growled, leaping over a broken chair and

onto the grand banqueting table. Tempest and Thomas followed.

The Storm Wolves swerved between smashed plates and squished food, kicking silver cutlery and soiled napkins from their path. Birds perched on candelabras squawked in alarm, newts and frogs and toads watched goggle-eyed from punchbowls and glasses, as the angry Fairies chased the Storm Wolves across the tabletop.

At last they were burned out completely and so was their magic.

Tempest felt like a weary husk of spent energy.

The Fairies circled, their forest of sharp fingers prickling like thorny branches. They grabbed Tempest, Thomas and Kwesi by the scruffs of their necks and grew in size, until it seemed like the three Storm Wolves were small as lapdogs. Tempest dangled from a huge hand, the floorboards, tiles and mud of the woodland spinning beneath her.

"*We've caught them!*" Auberon screeched.

"*Well done!*" the Fairy Queen commended, and she cast a quick Extinguishing Spell:

"Gutter, snuff, quench and douse. Put lightning, fire and flames out."

Immediately, the fires in the forested gallery stopped burning.

Then the Queen spoke a Reversion Spell:

"Change these children, Magicborn. Return them to their natural form."

Tempest found herself dropped on the floor in a tangle of now-human limbs. Coriel swooped down onto her shoulder. Kwesi touched his face in alarm. Thomas panted hard. They both looked exhausted.

The Fairies fenced Tempest, Kwesi and Thomas into the centre of the smoke-filled clearing. Tempest hadn't the strength or will to battle on. She needed to recover, to conserve her energy for what lay ahead – to face the Curse.

"*Fine,*" she said to her mother. "*Open the doorway. Take us back to Fairyland.*"

"*No need for that,*" her mother replied. "*We're already there.*"

At these words, the Heart of the Forest sprouted through the centre of the room and thrust its branches up into the ceiling of the gallery. It roots bedded deep in the floor, and mushrooms, bluebells and snowdrops bloomed through the dirt around it. Its limbs wove together into the roof above and sunlight spread through its leaves.

Tempest looked around. No trace of Kensington Palace remained. They were in the Fairy Palace in the Greenwood. And there was to be no more running – for how could you run from a mother and a Kingdom that could find you wherever you went?

23

Altered Curse

"Wraiths, boggarts, pixies, gnomes and elves," said the Queen to the raucous horde of Fairies, who were cheering to find themselves at home in the Fairy Palace once more. "We are gathered on the thirteenth Naming Day of my children, Tempest the Storm Girl and Thomas the Wild Boy, to fulfil the Curse. We've dreamed and danced away a hundred-and-thirty-three years. And now, at the chiming of the thirteenth hour, in the Fairy Kingdom's furthest corner, by the crossing of the paths of destiny, fate will claim a Royal Fairy life."

The Fairy hordes sang then, dancing round the Queen:

"Let them duel at the river, as the Curse demands!

The death of one will be at the other's hands!

Then your reign will continue, glorious and true!

And Fairyland will be born anew!"

Tempest felt sick. She was going to have to duel against her brother, her friend, Thomas.

She glanced at him. He looked as scared as she was.

She knew that there was no way she could fight him; she loved him too much. It would be up to her to save them both. She had to think of some way to challenge the Curse.

Coriel shifted on her shoulder. Kwesi and Thomas fidgeted at her side.

"Don't cry," said Lady Hawthorn, noticing Tempest's tears. "It's only fate. Remember, what is written on the tree is what must be." She smiled at Thomas as well. "I pity you both, poor little sacrificial lambs."

That last phrase riled Tempest, but the rest of her aunt's words seemed familiar.

Then she remembered why. The wily old Fairy had cast a Deception Spell over the words of the Curse.

"What did you say to us on our first Naming Day, Coriel?" asked Tempest.

"A terrible thing will happen to you on your thirteenth Naming Day, my whitethroat!" responded the red robin.

"No," said Tempest. "Not that! The other thing."

"I remember." Coriel perked up. "I said: They have

changed the Curse! She changed it!"

"Who do you mean by 'she'?" asked the Queen.

"Her." Coriel flew around Lady Hawthorn's head and up high into the sky. "On this day, thirteen years ago, she changed the Curse with her magic so she wouldn't suffer its consequences. She was the one originally named in the rhyme on the tree. The one sentenced to fulfil the Curse, but she put your children's names in place of hers, so the twins would take the burden instead."

"Untruths!" squawked Auberon, taking off and chasing her. "Fakery! Falsities!"

"The robin is lying," said Lady Hawthorn. "But what more would you expect of a stupid little hedge-bird."

"Or such sneaky children whose lives are at risk," Lord Hawthorn chimed in. "They'd say anything to save their own skins, wouldn't they, dear heart?"

Lady Hawthorn smiled at him, relieved to have one other defender.

"We're telling the truth, you horrible old butterworts!" screeched Coriel.

"And there's one way to prove it." Thomas stepped over to the Heart of the Forest and pushed its branches aside to reveal the hidden bower and the mossy trunk of the tree where the Curse was engraved. "Kwesi, can you help me?" he asked. "Can you cast your Healing Spell over this tree?"

Kwesi nodded. He put his hand on the words etched into the bark and spoke the spell:

"Fix, repair, heal, restore. Go back to how you were before."

The tree bark stretched and squirmed absorbing the healing magic, and when Kwesi took his hand away, everyone saw that one old hidden word had been revealed: sister.

The word twin was still visible too, slightly fainter, underneath, so the Curse now read:

At the chiming of the thirteenth hour,
At the plucking of the thirteenth flower,
On the hundred-and-thirty-third Naming Day...
In the Greenwood Forest,
By the Tambling River,
On the Stepping Bones...
The Queen will sacrifice a life
Of a single sister / twin
Born in strife
And given to her as kith and kin.
To save her Royal soul and skin,
She'll cry cold and bitter tears,
But will rule Fairyland for a hundred-and-thirty-three more years...

The Queen finished reading the Curse, and turned to her sister. "I'm sorry, my dear," she said, "but the Curse has spoken, and it always has the last word. You too will face elimination."

"That's not fair!" screamed Lady Hawthorn. "You were going to make Thomas and Tempest fight each other."

"Remember," answered the Queen, "'what is written on the tree is what must be.' You said as much yourself. But there's still an element of doubt." She paused thoughtfully and turned to Thomas and Tempest. "It says sister *and* twin. One of you will have to fight Lady Hawthorn. For that is what the Curse decrees."

Thomas opened his mouth. Tempest could see he was about to take up the challenge. She responded quickly, before her brother could answer.

"I'll do it."

"No!" cried Thomas. "I will!"

"Only one of each named party may face the trial," said the Queen. "Tempest volunteered herself first. The decision is made. So it shall be." She waved at Kwesi, Thomas and Coriel. "You three may advise her."

The Fairy Queen snapped her fingers and the doors at the far end of the gallery blew open. The Fairies danced in a long raucous line out through them, dragging Tempest and Lady Hawthorn through a clearing beyond, where candles in jars hung from tree branches, lighting up the Greenwood.

The Queen processed regally behind them. Thomas, Kwesi and Coriel dashed to keep up with her, along with Auberon and Lord Hawthorn. King George brought up the rear, shuffling along with the three rabbit princesses, hopping at his feet. He was followed by the crawling, leaping, slithering, flapping, creeping servants and masquerade guests.

The Fairy hordes threw petals, acorns and crab apples as they paraded the court from the edge of the woodland down a narrow path, past the pool and spring, and out towards the Tambling River and the Stepping Bones beyond.

Tempest glanced over her shoulder. Coriel and Auberon were flapping overhead. Thomas and Kwesi had made it to her side, and Hoglet waddled along behind them. Meanwhile, Lord Hawthorn had caught up to his wife.

Soon the long dancing parade of beasts and Fairies reached the shoreline and the Stepping Bones.

The great lumps of white rock stretched out from the shore in a rough T-shape and stopped abruptly somewhere in the middle of the foggy river.

The Fairy Queen cut a swathe through the centre of the crowd, and moved to sit down. As she did so, there, waiting for her, was a throne of stone.

Tempest looked away from her mother and stared out

across the river, to the spot where she'd almost drowned. The depths sucked the light away like tar.

She bent down, picked up a stone and dropped it into the near current. The stone disappeared at once, sinking without a trace, heavy as the fear inside her.

She straightened up and dusted her hands on her dress.

A few feet off, Lady Hawthorn stood calm and confident. The sun sparkled on her green dress, scattering sharp points of light like dropped pins over the slippery white T of the Stepping Bones.

Lord Hawthorn inched closer to his wife and Auberon flapped across and settled on Lady Hawthorn's shoulder.

They both began talking quietly, Auberon sweeping his beak this way and that to indicate various spots on the river, while Lord Hawthorn flicked through his Grimoire, pointing out spells to his wife.

They were giving her advice on the upcoming battle, Tempest realized with horror. With their help, Lady Hawthorn was bound to win. Anyway, how could Tempest defeat such a formidable opponent in the state she was in?

"I've made a terrible mistake," she told Thomas and Kwesi. "I can't beat her. She's too powerful!"

"I believe in you, little rock dove," chirruped Coriel, alighting on her arm. "Don't let panic cloud your mind."

"I believe in you too," said Kwesi. "Don't rush. Think carefully and do the best spells you're able."

"You're the Storm Girl," said Thomas as firmly as he could manage. "If anyone can beat her, you can."

"The trouble is," said Tempest, "I don't know if I have the energy to."

"Then we'll give you ours," said Kwesi.

His voice had a tired edge, and Thomas was swaying on his feet. Tempest wondered if the pair of them had enough energy left either. But then Kwesi and Thomas hugged her, and both whispered in her ear:

"Fix, repair, heal, restore. Be hale and well, just like before."

And Tempest felt what little energy they still possessed that night flooding into her.

When she pulled away, she saw they were both drooping like cut flowers, leaning on each other for support.

"Take this too." Kwesi pulled something from his pocket. "It's the fragment of Magic Mirror I stole from Lord Hawthorn's study. It may come in useful." He pressed the shard into her hand. "Fight well," he said. "And fight hard."

"Good luck, my storm sister." Thomas kissed her cheek.

They stepped away from Tempest. Coriel remained on her shoulder.

"I'm still scared to face her alone, Coriel," whispered Tempest.

"Then I will come with you," Coriel said. Instead of flitting away, she dropped secretly down into the hood of Tempest's cloak. The familiar warmth of the little bird nestled against Tempest's neck made the fear of the duel pale a little.

"I'll hide in here, as I always do," Coriel twittered softly. "No one'll see. It'll be you and me against the world, my little curlew, just as it always was."

"Thank you, Coriel," Tempest whispered.

She stared ahead at the Stepping Bones and thought of her brother Thomas and his wild spirit and bravery. Of Kwesi and his healing powers and courage. Of Prosper and Marino and their love and kindness.

The Bone Cloud and the Ferry Boat Talisman hummed loudly against her chest, mixing with the race of her pulse and the thud of her nervous heartbeat. She had her magic and she had Coriel. She'd need them both, plus her wits and strength, and the faith of her friends, to win the coming battle. She only hoped it was enough.

24

Magic Duel

Exhaustion flooded Tempest as she approached the first Stepping Bone. Her soul and head and heart ached and she felt scattered to the four winds. On the riverbank beside her, Lady Hawthorn looked relaxed and collected.

"Remember to step with care, little redstart," whispered Coriel from Tempest's hood. "The Stepping Bones are slippery."

Thomas and Kwesi jostled to the front of the Fairy hordes, who were arrayed along the riverbank, waiting for their Queen on her stone throne to speak.

"The Curse has decreed that these are the rules of the Magic Duel. On my count you will walk out onto the

Stepping Bones. When you reach the centre of the river, the place where the Bones fork away from each other, you will take as many steps as remain in opposite directions."

Tempest readied herself to begin, but the Queen held up a hand for her to wait.

"On ten," explained the Queen, "I will cast a spell that sends a flare of light high into the sky. That will be your signal to commence battle. And you will turn and attack with all the magic at your disposal. Is that clear?"

Lady Hawthorn nodded.

Tempest said nothing.

"Prepare to duel to the death," shouted the Queen.

The Fairy hordes cheered. The beasts roared. Thomas and Kwesi shifted apprehensively on their feet. King George stared dreamily ahead. Lord Hawthorn fidgeted in worried silence.

This is it then, Tempest thought nervously. She steeled herself as the Queen commenced her count. The river sluiced by at enormous speed. A single false move could see her tumble to the Dead Lands below.

"One," called the Queen.

Tempest and Lady Hawthorn climbed onto the first white rock.

"Two."

They leaped forward together along the narrow path.

Tempest felt the Stepping Bone floating beneath her, like an insubstantial cloud.

"Three."

She had to concentrate on putting one foot in front of the other. When she looked up, Lady Hawthorn was somehow already at the fork in the T.

"Four."

Lady Hawthorn began hurrying towards the end of the right-hand branch, muttering a spell. Tempest still hadn't reached the left-hand fork.

Nothing was coming. Her nerves flared like hot coals.

"Five."

Finally, she reached the fork and scrambled left along the rocks. She needed to reach the end and turn with a spell ready. But she didn't have one…

"Six."

Panic set in. Time was running out and Tempest didn't know what to do.

"Seven."

At least she'd saved Thomas from this terrible fate.

"Eight."

She glanced over at him, standing on the shoreline.

"Nine."

You had to fight for family, didn't you? Not run or hide like a coward.

"Ten!"

The Queen threw her arms up. A volley of bright light flew from her fingertips high into the sky and exploded in a flash of sparks. That was the signal to start.

Tempest turned and raised both hands and woozily tried to summon a spell...something...anything...

Lady Hawthorn was already bounding forward, spell-casting:

"Sparks fly. Fire light. Flames grow. Blaze ignite."

A fireball blasted at Tempest.

She scrambled out of its way, slipping about on the rough rocks. The fringe of her cloak was alight. She could smell it burning. Rapidly, she sang her mother's Extinguishing Spell to stop the fire.

"Gutter, snuff, quench, douse. Put the flames and fire out."

The fire fizzled and her cloak smoked acridly, but, luckily, it was only singed. It had taken all of her energy to stop it bursting alight with her inside it.

Lady Hawthorn was still reeling from throwing the fireball. Tempest couldn't give her time to cast something else. She tried to gather her thoughts, but they tangled like string. The battle had only just begun and already she was struggling to keep up.

Lady Hawthorn began readying a Lightning Spell:

"Static spiral, thunder crack, power thicken, lightning smack."

The power of it crackled in her hands as she gathered it into a jagged bolt, preparing to throw it at Tempest.

"What should I do, Coriel?" cried Tempest.

"Anything, my little puffin!" whispered Coriel in her hood. "No time to think! Just act!"

Tempest leaped forward onto the next rock, and felt the shard of Magic Mirror slap hard against her hip. That was it!

She whipped it out just as Lady Hawthorn threw the bolt of lightning at her chest.

The bolt bounced off the shard and ricocheted back at Lady Hawthorn, who had to dive to escape being hit.

"Quick! Cast!" screeched Coriel. "While she's down!"

A Snow Spell came to mind. Tempest spoke it swiftly:

"Snow. Hail. Sleet gather. Clouds come. Blizzards batter."

The blizzard slammed into Lady Hawthorn, knocking her back off her feet just as she was trying to stand.

"Now what?" asked Tempest.

"I don't know, my little rock dove," chirruped Coriel. "How about thundersnow?"

Tempest cast her Thundersnow Spell:

"Snow spiral, thunder clash, blizzard blow, storm crash."

Lady Hawthorn threw a hand across her face to protect

herself from the vicious shower of hail and ice. It gave Tempest a moment more to gather her strength. She needed another, but when she stopped concentrating on the thundersnow it dissipated as suddenly as it had come.

Lady Hawthorn began approaching fast. She muttered under her breath as she leaped from Stepping Bone to Bone, getting closer. It was a version of Thomas's Transformation Spell:

"Tail, snout, pelt, paws. Wings, fins, teeth, claws. Shake me, change me, magic art. Make me a creature dark of heart."

She became a terrible frightening beast, big as a bear, with needle-sharp teeth and claws, pointed horns and a spiked tail.

Tempest scrambled backwards, trying to escape her, but lost her footing in a crack and slipped. She panicked, flailing.

Thomas and Kwesi gasped from the bank as she teetered on the brink, just managing to keep her balance.

Lady Hawthorn barrelled into her like a hurricane. "You're not going to win, Storm Girl," she growled, snapping her teeth and slashing at Tempest with her claws, horns and spiked tail.

Tempest ducked and shimmied, slicing at Lady Hawthorn with the mirror shard.

But Lady Hawthorn was stronger. She marshalled Tempest back along the left-hand length of the T, muscling her towards the edge of its last Stepping Bone.

Tempest glanced down at the raging waters. They gaped like a snake's maw, hungry for over a century, waiting for their sacrifice to appease the Curse. She realized with a sickening surety it was going to be her. She had nothing left to give.

Suddenly the big beastly body of Lady Hawthorn jolted. She'd caught her tail in a crack on the far side of the rock.

This was Tempest's chance. She had to take it or else she'd lose Thomas, Kwesi, Coriel, and Prosper and Marino for ever.

She grasped the mirror shard, held it up and cast the Opening Spell:

"Open sky, open stone, open waters, open bone.

Magic Mirror in my hand, become the doorway to England."

The mirror shard shone bright in the Fairy darkness.

Through it, Tempest saw the blue River Tambling in England.

It was dawn there. The first rays of sun flashed from the mirror.

"Use the beam, little moorhen!" advised Coriel.

Tempest aimed the shaft at Lady Hawthorn.

The sparkling bright light flooded into her beastly eyes, blinding her. Lady Hawthorn roared and shrank away, her tail thrusting deeper into the crack.

"Cast again, my hoopoe!" cried Coriel. "You've got her on the back paw!"

Tempest nodded. She was about to put the shard of mirror away, when she saw something else in it. Ferry Keeper's Cottage, on the far bank. Her home, with Prosper and Marino. Suddenly, she remembered their words:

"Some difficulties can feel immeasurable on the surface," Prosper had said, "but in your depths you carry something stronger: stillness."

"Own that stillness," Marino had advised. "Let it fill you with power. Then you'll know the truth of who you are."

Tempest put her free hand up to her chest and felt the humming of the three figures in their little wooden boat. It was her true Talisman, given with love. She'd almost forgotten it. Forgotten Prosper and Marino, forgotten who she was. But now she remembered.

She realized she didn't need to be scared any more. She took a deep breath and surrendered, letting the panic, anger, worry and fear wash over her in a wave.

Almost as soon as she let them in, the stormy feelings slipped away like a heavy overcoat and were gone, sinking into the river.

Then she felt as light as a feather and filled with raw power.

The roaring beast of Lady Hawthorn had freed her tail and was coming at her once more – head down, claws out, teeth bared and spiked tail poised to attack.

Tempest reviewed the enchantments she'd been taught. They seemed old. Not her own. She needed to conjure a new magic with words that flowed. She clutched the humming Ferry Boat Talisman and the shard of mirror. I am the Storm, she thought to herself. I am the Stillness.

And in that moment a fresh, unknown, improvised spell came, spun from thin air. The words tasted clean and clear on her tongue, and they tumbled from her lips in a handful of heartbeats.

"I am the storm and I am the wild.
I am the stillness, the calmness, the mild.
I am the fog, I am the river.
I am the sky, the maker, the giver.
I am weather, inside and out.
The summoner of storms, and the bringer of drought.
Child of a Fairy, and the Green Man,
The heart of the ocean, the soul of this land.
I speak to you now, each drop of water.
I am your sister and I am your daughter.

To the sky and the lightning and each cloud that's free.
Heed my request, and please... save me."

It was the longest spell Tempest had ever spoken and it came from the heart. She felt the midnight-dark waves rise up inside her and saw the beastly Lady Hawthorn leaping in slow-motion across the last length of Stepping Bone. Quickly, she finished the spell, adding the line she'd used to raise the river:

"Tide rise. Clouds gather. Floods come. Rain batter."

The black water snatched Lady Hawthorn up mid-leap and pulled her off course.

She hit the surface of the water with an almighty splash. At once, the river doused her magic and she became herself again. The current seemed to sense her weakness. It snapped and sucked at her, dragging her down.

"Help me!" screamed Lady Hawthorn, and Lord Hawthorn jumped into action.

Startling Auberon from his shoulder, he leaped over the Stepping Bones, towards his wife.

Brushing past Tempest, he dropped the Grimoire and fell to his knees and grasped his wife's hand.

"Don't let go, dearest!" he ordered Lady Hawthorn as she gripped his wrist.

Lord Hawthorn began muttering spells, trying to yank

his wife back onto the Stepping Bones, but the magic Tempest had poured into the current was stronger. He looked around wretchedly and shouted at his remaining apprentices on the riverbank.

"THOMAS! NOAH! GET OVER HERE AT ONCE!"

Thomas didn't move.

Neither did Kwesi. "My name's not Noah," he said with quiet resolve. "It's Kwesi. The name my mother gave me, when she told me that my courage and magic would set me free."

Lord Hawthorn looked like he was about to answer, but the current pulled him off his feet and he tumbled into the river. He flailed his arms in desperation, sinking, as Lady Hawthorn splashed frantically beside him.

Tempest wondered for a second whether she should try and save them, but then realized the waters would take her too. She glanced round for Auberon, but he was not flying to their rescue either – instead he was perched on a tree stump. He watched in disdain as his master and mistress were swept away downriver.

Soon the Hawthorns were little more than tiny specks on a distant stretch of water. Finally, they bobbed under and were gone, sinking down to the depths and the Dead Lands beyond.

Don't Look Back

"Well done, little grebeling!" twittered Coriel, turning joyful somersaults in the hood of Tempest's cloak. "We did it!"

They had, hadn't they? But at what cost? Tempest stared in a daze at the rough surface of the Stepping Bones, her heart pounding with an unquenchable sense of relief. She had won, with help from her friends. Beaten the Hawthorns at their own game. They were gone. Sunk to the Dead Lands. And she had overcome the Curse.

A few raindrops spattered the white stone beneath her feet. The last of her great magical storm. Except they weren't raindrops, Tempest realized. They were tears. She brushed her eyes and raised her head. She could see clearly now, in both directions.

On one side of the river was the Fair Isle, where her friends waited. Along with the King of England, hordes of beasts and Fairies, and her mother, who no doubt was expecting some kind of triumphant return.

On the other, unseen, was England and the little pier that led to Ferry Keeper's Cottage, Prosper and Marino and her home.

She could go back there at once, if she wanted. Nothing was holding her to the Fair Isle any more. But first she had to confront her mother and collect her brother Thomas and her friend Kwesi.

She replaced the shard of mirror in her pocket and saw Lord Hawthorn's Grimoire resting at her feet. It was a vile dangerous thing and for a second she considered throwing it in the river. Then she remembered all the spells it contained and how valuable they were. Who knew how many people she could help with its magic? she thought. And perhaps against her better judgement, she decided to keep it.

She bent down and picked it up, clasping it nervously to her chest as she crossed the Stepping Bones towards the Fair Isle.

The river shrank back, revealing a safe passage. She

stepped along its path, feeling the rocks she had known so well in the past, strong and steady, beneath her feet.

As she hopped from the last Stepping Bone onto the shingle, Thomas and Kwesi cheered loudly. They rushed over and hugged and kissed her in blessed relief. Even Coriel trilled in delight, and took off and looped the loop happily around her head.

The beastly crowd brayed and barked and the Fairy hordes whooped and whistled and parted to make a path for her to her mother's throne. Auberon on his tree stump looked unimpressed. King George snored loudly. In his hypnotized and dreamy state, he had sat down with his back against a tree and fallen asleep.

Her mother stood as Tempest approached and clapped a polite round of applause. "I knew you had it in you to defeat my sister, little Storm Girl," she said, with a smile. "And that dreadful husband of hers. Well done." She tried to take Tempest's hand, but Tempest snatched her fingers away.

"No," she said flatly.

The Queen's face fell, and her eyes were filled with surprise. No one had ever successfully defied her before. Not in centuries. Not until this night. She always got what she wanted. But now the Curse was over and still her daughter was standing in front of her with fire in her belly, ready to refuse her wishes.

Tempest realized the Queen had held a little piece of her heart these past thirteen years – a piece that she'd left behind when she'd run off to England and forgotten everything. In all that time, Tempest had ached for her old home. Yearned to see where she was from and who she belonged with. But there was no room for her here. Not any more. The Fairy Court was another theatre of lies. It was the same as Kensington Palace in that respect.

"You're no different to Lord and Lady Hawthorn," Tempest told her mother. "Or this terrible English King." She gestured to the sleeping George in his mud-spattered lion costume. "You kept Thomas and me trapped and in the dark for years, knowing that one day we'd have to face the consequences of the Curse and this deadly duel."

"That's over, my Storm Girl," said the Queen. "You can tell your piteous heart there's no harm done. I promise, there'll be no more tricks or curses, no more tribulations. You've earned the right to stay in the Fairy Court for ever, both of you. Earned your titles as Prince and Princess of Fairyland." The Queen glanced down at the sleeping King. "Perhaps I will keep him," she said. "Though he barely looks a lion. More a donkey." She laughed. "I might give him an ass's head and a tail for his bottom. I think that would suit him, don't you?" She smiled at her children.

"Do what you like," said Tempest. "We will no longer be

a part of your Fairy Court, Mother."

"Or your Royal family," added Thomas. "Wildflowers need meadows to grow, not forest prisons."

Their mother sighed.

"Please," Tempest said, "let us go."

"Where?" asked the Queen sadly.

"To our new family," Tempest replied. "To Prosper and Marino. They saved me and Coriel. And I don't mean from drowning. They save me every day, and I them. They always wanted a daughter, and they found enough love to care for me. And there's plenty of space in their hearts for more children," she added, glancing at Thomas and Kwesi. "It's what they yearn for. That's why I wish to return to them, and to take my brother Thomas and my friend Kwesi. Perhaps there could be a home for us all there, at Ferry Keeper's Cottage. We won't know until you let us go. And you really should. At the very least, you owe us that much after all you've put us through."

"I understand," said the Fairy Queen, begrudgingly. "You may have your wish. You are free to leave, all of you."

"Thank you." Tempest took her mother's hand at last and kissed it.

As she backed away, she felt a sudden sense of relief. It was as if she had been holding her breath for the entire confrontation, and at last that feeling was gone.

"You can visit us if you like," Tempest said. "At Ferry Keeper's Cottage, in Tambling. But you have to promise it will be on our terms."

"I promise," said the Queen, giving them a gracious curtsy. "If you hold up your shard of Magic Mirror, I will open a doorway to England for you. A new way out."

Tempest did as her mother had asked, and the Fairy Queen muttered a few words and drew a silver shape in the air around the shard of glass.

Threads shifted beneath the Queen's fingertips as if she was moving the very elements. And magic coalesced in the shard of mirror in the palm of Tempest's hand. Soon it separated from the mirror and became a wide-open doorway that floated by itself a single step above the riverbank.

It was just wide enough for three children to pass though shoulder to shoulder.

"Goodbye, Mother," said Tempest. Putting the shard of mirror safely back in the pocket of her red cloak and clasping Lord Hawthorn's Grimoire under her arm, she beckoned to the others.

Kwesi and Thomas joined her, while Coriel rode on her shoulder.

Together, they turned and marched through the doorway, away from sleeping King George and the beasts of the English Court, away from the Fairy hordes and courtiers and their mother, the Queen of Fairyland, and onwards, through the doorway to England.

On this occasion, Tempest remembered Coriel's wise words from the first time they left, and she did not look back.

26

Homeward Bound

Tempest, Thomas and Kwesi stepped through the magical doorway the Fairy Queen had made for them and stumbled across the threshold onto the riverbank. Whereas in Fairyland it had been approaching evening, in the English Greenwood it was early morning. The sun was barely high enough to burn away the fog that hung around the trees and was glistening on the surface of the river.

"*We're back in England, my little waxwing!*" Coriel twittered from Tempest's shoulder.

"So we are," Tempest said.

They walked upriver, following the bank along the edge of the forest.

At last, there was the hut. The place where Kwesi and Tempest had first talked, and where Thomas and Tempest had first found each other in this world.

Beyond the hut, at the end of the pier, was the bell on its rope.

And beyond that, on the far side of the Tambling River, Tempest's home, Prosper and Marino's cottage. The shape of it was vaguely visible through the fog.

Tempest hurried along the pier and rang the bell to summon her fathers, the ferry keepers.

Then they waited.

It was a little frosty. But they did not wait in the hut. Tempest wanted to see Prosper and Marino as soon as they came into view. And, besides, the sun was rising, and the sky was clear. Soon the fog would burn away, and it would be a splendid warm spring day.

Thomas sat down by the edge of the jetty and Kwesi stamped his feet together to ward off the cold. Tempest sat on the heavy Grimoire.

"What will you do when we get to Tambling Village?" she asked Kwesi. "Are you going to stay with us?"

"Maybe for a while," Kwesi said, hugging his arms. "At least until I'm rested and recuperated and can decide what I want to do with my life. It's a good feeling to know that my magic is mine alone, and that, at last, I'm in charge of my own destiny and free to do as I please."

At last they heard the splashing of oars. And there, rowing through the last wisps of fog like they were being floated across the water by a magic spell, were Prosper and Marino in their little ferry boat, *Nixie*.

Kwesi stood bolt upright and uncrossed his arms. Coriel flapped down beside Thomas, who'd fallen asleep beside the hut, and pecked lightly at the crown of his head to wake him. The three of them hurried to join Tempest, who'd already picked herself up and her things, and was racing to the end of the pier to meet her fathers as their boat came in.

Prosper saw her first. "TEMPEST!" he shouted in shocked delight. Then he spied the Grimoire under her arm. "What've you got there?"

"Just a book," she answered.

"We've searched everywhere for you!" Marino called out.

"Where were you?" Prosper said. "Where have you been all this time?"

Tempest couldn't reply. Her heart had leaped into her throat, blocking all the things she wanted to say. Even after she'd recovered her breath, she could not think of the perfect words to express how much she loved them. Or how happy she was to see them again. So she simply said:

"Dear fathers, we were waiting for you to come and take us home!"

"We?" Marino asked, as Prosper manoeuvred *Nixie* alongside the pier.

"Yes." Tempest caught the mooring rope with her free hand and tied it to a post. "This is my twin brother, Thomas, and this is my good friend, Kwesi. I promised them they could stay with us for a while. Is that all right?"

"Of course." Prosper climbed onto the pier and hugged Tempest, then Thomas, then Kwesi. "You're welcome to stay for as long as you need," he told them both.

"For ever even, if you like," Marino added, kissing their cheeks.

Tempest laughed. It was exactly what the pair had said to her the day she'd first arrived, though it had taken her weeks to understand it.

"Everyone row together," Prosper suggested, when they were all seated in *Nixie* and the little ferry boat had finally stopped rocking.

Tempest, Thomas and Kwesi took one oar, Marino and Prosper the other, and they cast off from the Greenwood jetty.

Coriel sat on the prow, directing them back across the river. It was a sparkling spring day and the strong breeze at their backs helped them along. Tempest may have been an expert at weather spells, but that morning she felt as if the wind was working for her unasked. They barely had to use their oars, except to steer occasionally.

Tempest put her free hand in the current and let the water drift over it. Thomas pointed downstream towards the estuary mouth, where the sea and river mingled. "What's out there?"

"The sea," Marino said, looking up from his oar. "Can you smell the ocean on the wind's breath?"

Thomas nodded.

"Could we go and take a look?" Kwesi asked.

"Maybe tomorrow," Prosper said.

Tempest smiled and breathed in salt and cold, the smell of the deep blue stretching off into nothing, as far as the eye could see.

She glanced at Coriel on the prow, then at Prosper and Marino and Thomas and Kwesi radiating joy beside her.

"*This river and the wide blue sea,*" Thomas said. "*Their waters hold much power. They're not just a barrier between worlds. They're also what ties them together.*"

"That's true," Kwesi replied. "There's a flowing spirit in such wild waters that can be healing."

"It will be a good place to recuperate," Thomas said.

"For me too," Kwesi added. "Until I can meet your friends, Tempest, and am ready once more to begin my travels. With their help, and my magic, I'm sure I'll be able to find my way home."

Tempest couldn't have agreed more. She dearly hoped Kwesi would be successful. She looked up and found they were approaching the far riverbank. And, there, just beyond where Coriel was perched on *Nixie*'s prow, at the end of a rickety old pier, was Prosper and Marino's Ferry Keeper's Cottage.

Her home.

This is the end. Almost. In another way, it is just a beginning. On a spring morning, at the twelfth stroke of midday, in a small boat, on a magical river that winds through many lands, three brave children, an enchanted robin and a pair of loving ferry keepers are rowing onward, their hair tussled by the wind and their hearts buoyed by the clear, clean smell of the ocean.

After Wood

There's one last stump of this tale, which tells of what happened when the Fairies left the Greenwood. It is called the After Wood.

One foggy morning, almost a month after the great Magical Duel, a ragged Wild Man in a mud-spattered lion-skin coat appeared in Tambling Village, beside the river.

He meandered up Fairport Lane and was discovered by an old charcoal-burner, who brought him to the village hall.

The Wild Man spoke a mixture of English and German to the villagers who gathered to see him. He claimed to be the King of England. He maintained he'd been at a Masquerade in Kensington Palace with his servants, granddaughters and a hundred noble guests, when they were all kidnapped by Fairies.

The wreath of withered birch branches round his head he said was Titania's crown and a gift from the Fairy Queen. As well as that, he suggested the Fairy Queen had cursed him with an ass's head and tail and forced him to roam the forest until the next full moon.

Eventually he'd somehow got his old head back, made his way to the river and crossed a shimmering Bone Bridge that magically appeared. The rest of his party, he proposed, were still on far Fair Isle, hiding in the Greenwood.

There was no bridge, of course, and there hadn't been one for one-hundred-and-thirty-three years.

The townsfolk sent for the two ferry keepers, Prosper and Marino, and the three children who were living with them, Tempest, Thomas and Kwesi. All five crossed the river regularly, in their little boat, *Nixie*, on errands and so were asked what they thought about the Wild Man's story.

The two ferry keepers and the three children said they'd seen nothing on the Fair Isle to suggest the Wild Man's tale was true.

The Wild Man got very angry and shouted that they were lying. He recognized the children from his palace, he said, as well as a red robin perched on a nearby twig, who he was certain they could talk with.

The children told the villagers the Wild Man was spouting nonsense. They'd never seen him before in their lives. They didn't have any idea who he was or where h came from. Perhaps, they posited, he had got lost in the woods and a strange hallucination had come upon him.

As for the real missing King, the country searched for him far and wide, for a year and day, but he was never found. Neither were the Princesses, or the Prime Minister, or a great many other consequential people.

Apart from the Wild Man, who departed soon afterwards, no one ever came forward to tell of what happened to those who had disappeared. And they were never seen or heard from again.

It became the most famous unsolved mystery of the age. But no one imagined in their wildest dreams that it might have something to do with Fairies. Not even the King's head servant Mehmet, who came to Tambling to help Kwesi return to London so he might meet friends of Prosper and Marino's named Adofo and Yaba Fremah. Nor did Lady Hawthorn's maid Molly, who, along with the rest of the King's servants, remained working at Kensington Palace long after His Majesty was gone.

In 1727 the King's son, who'd been acting Regent, was finally crowned. He was the second King George and, along with his wife Queen Caroline, ushered in a new age of science and reason.

A handful of people in Tambling still believed the Wild

ıan of the Greenwoods had been the old King. But most told themselves those were just stories. Myths. Legends. Old wives' tales. Only the two remaining children Tempest and Thomas, their robin Coriel, and their ferry keeper parents, Prosper and Marino, knew the truth.

Sometimes, in the woods, Thomas and Tempest would come across a few rabbits who looked awfully like the missing Princesses, or a squirrel that resembled the missing Prime Minister, Mr Walpole. A fox that bore a likeness to the missing court composer Mr Handel. Or a pair of old grey-whiskered badgers that were the spitting image of the missing writers Mr Daniel Defoe and Mr Jonathan Swift.

They never told anyone this. Nor did they use their magic to change the creatures back. For it seemed to them that so much time had passed, what would be the use? By now everyone probably preferred their animal forms, and many of them seemed more likeable that way anyway. After all, as a wise Storm Girl once said: not all who wander in the Greenwood are lost. Some are there because they call it home.

All this is as true as the day is long. And if you go down to the woods today, you'll see those creatures. Only, be sure not to go alone, or else the Fairies might get you.

Q + A with Peter Bunzl, the author of *Magicborn*

***Tell us a little bit about your inspiration for* Magicborn?**

One day, when doing a school event at Kensington Palace, I was taken to see an amazing mural painted in 1726 by William Kent for King George I. There are forty-five people in the painting and it is believed to show George I's favourite servants and courtiers. I was intrigued to learn more about the subjects in the painting and kept imagining things about them. Included in the scene is a young white boy with brown hair in a green coat clutching a handful of oak leaves and acorns. His name was Peter the Wild Boy.

There is lots of research on Peter, and some historians suggest he had Pitt-Hopkins syndrome, a rare genetic disorder first identified in 1978. People with conditions like this were treated very badly in Peter's time, and I wanted to let his memory rest, rather than try to write his story. But I was fascinated by the idea of what it might mean to be a child in the Royal Court, a place filled with powerful adults. So I decided to write a story of two children, Thomas and Tempest, who are Magicborn, and taken into the Palace in unusual circumstances. From there, the dual world of *Magicborn* was realized.

hat are your favourite fairy stories?

When researching Kensington Palace, I was amazed to learn Peter Pan has roots there. The author J.M. Barrie was inspired to create the story of a boy who could transform into a bird while walking in the palace gardens. Suddenly, I began to imagine my character Thomas as a shapeshifter – who could switch into animal forms and who carried an innate magic in him. Thomas's Fairy twin sister was named after Shakespeare's *The Tempest*, a play about a father and daughter shipwrecked on an island full of magical beings.

Tempest became the Storm Girl to Thomas's Wild Boy. A character with her own powers who shared Thomas's forgotten past. She lived on the Tambling River, named after one of my favourite folk tales: *Tam Lin*. Just like Janet in *Tam Lin*, Tempest must overcome her fears and harness her powers to save the ones she holds dear.

Fairy tales often show the forces of good versus evil and I knew this was something I wanted to examine in *Magicborn*.

What would happen if Malkin from* The Cogheart Adventures *and Coriel from* Magicborn *were to meet?

I love animal sidekicks! They are engrained in our myths and fairy tales. Malkin is a mechanical fox and unlike a real fox he can talk. But just like a real fox, if real foxes could talk, he has high-minded opinions about everything.

Coriel is also a little bit on the snarky side, and like

Malkin, they both get away with this because they are such lovable rogues. Malkin and Coriel also protect their friends fiercely, so I think they'd definitely become firm friends – but let's not tell them they are sidekicks!

What research did you do for the novel?

I read so, so many books on Georgian England. In this adventure we also meet Kwesi, who is misnamed and mischaracterized by the Royal Court. He was inspired by another figure in the staircase mural: a Black pageboy climbing over the balustrade. Kwesi's story was influenced by the childhoods of Francis Barber, born Quashey, and Ignatius Sancho; two famous Black figures from Georgian history who grew up enslaved and became free men.

Barber was a slave who ran away to sea, but returned, went to school, and became Samuel Johnson's secretary, helping him revise his dictionary. Sancho was born on a slavers' ship and brought to London, but after escaping became a shopkeeper and musician; a writer of essays, plays, books and music. Thought to be the first Black Briton to vote, he wrote many letters advocating for an end to slavery.

Authors often write stories to show the world not as it is, but as it should be, and I used real life history, myth and folk tales to inspire *Magicborn*, but like all good fairy stories I hope it also has a deeper message: we can't change the past but we can be active in the present.

Acknowledgements

This has been an epic battle of me versus the page. Writing through covid times has been especially challenging. I would like to thank everyone whose wit, wisdom and sage advice helped birth these magic words…

My partner, Michael. My editors, Rebecca Hill and Becky Walker. My agent Jo Williamson. Designer Katharine Millichope and Sarah Cronin, and illustrator Maxine Lee-Mackie for their stunning artwork. Copyeditors Sarah Stewart and Anne Finnis. Publicist Katarina Jovanovic. Marketeer Hannah Reardon Steward. Historical reader Dr Jackie Collier. Authenticity and sensitivity readers Jasmine Richards and Charlotte Forfieh. Everyone at Usborne Rights, Publicity and Fiction who worked tirelessly on the book. Chitra Soundar for collecting fairytale openings. Catherine Johnson for contacts. S. I. Martin for generously reading early chapters. Black History Walks for historical information. Yaba Badoe for advice on names and for letting me steal hers. Michelle Harrison and Abi Elphinstone for agreeing to read early proofs. Lorraine's Lady Writers, The Juvenile Literary Society and The Forester Writers for your online cheerleading in desperate times. Saul Argent and Pop Up Projects for inviting me to do the school event at Kensington Palace that started all this. And most especially Gail Cameron, the Learning Producer at Historic Royal Palaces, who introduced me to Peter the Wild Boy. His story mixed in my mind with folklore, magic, myth and fairytale and sparked the beginnings of this book.

I hope you have enjoyed it, dear reader!